CHRISTOPHER NICHOLSON

❧ ❧ ❧

WINTER

FOURTH ESTATE • *London*

Fourth Estate
An imprint of HarperCollins*Publishers*
1 London Bridge Street
London
SE1 9GF

www.4thestate.co.uk

This Fourth Estate paperback edition first published 2015
First published in Great Britain by Fourth Estate in 2014
1

ISBN 978-0-00-751608-7

Typeset in Fournier MT by Palimpsest Book Production Limited,
Falkirk, Stirlingshire

Printed and bound in Great Britain by Clays Ltd, St Ives plc

MIX
Paper from
responsible sources
FSC www.fsc.org **FSC™ C007454**

To Kitty
(1958–2011)

PART ONE

✻ ✻ ✻

PART ONE

CHAPTER I

❈ ❈ ❈

One of the old roads leaving a well-known county town in the west of England climbs a long slope and finally reaches a kind of open plain, a windy spot from which a wide prospect of the countryside is available. Fields of corn occupy the near and middle distance, while the rolling downs further off are grazed by numerous flocks of sheep. Much closer at hand there stands a clump of pines and other trees, the branches of which overhang a brick wall surrounding a dwelling of some substantial kind. Chimneys and a roof may be glimpsed especially in winter, but the wall is of sufficient height to obstruct the gaze of any pedestrians on the road, and the house remains as well hidden as if it were deep in a wood. Most wayfarers pass by scarcely aware of its existence. Yet a few curious souls, noticing a white entrance gate set in the wall, occasionally linger to ask themselves who may live in such a secluded, lonely place.

On a blue November dawn, not long before the present time, an old man might have been observed walking down the short drive that led from the house to the gate. He walked slowly, with a slight stoop, and carried a stick in his right hand. A small dog, a wire-haired terrier, accompanied him, snuffling at the vegetation on either side of the drive.

The drive was flanked by trees, and the depth of shadow beneath their boughs was such that the old man seemed to emerge by degrees out of a dim obscurity. He wore a tweed jacket, a wool tie and trousers of a nondescript colour, and on his head sat a wide-brimmed hat. When he reached the gate he halted, leaning on its top rail and scrutinising the world beyond. His moustache and eyebrows were pale, his face lined by a lifetime of experience and thought. While the down-turned nature of his mouth suggested a deeply ingrained scepticism, his eyes were keen and sharp and the wrinkles at each corner seemed to contain a distinct humour.

So, at least, he imagined himself. Not that bad for eighty-four, he thought, with a certain touch of vanity.

The road itself was empty, little traffic using it at this early hour on a Sunday. An erratic breeze blew, stirring the pines above his head. In the air hung a damp, resinous fragrance often encountered in wooded parts of the countryside in the last stages of autumn. This was, with the possible exception of spring, the old man's favourite season, the year quietly burning down and the steady passage of time made visible by the lowered sun and shortened days.

There was no sun today, or none visible, but the light was gradually increasing and the sombre blue of the air had turned to a dull grey as he retraced his steps. The drive curved around a thick shrubbery and brought the front of the house into view. A handsome brick edifice, it had been built to his own design, and he was as proud of its dark slate roof, imposing porch and low turrets as he was of some of his literary works. The piece of land on which it stood had formerly been nothing but a bare pasture exposed to the full force of the prevailing westerly wind, and the trees that now encircled and protected it had taken forty years to grow to their present height. Inspecting the garden always gave him considerable satisfaction, and he strolled here and there, occasionally turning his head to follow the progress of the dog or to listen to the song of some bird. The lawns were thick with freshly fallen leaves. After a time he retired indoors, leaving his stick in a corner of the porch and hanging his hat on a wooden peg.

The house was too far from the town to be supplied with electricity, and all artificial light came from oil-lamps. One such had been lit in the dining room, where the old man ate breakfast in the company of his wife, Florence. He had married her a decade earlier, his first wife having died unexpectedly. They sat at opposite ends of the table and by mutual agreement talked very little; early morning was never a good hour for conversation. It being a Sunday, the newspaper had not yet been delivered, and she seemed content to read a book while sipping her coffee. The room was rather chilly, and around her neck she wore a fox stole. The head of the fox, with its glass eyes, dangled over the book.

She had a round face, dark brown hair tied in a bun, and heavy-lidded eyes that gave a powerful impression of melancholy. The old man wished it could have been otherwise, for his own personality had melancholic tendencies which would perhaps have adjusted to some counterbalancing force. Still, one was what one was. His outlook on Life, his essential philosophical beliefs, had been formed long ago. At his age he could hardly expect himself to change.

He drank tea, and ate bacon and toast. The dog sat by his side, saliva spooling from the edges of its mouth, uttering polite whines. 'Wait, Wessex,' the old man chided. 'Now now. Where are your manners? Stop begging.' But the begging was a regular part of breakfast, and as happened every day the whines grew more urgent and insistent until the old man at last dangled the bacon rinds above the dog's nose. 'Gently. Gently. Don't snap. There.'

Once he had finished he wiped his fingers on his napkin and drained his tea. As he rose from the table Florence looked up with an anxious expression and appeared on the point of speech, but then chose to remain silent. The old man was relieved: her anxieties were almost always unnecessary, and at this hour of the day his mind was on his work. But, out of kindness, he felt obliged to say something.

'How are the hens laying?' he asked.

The abruptness of his inquiry seemed to startle her, and it took a moment before she gave the reply that they were laying well. 'I think they are laying well,' she corrected herself, as if experiencing a degree of uncertainty on the matter. But the old man's interest in the hens was limited and he was disinclined to be drawn into further talk. He nodded and left her, the dog trotting at his heels.

Adjacent to the dining room lay the hall. It was simply furnished: a grandfather clock stood and ticked by the side of a flight of stairs, a black telephone gleamed on a small table, and a barometer in a mahogany case hung on one wall. The old man went up the stairs, turned right along a short corridor and entered the study which was his daily refuge, even on Sundays. Wrapping a woollen shawl around his shoulders he settled at his desk, while the dog curled up on a rug.

The observance of an unvarying routine was one that the old man valued highly and that, he believed, contributed in large measure to his productivity as a writer. For many years he had begun each day with a walk around the garden, in the belief that the fresh air invigorated his brain; likewise, for the same indeterminate number of years, he had withdrawn after breakfast to his study, where he remained for the whole of the morning and the greater part of the afternoon. The chair on which he now sat had served him for much of his life, and the worn condition of its tapestry seat – the once bright floral design now chiefly bare sacking – bore testament to the thousands of hours in which he had been engaged in literary endeavour. The desk itself had also done long service, and despite its inanimate nature stood in the category of a friend. The shawl draped over his shoulders he held in the same affectionate regard.

When seated here, pen in hand, he did not feel old. Physically, he was aware how much he had declined – he no longer felt safe on a bicycle, and it was many years since he had danced – but in his mind he felt as strong and vigorous as he had done in his youth. Yet he was aware that he did not always achieve very much. This was particularly so in the last few months; some days he made no progress at all, and spent long periods staring at a blank page or making inconsequential notes. However, routine was routine, and if he did not try to work he would achieve nothing at all. Behind him lay a string of novels and hundreds of poems, and to break with the habits of a lifetime merely because he happened to have reached a certain age was impossible. Even if he had received some authoritative assurance that this day was his last on the planet, he would have spent it in the same fashion, writing as best he could. Perhaps he might have drunk a glass of champagne at lunchtime, and perhaps if the weather had been good he might have taken a short stroll; but it would not have been in his nature to have done anything out of the ordinary. When it came to a consideration of possible ways of drawing to a close his earthly sojourn, the thought of being at his desk, with the ink drying on the last words of a final poem, was an altogether agreeable one.

This morning he found himself singularly lacking in inspiration, and he knew the reason well enough: in the afternoon he was expecting a visitor for tea, which was the meal he nowadays preferred for social intercourse. In its favour, above all, was its brevity; guests who came at four had generally left by five. Visits of any longer duration tended to leave him exhausted.

She was a young woman by the name of Gertrude, although in his mind he always called her Gertie. He had been thinking of her visit for days, not only because he always enjoyed her company but because there was a certain proposition that he intended to put to her and he was interested to see how she reacted. He admired her greatly. The daughter of a local tradesman, she was in every way a product of the Wessex environment and yet she possessed qualities that, in his mind, put her on a superior plane. He remembered how disconcerted he had been when, some years earlier, he had heard of her impending marriage to a man who came from the town of Beaminster. Beaminster lay in the far west of the county, and men bred there tended to have the slow, plodding qualities of the oxen that had once been used to plough the heavy soils found in the surrounding countryside. Love blooms in the most unlikely of places, but he could not entirely repress a feeling that, as the saying goes, she might have done better for herself.

He wondered what she would be wearing. She always dressed with remarkable style and taste, yet it was perhaps true that she would have looked elegant whatever her dress.

Preoccupied as he was, the morning was an undoubted failure from an artistic consideration, and when after a frugal lunch he returned to his desk he was again unable to write anything of any worth. His impatience grew, and after the grandfather clock in the hall had struck three he changed from his old trousers into a pair of more respectable tweeds. He watched for her from a window, stroking his moustache as the sky behind the trees grew darker. Below him, Mr. Caddy, the gardener, could be seen plying his rake on the lower lawn, barrowing up leaves and wheeling them away.

The dusk was already thick when he discerned her figure on the drive. For fear of being observed at the window he stepped back a pace, and when he heard the ring of the bell, immediately followed by a volley of loud barking from Wessex, he hurried back to his study. Then there came a knock on the study door from one of the maids. The house had two maids, one called Nellie, the other Elsie, so similar in manner and appearance that he often mixed them up.

'Mrs. Bugler has arrived, sir. And Mrs. Hardy told me to say that she is not feeling well, sir. She hopes you can manage by yourself.'

The old man was neither displeased, nor very much surprised. Probably a head-ache, he thought.

'Is there a fire lit?'

'Yes, sir.'

He stood up and collected himself. Upon checking his apparel he discovered that at some point during the previous hour the top three buttons of his trouser fly had mysteriously unbuttoned themselves. He fumbled them shut, stepped into the corridor, descended the stairs and crossed the hall.

Gertrude Bugler was at this time in her mid-twenties and at the height of her beauty, although varying opinions as to the source of that beauty might have been put forward. Her hair was a conspicuous feature; thick and very black, with tresses that shone in the light of the fire, it was the kind of hair that in a former age might have adorned the head of a Cleopatra or a Helen of Troy, and a man with an imaginative cast of mind might have wished himself transmuted into a comb, merely for the pleasure of being drawn through its length. Yet another admirer might have noticed her lips, which were perfectly shaped, full and generous and red, with just the hint of a pout, and a third have chosen her face, which was faintly oval, her complexion smooth and pale. Her eyes were what most men noticed. Wide and innocent, with a bright, liquid sparkle, they hinted at a great depth of emotion and sensibility.

She was by the fire in the drawing room, tickling Wessex, who was flat on his back with his paws in the air.

'How good of you to come.'

She straightened, smiling.

'I am afraid Mrs. Hardy is unwell, but she sends her best wishes.'

She was wearing a green skirt with a white blouse and long grey cardigan, and despite the best efforts of the wind not one hair of her coiffure was out of place.

The old man drew the curtains. 'And your baby is in good health?' was his next inquiry, for he knew how women always loved to be asked about their children. 'What is her name? Diana, is it not?'

She agreed that it was. 'She is very well, though she doesn't sleep very regularly at night. She always wakes up about two o'clock, bright as a daisy, which is a little inconvenient.'

'What do you do when she doesn't sleep?'

'I sing to her, but it doesn't always work. Sometimes I bring her into my bed, but she kicks.'

'I am sure she is very beautiful, if she is anything like her mother.' His success in managing this compliment delighted him enormously. 'You should bring her here some time. I should love to see her. Mrs. Hardy and I never see enough children,' he added a trifle wistfully.

After a quick knock the two maids came into the room together, each bearing a tray – one with a teapot and crockery, the other with a plate of tiny white sandwiches from which the crusts had been cut. They put the trays down on a small table. With Florence not there, Gertie played the part of hostess and poured out the tea.

Once they were settled, they began to discuss theatrical matters. Gertie was a member of a local amateur dramatic company, and was currently playing the leading role in a play that would be performed in less than three weeks' time in the town's Corn Exchange. The old man was intimately involved, being the author of the play, a dramatic version of a novel that he had written some thirty years earlier, and he asked her a series of questions: how rehearsals were going, whether the actors and actresses knew their lines, and whether any of them had seen their costumes yet. Her answers were that, in general, all was going well – although one of the actors was growing a moustache that was still not particularly convincing. The old man, amused by this, stroked his own moustache, and sipped his tea. Then he came to the point for which he had been waiting.

'Over the years,' he said, 'various people in the theatre business have asked permission to stage the play in London. I have always been rather opposed to such an idea, but lately I have been approached by Mr. Frederick Harrison – the manager of the Haymarket Theatre. The Haymarket is one of the best theatres in London, and Mr. Harrison seems very enthusiastic.'

He was aware of her attentiveness. She was sitting on the sofa, very upright, with her cup of tea on her knees, but her eyes never left his face.

'Of course, if the play is to end up on the London stage, the question of who should play your part – the title role, the part of Tess – arises. There are a number of well-known actresses who have expressed considerable interest. However, some while ago, if I remember rightly, you asked me about the possibility of acting in a professional capacity, and I feel that you should have first refusal.'

His voice could not have been more cautious, but she answered immediately that she would love to play the part.

'It is very uncertain,' he told her. 'Nothing is definite. The reviews may not be good enough. But Mr. Harrison's plan, as I understand it, is to put on a production next spring, or in the early summer.'

'What of the rest of the cast?'

'They will be professional actors, of course.'

She seemed momentarily overwhelmed. Her lips were slightly parted; her teeth shone. He could sense the excitement running through her body. A slight flush even spread over her face.

'You must think about it carefully,' he advised. 'Talk to your husband. It would involve staying in London for some time.'

'O, but my husband won't mind, not at all!'

'Perhaps. But there is also your baby to consider. If, after consideration, you are sure you would like to do it, I will write to Mr. Harrison. I am neither encouraging nor discouraging you, although I can see you on the London stage. You would be a great success.'

The old man believed this sincerely. She was an actress of great expressive talent, and not only in his own estimation: London critics who had seen her perform in previous local productions had showered her with praise.

'I don't know how to thank you,' she said.

He modestly disclaimed all influence. 'There is no need to thank me – it is nothing to do with me, and it may come to nothing.'

They talked of it for some time. Seeing how much he had raised her hopes, he repeatedly counselled caution, telling her to look at it from all aspects. Acting in a professional company would, he said, be very different to acting with amateurs and he would entirely understand it if in the end she decided against going to

London. 'As I say, there are other actresses willing to play the part – including Sybil Thorndike, I believe,' he added dryly, unable to resist dropping the name of one of the most famous actresses of the day into the conversation.

Gertie was barely listening in her excitement.

'As early as the spring? How long will it run for?'

'I imagine that depends on its success. You must meet Mr. Harrison. He may well come down to see the play here – Wessex! Wessex, do stop that! Stop dribbling!' he said, for the dog was pestering her for a sandwich.

'May I give him one?' she asked.

'If you like.'

He watched as she held out a sandwich. Wessex took it from her fingers with remarkable delicacy, given his usual propensity to snatch. She smiled.

'I believe you spoil him.'

'Ah, he is an old dog. He is too old to be spoiled.' The old man was vaguely conscious of a desire to be in Wessex's position, licking her fingers. 'He likes you,' he said.

'I feel honoured,' she said, 'even if it is cupboard love.'

He tossed out another compliment. 'You are a favourite, Gertie. He likes you more than anyone else.'

She left a little later, thanking him again as she put on her coat. From the porch he watched as she disappeared into the darkness.

Once he had shut the door the house seemed unusually quiet, as if reflecting on what had passed. He stood by the grandfather clock, listening to its slow, measured ticks and the intervening silences, frowning slightly. He was conscious that he might have started a fire that would be hard to control. Should he have waited until the play had been performed at the Corn Exchange? What if it received poor reviews and Mr. Harrison changed his mind?

Then he remembered his wife. Reluctantly he went up the stairs to her bedroom. Florence was lying on her bed, with the curtains undrawn and the lamp on the bedside table casting such a feeble light that only her head and shoulders were visible in the general darkness. Her back was turned to him, and as he stood in the doorway and regarded her still shape he wondered if she was asleep. But she became aware of his presence. She turned with opened eyes.

'Has she gone at last? She stayed a very long time; it's nearly six o'clock. You must be worn out. Did she bring her baby?'

'No.'

'I couldn't face meeting her. She is always so healthy. I feel unwell even seeing her.'

The old man gave a grunt. 'She is much younger than you.'

This was true, for Florence was a score of years older than Gertie, but it was also true that Florence's health was far from good. She had a weak constitution and suffered not only from headaches and recurrent toothache, but also from neuritis, a condition caused by undernourished nerve endings, for which she took some large pills manufactured by a chemist in the town. Nor was this all: less than a month earlier, in London, she had had a surgical operation to remove a lump from her neck. It was to hide the scar that she had taken to wearing the fox stole, an object that the old man had never much liked.

She was wearing it now. She sat up, pulling it tight round her neck. 'It's very cold in here,' she complained. 'What did you talk about?'

'Nothing. Nothing of any consequence.'

'Who was on the telephone? Someone rang.'

'I didn't hear it.'

'It rang several times.'

'One of the maids must have answered it. I never heard it ring. Perhaps it was a bird,' he said, rather improbably.

'Thomas, it rang at least four or five times, about an hour ago. Of course it wasn't a bird. It was nothing like a bird.' Her voice was suddenly severe. 'I certainly didn't imagine it. I must ask the maids.'

'I'm sure you didn't,' he said hurriedly, not wanting to upset her.

There was a silence between them.

'I can't think who it can have been,' she said. 'Maybe it was Cockerell. He sometimes rings.'

'Why would he have rung?'

'I don't know. He does ring.'

The conversation was going nowhere.

The old man returned to the drawing room. The fire was burning down – let it burn, he thought, she had gone, she was on her way back to Beaminster, there was no point in wasting more coal. Yet something of her presence remained, even now. The cup from which she had drunk still sat in its saucer, and the faintest smudge of red was visible on the rim. There it had touched her lips – and there she had sat! There – one of the sofa cushions was indented – she had sat only minutes before! Something else caught his eye. On the sloping back of the sofa lay a long black hair.

With some difficulty he grasped it between finger and thumb and held it to the firelight. It trembled and swayed, stirring in the current of his breath like a living thing.

One of the maids entered with a tray. She stopped short at the sight of him.

'Excuse me, sir.'

'No, no, go on.'

He watched without a word as she cleared the tea things. Then he went upstairs to his study. He spread the hair on a sheet of white paper and turned up the lamp so that it shone as brightly as possible. In its light the strand of hair gleamed, thick and strong. A hair was merely a hair, but it was the kind of token that, in a romantic age, a secret admirer might have treasured – might have put in a locket and worn on a chain around his neck, and examined now and then when unobserved. According to the common view of such matters he was many years too old for that sort of thing, yet he was reluctant to throw it away. Why throw it away? Only a short space of time ago it had been part of her.

On one of the book-shelves in his study was a small volume bound in green leather, containing the collected poetical works of Percy Bysshe Shelley. Of English poets, there was no one whom he admired more than Shelley, a man of blazing courage and single-mindedness, ready to defy the narrow morals and social conventions of his age. The old man pulled down the book and turned its leaves until he reached the title page of a poem entitled 'The Revolt of Islam'. A long and obscure work, little read nowadays but breathless in ambition and beauty, its opening section was a passionate address to Shelley's young wife Mary, with whom he had eloped not long before. The section concluded with an image of the two lovers as a pair of tranquil stars, shining like lamps on a tempestuous world. It was on these last lines that the old man placed Gertie's hair.

As he closed the book and replaced it on its shelf in the book-case he was conscious of a certain absurdity in what he had done. He was eighty-four! Too old! What a thousand pities that he and she had not met when they were both young. Had she been born earlier, or he later, 'had time cohered with place', what then might have ensued? How different their lives might have been!

It was the type of reflection that often appealed to the old man as the subject for a poem: how different lives might have been in different circumstances. Picking up his pen, he dipped it in the ink-well and began to write freely.

The old man's interest in Gertrude Bugler was a complicated one, and he frequently found himself dwelling on her in the damp days that ushered in the start of winter. At one level, it might be said, he had always been an admirer of feminine beauty, and she was, without question, a radiant member of that company, young and healthy and full of *joie de vivre*. Yet, as he was well aware, there were other reasons that lay behind his sentiments towards her, and these had their origin in an incident that had occurred many summers earlier, on what he remembered, whether correctly or not, to have been his forty-seventh birthday.

He had spent the day at the house. During the morning he had worked hard on the final draft of a novel, and during the afternoon he and Emma, his first wife, had taken tea in the garden. The sun shone, but he had been in a reflective mood; birthdays always filled his consciousness with a sense of the brevity of life. How many years were left before Death laid its cold hand upon his shoulder? How much more had he to do before he could feel that he had accomplished his life's aims? True, he came from a long-lived family, but longevity was not something upon which anyone could count with certainty. He was not yet financially secure; and the house was proving much more expensive to run than he had originally anticipated. What if he were to fall ill, or what if, for some reason, his novelistic powers were to leave him? He felt no waning of ability, but there were many examples of writers whose once bright careers had ended badly. Such were the thoughts that came to oppress him, that summer's afternoon.

There was another reason for the cloud that hung on his spirits. His relations with Emma, which for so long had been excellent, had undergone a sharp turn for the worse. It was not largely his fault, or so he felt. Not long before, she had claimed – he recalled this distinctly – that he loved his mother more than her. This charge had caught him by surprise, although in an earlier novel he had written about just such a problem – there one of the central characters had been fatally torn between the demands made by his mother and those made by his wife.

He had considered Emma's words – which had struck a gaping wound in his heart – and rejected them. It seemed to him that she was asking him to choose between her and his mother, when no choice was necessary. Surely, he had said to her, it was possible for a man to love and respect his mother, and also to love and respect his wife. The one did not make the other impossible. But this careful, emollient response she had immediately and wilfully misinterpreted as confirmation of his elevation of his mother above her.

In truth, this dispute was merely a symptom of deeper division. They talked less to each other than they had once, and laughed even less. She was dissatisfied here in the country, and lately had begun to make disparaging remarks about the house: 'an ugly, misshapen house, on the edges of a narrow, ugly, superstitious town'. Such words, never to be forgotten! Now, this very day – his birthday – as they sat over tea, she had gone further, saying that they should sell up and return to London, where they would be among people of their own class and education.

Everything in this offended him deeply, even if he took care not to show it. The house did not, he thought, merit such an attack, and nor did the worthy folk of the town and its surrounding villages deserve to be dismissed in such terms. Among them were old friends and acquaintances, not to mention relatives, whom he had known his entire life; to him they were intensely interesting.

As for returning to London, he could scarcely have been more strongly opposed. True, there was a good deal to be said in favour of London, but even more on the other side. When he and Emma had last made their home in the city, when they had lived in the convenient suburban locality of Tooting – their house overlooking the Common – he had fallen so gravely ill that for a time the doctors, who seemed unable to decide whether he was suffering from a kidney stone, an internal haemorrhage, or some altogether different malady, had doubted that he would live. As he lay in what might have been his death-bed, with a strange glare of light in the room from the snow which, although it was October, had fallen a few days before and was now slowly melting, the countryside had beckoned him with a series of alluring, radiant images and he had understood that he and the city, for all its glitter, would never be wholly reconciled.

Emma had felt the same; she had been delighted to move back to Dorsetshire. Now, it seemed, she had changed her mind! The fickleness of women! Well, he had no intention of leaving. Here he was, and with quantities of novelistic material at hand. Even now, he was brooding on his next story – that of a beautiful young countrywoman destroyed by Fate – which, he thought, might be his best yet. To return to London would be fatal.

Thus the tea which he and his wife took that birthday afternoon on the sunlit lawn, and which, to an observer positioned some distance away and having no knowledge with which to interpret the scene, would have seemed an expression of a warm and harmonious marriage, was in reality a chilly affair in which few words were exchanged between the man and woman.

Towards the end of it Emma had returned to the subject that divided them.

'I must ask you to change your mind, Thomas,' she had stated in a peremptory tone.

'If by that you mean that we should move back to London, I cannot,' was his reply.

'Then,' said she, 'you are no longer the man I married.'

On this melodramatic note she had left him, stalking across the lawn to the house; and when, that night, he betook himself to bed, he found that she had moved to a room in the attic. Well, he thought, if he was not the man she had wed, neither was she the woman he had met at the altar. 'Marry in haste, repent at leisure' – that old saying was as true nowadays as it had ever been – and it struck him, not for the first time, but more forcibly than it had ever done hitherto, that the vows of lifelong love made by each party in the solemn rite of matrimony ran contrary to nature, forcing husbands and wives to endure each other's company when the fire that had brought them together was naught but ashes.

He slept badly. Waking before dawn and in need of a space of further reflection, he decided on a walk. He took a familiar path, one that crossed the low-lying meadows by the river and that, if followed long enough, led to the little church at Stinsford.

It was one of those lovely dawns often encountered in the Wessex countryside in early summer. The sky was a clear grey-blue, the air deliciously clean, and the birds were singing loudly. A still mist had risen from the damp earth and spread itself like a white lake over the meadows, and as he descended from the higher ground into this thin, gaseous stratum he found his feet, legs and waist swallowed up, while his chest and head remained clear. The pollarded crowns of the willows on the river-bank floated on a bed of nothingness, the rising sun shone brightly on the dancing particles, and the cables of a thousand spider webs swayed and shimmered. How, he asked himself, can I possibly leave this Eden for London?

The path took him close to the buildings of a farm, and he heard light female voices penetrating the vapour. Presently the luminous shapes of the dairymaids, five in number, each one carrying a stool and a bucket, came into view as they made their way from the barton towards the river. To his gaze, they seemed to him as much spiritual as physical beings; humble country lasses, but also angels, he thought to himself. Among them was one whose beauty stood out from the rest, and who fastened on his mind with the power of a dream: a girl with long dark hair and pale features. She and the rest passed down the slope without even a glance in his direction, entirely taken up with their own chatter.

Not being in a hurry, he followed them as they receded into the lake of mist. At first he was frustrated to find that the girl who had so engaged his interest seemed to have vanished. Then she reappeared, only to duck behind the body of one of the cows. He waited, hoping that the uneven textures of the mist might thin enough to afford him a further view of the maiden, and was presently rewarded by another vision of her face, revealing a full mouth, dark eyebrows and large eyes.

She was a type of womankind to whom he was particularly

susceptible. When, in thought, he used to picture his ideal woman, the face that he conjured was very like that of this innocent young Madonna of the meadows. How is this possible? he thought. Why has it taken until now for me to find her? What shall I do?

She and the other maids were now settling to their work, each one setting up her stool, and with the commencement of the milking a quietness settled on the scene. He imagined as much as saw the bevy of girls with their cheeks pressed against the smooth bellies of the cows, and seemed to hear the purring sounds of the streams of milk as they struck the sides of the pails.

A conversation between the maids began. Although he could discern neither the exact words, nor even the general sense, he was occasionally able to make out what, from its tone, he took to be a remark addressed to one of the cows. He then became aware, from the looks sent in his direction, that some of the girls had noticed him. Now, had he been younger, he could and would have walked up to them, engaged them in conversation, amused them with some light remark, impressed them – or, rather, impressed her, the maiden of his dreams. But he was middle-aged and balding, and more significantly – for the aforementioned particulars might not have been an insuperable obstacle – he was married. Well, there it was. Destiny had failed him by thirty years.

He left, walking on briskly, but the seed of the vision had germinated. Later that day he had to catch a train for London. He chose a window seat, and as the train left the town he was afforded a distant view of the meadows. The dawn was long past, the mist had evaporated, the milkmaids were gone, she was gone. Unheeding, the train bore him eastwards and finally deposited him in the dirt and noise of the great metropolis. He stayed the night in a small and unremarkable hotel; the next morning, as he walked down the great thoroughfare of Kingsway, crowded with pedestrians on their way to their places of toil, his mind was far away. He seemed to see what he had not actually seen: the girl with her cheek turned against the dappled flank of the cow, her hands kneading the teats and the milk squirting into the pail in alternate streams. A heron rose from the mist, its wings creaking faintly, a scatter of silver droplets falling from its stiff legs. He was so blind to his surroundings that he stepped into the traffic, and narrowly avoided being run down by a cab.

Back home, he made careful, roundabout inquiries of the farm manager, and discovered that her name was Augusta. She was the daughter of Jack Way, who ran the dairy. He knew Mr. Way, of course: a big, busy man whose loud voice often rang out as he bawled at the cows. He had seen Mr. Way wielding a heavy stick, clouting the rumps of cattle that lingered too long.

He made no attempt to contact her, having no possible pretext; besides, he knew himself too well not to fear that, were they to meet, he might be disappointed by what he found. It was better for Augusta to remain as he had seen her that dawn in the mist, a quintessence of unattainable, unapproachable beauty, never to be forgotten. It was she, he now thought, she and no one else, for whom he had been searching for so long; she who would become the model for Tess. The vision of his heroine grew out of the vision of the milkmaid.

A further thirty years had elapsed, and the beauty of the maiden to whom he would never speak had continued to haunt him. In those years – years that included the death of Emma – time had creased and leathered his skin, but she and the scene that she had inhabited so briefly remained unchanged. He associated her with all that pertained to the freshness and serenity of those early mornings in the water meadows: the profusion of pale pink flowers, the clumps of bright yellow kingcups, the dew-soaked grass. Details accrued, without his willing: the occasional squawk from some disgruntled coot on the nearby river, the distant call of a cuckoo.

In old age, naturally, these visions became rather less frequent than they had been hitherto. Then, some years ago, he had attended a rehearsal of one of his plays in the town, and she had appeared once more. He recognised her immediately. 'Who is she?' he had asked Harry Tilley, who was directing the play, and Tilley told him that she was Gertrude Bugler, daughter of Arthur and Augusta Bugler, who ran the Central Hotel in South Street. His heart had turned over. His mind was so confused he hardly knew what else Tilley had said, although he seemed to remember one remark: 'It'll be a lucky man who ends up putting a ring on her finger.' He watched her in rehearsal after rehearsal. He scarcely noticed the other actors and actresses, and when he talked to her, her attentive eyes left him half dumb. He found her sympathetic, interesting, eager – everything a young woman should be.

He had never bothered to unfold this history to Florence, when there had been no reason for so doing. A suitable moment had never presented itself, and besides, experience had taught him that in general it was best not to talk to her about private matters, especially those which lay deep in the past; she was easily upset, and inclined to misinterpret things.

Three evenings after Gertie's visit, he was in his bedroom on the first floor of the house. Wearing night-shirt, dressing gown and slippers, and holding a glass of whisky, he was seated on a wooden chair. He had a small woollen blanket over his legs. Two oil lamps were lit, one stationed by the bed and the other on a side table, and in the pool of light cast by the latter, Florence, seated in another chair, was reading aloud. She too was in her night-clothes, and in addition to a blanket over her legs she had the fox stole wrapped round her neck. Wessex, deep in sleep, one of his sandy-brown ears flopped over an eye, lay on the floor between them.

Ever since the start of their marriage she had read to him at night, usually for about an hour, occasionally for longer. It was part of the routine of their existence together, and an agreeable way of bringing the day to a natural close. Sometimes she read a novel, sometimes from a volume of poetry, so long as it was not too modern. The book that she was presently reading was one of the novels of Jane Austen, 'Pride and Prejudice', and for once it was her choice, not his. The old man was enjoying it a great deal. When he had read it last, a very long time ago, he had found Miss Austen a little narrow and strait-laced, but now she seemed to him an adroit observer of the human scene, and he was particularly amused to discern in himself a certain resemblance to the character of Mr. Bennet, the distant and reserved father of Jane and Elizabeth. In a pause between chapters, he said as much: 'Do you not think I resemble Mr. Bennet, to a degree?'

Florence saw the likeness instantly. 'Yes – you do, a little. Quite a lot, in fact.'

He nodded, pleased.

'I very much hope I do not resemble Mrs. Bennet,' she responded.

'Not in the least.'

'She is such an empty-brained chatterbox.'

'You are not in the least like Mrs. Bennet.'

'Thank you,' she said. 'What a relief! Shall I go on?'

'If you like.'

Moments such as this, the old man thought, were part of the success of his life with Florence. She was a good reader, sympathetic to the cadences of the prose, with a gentle, soothing voice. When she had been up in London for her operation, when he had been alone, he had tried reading to himself, both silently and out loud, but it had not worked. Late in the day his eyesight was not good enough to follow the print easily, and in any case it was not the same; just as tickling oneself fails to amuse the tickler, so reading to himself seemed a less than satisfactory affair.

He reached out for the glass of whisky, an inch of which he always drank at night and which helped him sleep. Florence never seemed to sleep that well, although he suspected that she slept better than she claimed. He watched her as she bent over the book.

Her hair lacked lustre, her complexion was dull, and she had bags under her eyes. This neuritis — and then the lump in her neck! Despite the operation, she seemed as frightened as ever. Why else did she keep it perpetually wrapped up?

The doctors, he was sure, had not helped. The old man had a natural distrust of doctors that probably went back to the days of his youth, when the English countryside was home to travelling quacks who sold medicines that upon chemical examination were found to consist of no more than flour and water. Although those disreputable pedlars no longer existed, it remained the case that doctors made their livelihoods out of the illnesses of their patients, and a cynic might have suggested that it was in the interests of doctors that their patients should remain unwell as long as possible. The old man sometimes felt that there was more than a little truth in the notion. Florence seemed to derive such pleasure from her visits to her London doctors.

It was inevitable that the contrast with Gertie, who was such a picture of health, should cross his mind. Of course, he reminded himself, she was younger than Florence by perhaps two decades. Florence was forty-five. How old was Gertie? Twenty-four, twenty-five? In a trick that no doubt came from his long career as a writer, he slipped into a kind of trance in which he pretended that she, not Florence, was sitting here now, reading to him.

'Thomas!' she broke into his reverie. 'Do you want me to go on?'

'If you are happy to.'

'I thought you were asleep.'

'I was listening. I was thinking of Mr. Bennet.'

'What were you thinking about him?'

'O . . . nothing much.'

She read on awhile, and he did his best to pay attention, or to seem to do so, but his thoughts came and went of their own accord. He noted the sparkle of the whisky as he turned the glass; he noted the gleam of Wessex's nose; he noted the shadows moving on the wall by his bed, among them two of Florence, each cast by a different oil lamp, one darker and stronger than the other. There was also his own double-shadow, shifting. It was common enough to see shadows as reminders of death, but what if they were more than that? What if shadows were owned not only by the quick but also by the dead, or if attached to one side of a shadow was the body of the living man, and to the other his dead self?

He explored the fancy that shadows lived outside time, possessing knowledge and consciousness; that they were not mute but had tongues, and could whisper what they knew of the invisible country beyond. It was a possible subject for a poem, the shadow soliloquising on its corporeal self, and if he had had the energy he would have fetched a pen.

Curious ideas such as these often entered the old man's mind when Florence was reading. They were like clouds drifting in a clear sky; he enjoyed looking at their shapes and structures, without any sense that they had any great significance.

'I think I shall stop now. Her sentences are so long.' She put her hand to the stole. 'My throat is a little painful tonight. I sometimes feel as if there is something still there.'

'You should try whisky.'

'I hate whisky. You know I hate the taste of whisky.'

The old man saw that he had said the wrong thing, or the right thing in the wrong tone. He kept quiet, which seemed the best course.

'You don't think there is anything still there?' she asked anxiously.

'I am sure there is not. If there were, the doctors would have found it.'

She closed the book and got up from her chair. She smoothed the front of her night-gown, turned down one of the oil lamps and seemed about to leave for her bedroom. Then she paused.

'Thomas,' she said, 'I have been thinking about the trees. We must get them cut back this winter. This is the time to do it. This is the time.'

Although it was far from the first occasion on which she had spoken to him about the trees, the old man was perplexed. Why mention it now?

'They are so oppressive,' she went on. 'Some of them are so big, when they sway in the wind they are so worrying. Imagine if one came down on the house. And they make the house so dark. They shut out the light, even at this time of year. We never see the sun!'

This was a very considerable exaggeration. The sun was low in November, but not so low that the trees hid it for the entire day.

'They are not at all dangerous,' he said. 'I know they make a lot of noise, but they are in excellent health, according to Mr. Caddy. You shouldn't worry about them; there is no need. They are perfectly safe.'

'Thomas, they are getting bigger and bigger, they are so much bigger than they were. You can't deny it. We are almost engulfed!'

Trees were fine things, noble things, thought the old man; he simply did not understand the problem.

'My dear, this is a very exposed, draughty spot; if there were no trees, imagine what it would be like. I remember it when Emma and I first came here, before the trees were planted. She was always complaining about the wind. If there were no trees, we should be blasted.'

'I am not talking about cutting them down, it is a matter of cutting back. They are so big. They take so much light. And the spores . . . the spores are so bad for one's health.'

She was becoming upset; this was what the neuritis did to her. 'Let us talk about it another time.'

'When?'

'In the morning. Now is not a good time. Has Wessex been out? Wessex? Have you been out?'

'Yes, he has,' she said.

They wished each other good night and she departed for her bedroom, where she no doubt took one of the pills that were meant to improve the blood supply to her nerves.

He forgot about the trees straight away. Instead, as he finished his whisky, he again allowed his mind to be occupied by thoughts of Gertie, with her pale complexion, oval face and liquid eyes. Fifteen miles of dark countryside lay between here and Beaminster, but he had no difficulty in bringing her to life. He saw her in her little cottage, standing by the fireside, hoisting her skirts to warm her legs. He saw her red lips as she yawned, and the white of her teeth, and the skin shining on her arms, just as he had once imagined Tess yawning, red-mouthed, arms shining like satin. Gertie was the very incarnation of Tess.

Sighing to himself, he wondered whether he would ever have the opportunity to explain how close she was to his heart. The discrepancy in their ages seemed to make such a disclosure impossible; nonetheless, between them there was a perfect reciprocity of thought and emotion, or so the old man felt.

CHAPTER II

✿ ✿ ✿

Last night I asked him, not for the first time, for indeed I have asked him a number of times, if we could have a few of the branches taken down as the house is now in shadow for much of the day. The problem is most acute in the summer, when we are engulfed by foliage, but even now, with winter almost upon us, the trees are an oppression. They oppress me, they darken my life. This is a dark house. He would not discuss it. I tried again this morning.

'Thomas,' I said, 'forgive me for mentioning it again but we must talk about the trees. I know you are very preoccupied, but this is the right time of year – this is the time for tree work. The birds are not nesting now.'

We were at the breakfast table, and he said nothing, not a word, he looked elsewhere as if he had not heard me. He looked at his toast. He studied his toast. I wondered if I had spoken or if I had merely imagined speaking. Had my senses deserted me? Had my words left my mouth or had they stuck in my throat?

I drew a breath. I pressed on. 'You said in the summer we could not cut back then, because of the birds, and now it is nearly winter. The servants agree with me – they agree entirely. Mr. Caddy agrees too, I have spoken to him. The trees have to be cut back sometime. And the ivy, too,' I added, aware that I was annoying him by my persistence, that he would prefer me not to mention the subject.

He looked at his toast as if it was burnt. He fiddled with the handle of his tea-cup.

He believes that the trees must not be touched for fear of wounding them. Can trees be wounded? Trees are not sentient creatures. He talks of mutilation and disfigurement. To care for the feelings of birds and animals is one thing, yet to believe that trees are capable of suffering as human beings suffer is quite another. What of my suffering? I am still not well, I know I am not well. The doctors say that on all accounts I must avoid straining my nerves. Can he not see how the trees are hampering my recovery? Can he not see how I suffer?

'This is such a dark house,' I said. 'I feel everything would be different if there were more light.'

He raised his eyes to mine. 'Later, Florence, later,' he said, softly. 'Not now. I am thinking.'

I fell silent. I could say no more, for the moment. He was thinking; that is, he was thinking about his work; a poem was possibly taking shape inside his head. How should I know what shapes form inside his head? All I know is that on account of the trees I am condemned to shadow. I wish he would understand how dark and gloomy they make the house, and how much the absence of sunlight oppresses my spirits during the winter months, but this it seems is of no consequence when set against the supposed feelings of the trees and the nesting birds.

This is how our breakfasts always are. I am not meant to speak and therefore I do not speak, although in the spaces that might be occupied by speech I often address him with silent questions. When were you ever happy? Were you happy when you were a boy? What could make you happy now? Should we not be happy? Is it not in our natures, is it not part of our beings, to strive for happiness? Has your writing made you happy? Would you not be happier if you were to say, I have written what I have written, enough is enough, and to put down your pen? What iron compulsion makes you continue? Thomas?

My life is full of these unanswered questions.

What irks me, more than anything, is that he is perfectly capable of gaiety. When guests arrive for tea it is as if an electric light were switched on (not that we have any electricity here!): suddenly he becomes a different human being. He chats and jokes and entertains, and reminisces about his childhood and tells confidential witty anecdotes. He performs. None of our visitors has any idea what he is truly like. They *marvel* at him! 'What a marvel he is!' they confide in me as they leave. (O that word, 'marvel'!) 'So sprightly! So spry! Such vigour!' I nod in agreement. As soon as they are gone, the light switches off; he relapses to his former self.

The truth is, he cannot be bothered to make an effort for me, his wife. I who do nothing but make an effort for him, I whose whole life is devoted to him, I who tiptoe after him, lay out his clothes, help him dress, read to him for hours every evening and do all that is humanly possible to make him happy, I am not worthy of the performance.

He left, with Wessie at his heels. O Wessie, Wessie, stay with me, I beseeched him silently, do not leave me now – it was all I could do not to call him back – but they were both gone. I remained at the table with my feelings, my words which I may or may not have uttered. The door closed. My hand shook as I tried to drink my cup of coffee.

I am not suggesting that all the trees should be cut down, merely that those nearest to the house should be thinned. Is that so much to ask? To thin the trees so that light, blessed light, will once again shine freely into the rooms? Was this not his intention when he built the house, forty years ago? The house faces south; it should be filled with sunlight, and yet it is dark. But there is nothing to be done, until later; later, later, it is what he always says; and so the matter is forever postponed, and meanwhile the trees grow ever nearer. The branches are nearly scratching at the panes of the windows, and the gutters are blocked with autumn leaves, and the chimneys are covered in ivy. The air is damp. Even the lawns are affected: they are thick with moss and ugly worm-casts.

I cannot feel that trees are necessarily friendly creatures. In the right situation, I admit, they are pleasant enough. Here they are hostile. Left alone, they will overwhelm the house. This is how I choose to begin my account, which I tell to myself, since there is no one else to tell.

I am busy, too; I have my daily round of tasks. There are the hens to let out of their coop. They have a little field to the side of the garden, away from the trees, in sunshine. I bought this field with my own money, four years ago, since he would not buy it, although he has so much more money than I, although he may well be, according to Cockerell, the wealthiest writer in the entire country. Is that possible? How does Cockerell know? I waited to see if he would offer to buy the field for me, but it did not seem to occur to him. If it did occur to him, he gave no sign of it having occurred to him. I might have asked him directly, but I have my pride. Thus I had to raid my own small savings. That is how things are. That is the way of things.

I open the door of the coop and out they come; seven lovely hens. 'My beauties, my darlings. How are you today?' I love my hens and I talk to them in a particular voice which I persuade myself – with what truth I cannot say – they recognise. O, but I am sure that they do. I have names for them all. This is Betty; this is Jess; that is Hetty. Dear little Hetty! That one is Maud.

In the low sunshine they glow with light. Their feathers shimmer. 'Patience, patience,' I say to them, 'patience, my dears.' They fuss and cluck as I hold up the bag of grain, and then I dip in my hand and throw out the seed. They make a quick rush and begin to peck and stab, and as they do so wheedling sounds of gratitude come from their throats. Even when they are eating! How sweet and contented they are!

It does me good to see such contentment, I who feel so little contentment. It does me good to be in the sun, away from the long shadows of the trees.

I scatter four handfuls of grain. Some of the hens – Betty, and Alice, particularly, are bigger and more forceful than the others. Please, please, I beg you, be patient! I have enough for you all.

They are laying well at the moment. Yesterday, I collected three brown eggs; today, three more, which will do very well for this evening's dinner. I admit that there are times when I think that I should be kind and allow them to keep their eggs, to sit on their eggs. Would that be kinder? But the eggs would not hatch, there would be no chicks, they would sit and sit and nothing would happen, which would be dreadful for them, they would be perpetually disappointed. I think it is better that I take the eggs, to spare them that disappointment. They are fond of me, they do not care whether I take the eggs.

The sun shines over the field, the birds sing – O, I admit, my ownership of the field does afford me a certain satisfaction, for almost everything else is his. The house and its contents belong to him; they were his long before I became his wife. I live in the shell of his ownership. The field is mine, however, and therefore perhaps, upon further consideration, I am glad that I bought it with my own money, that he did not buy it for me. Yes, I am glad, I think, although I would have liked him to have offered to buy it for me, as he might easily have done. I am not saying that he is miserly but, if I may draw the distinction, he is very careful; he does not realise how much money he has and does not believe it, even when he is told. He avoids conversations about money, just as he avoids conversations about the trees. These are not matters I am able to talk to him about, among so many other matters.

Obstinacy is ingrained into his very nature. It blinds him to common sense. It makes him deaf to all persuasion. Was he always like this, or has his obstinacy grown over the years? He cannot have been like this as a young man. But then, how do I know? I did not know him when he was young. Even though I have seen a number of paintings and photographs, to relate the young man there with the old man now defeats me. Inasmuch as I am able to imagine it, he was exactly the same then as he is now.

To give one instance of his obstinacy: the telephone. I could not understand the nature of his objection, although it seemed to be based on some irrational fear of the instrument. He murmured vaguely: 'Human beings have succeeded in communicating for centuries without the use of a telephonic apparatus; I do not understand why it must suddenly become a necessity.' – 'Thomas,' I said, somewhat exasperated, not least by the absurdity of the phrase 'telephonic apparatus' in this day and age, 'of course, it is not a necessity; it is a convenience. It would be very convenient to have a telephone here. It would be convenient for ordering groceries, and coal, and for visitors.'

I went on to say that it was becoming odd for us, in a house this size, not to have a telephone.

'There would be wires everywhere,' he said. 'They are very ugly.'

'We will soon be used to them,' I countered.

He became a trifle petulant. 'Florence, I do not want to be used to them. Merely because the world happens to have moved in a certain direction, it does not follow that we have to move with it. Besides, there is the cost.' (As if he would even notice the cost, when he is so wealthy! The wealthiest writer in the entire country!)

Later, he said that the press would discover the number and that the telephone would never stop ringing. The noise would be an intrusion and would prevent him from working. 'And what if it rings in the night?' he went on. 'Imagine that; we shall be woken by it ringing and you will hurry out and fall down the stairs and break your neck.' I did not know whether to laugh or cry. 'Is that likely?' I asked. 'Who on earth is going to ring in the night?' He gave me a particular look, a look that I have come to know well, intended to convey the message that he was impervious to all argument, however reasonable.

I enlisted the help of Cockerell, when he next came to stay. He always pays greater attention to Cockerell than to me, although I am his wife. I took Cockerell aside and asked him whether he had had a telephone installed at his home in Cambridge, and he said that he had had one for four years and that it had come in jolly handy as it was so much quicker than the post and capable of carrying so much more information than the telegraph. Exactly! 'Well,' said I, 'if you would persuade Thomas, I should be very grateful.' So he said he would – that is, he would try – 'But, Florence,' he said, 'your husband is a very hard man to bring round, once he has set his mind against something.' – 'Sydney,' said I, 'he is an ox! He doesn't like anything new; he would like the world to be as it was in eighteen fifty! The world has changed, like it or not. But, please, don't tell him that I asked you to say anything; if you do, he will set himself against it on principle. He is so prickly nowadays.'

The argument that Cockerell employed was that, if my husband were to fall ill and to need a doctor, a telephone would be immensely valuable and might even save his life. I had told him that much myself, had advanced the self-same point; he had paid not a farthing of attention. Once the point was made by Cockerell, however, it carried more weight; he nodded.

'Is it not the case that, sometimes, the apparatus remains alive when it should not?'

'How do you mean, alive?'

'It is still alive. It listens when it should not.'

'Thomas –' I broke in – 'a telephone is not alive; it is a machine.'

'What I mean,' said he (to Cockerell, not to me; although I had spoken, it was as if I had not spoken), 'is that the line remains open when it should not. The operators at the exchange have the ability to eavesdrop on one's private conversations, without one's knowledge.'

'Where on earth did you hear that?'

'I believe that it occurs very commonly.'

'I doubt it very much,' Cockerell told him. 'I doubt it very much indeed! The operators are far too busy to spend their time eavesdropping on people's conversations. Is that truly your main objection to the telephone?'

'It is one of my objections. If something is possible, then, human nature being what it is, it is likely to happen. You don't have newspaper reporters poking about all the time, trying to discover details of your private life. It is different for me.'

'That may be true,' Cockerell agreed. 'But I hardly believe –' he stopped. 'You see, I never use the telephone for conversation. It is simply a very handy little thing to have, for contacting people, in emergencies. You don't have to use it yourself.'

Eventually my husband gave way, which pleased me, although I admit that I was slightly aggrieved that Cockerell had succeeded where I had failed. The truth is, he trusts Cockerell's judgement but does not trust mine; that is the truth.

On the day the telephone was installed, and for several days afterward, he was very irritable and claimed that he had been unable to write a word on account of it. 'But, Thomas,' I said, 'no one has rung! We have not had a single call!' – 'No,' said he, in a very melancholy voice, 'but I am thinking of it waiting to ring. It will ring sooner or later. It is there, in my mind; waiting.'

Mr. Caddy is wheeling his barrow past the vegetable garden. Mr. Caddy has been gardener here at Max Gate for a long time. He is a man of about fifty, entirely bald, with wide ears, and a ruddy face which comes not only from working all his life out-of-doors but also, I suspect, I suspect strongly, from drink. At my approach he drops the handles in order to touch his forehead.

'The gutters need unblocking,' I tell him. – 'Yes, ma'am.' – 'Could you do it soon, please?' I ask. 'Before the next storm, if possible. It is almost winter. Winter is almost upon us.' – 'Yes, ma'am.' – 'And if you could pick up some of these twigs and sticks, and rake the drive.'

He nods and yes ma'ams me for a third time, a little slowly, as if behind his respectful exterior he is laughing at me. Yes, for some unaccountable reason I feel sure he is laughing at me, and that my stole must have slipped. He is staring at my scar. A terror seizes me, it is all I can do not to break down on the spot and gibber like a mad-woman. What has become of me? Pull yourself together, Florence, I tell myself, remember who you are. You are mistress here.

I hold his eye and say: 'I very much hope we shall be allowed to cut back some of the trees this winter.'

'Yes, ma'am.'

As I walk on I adjust the stole which, it turns out, has not slipped at all, but I am quite sure that he was thinking of it. Mr. Sherren, the surgeon who performed the operation, said that it was a very neat job and that the scar would fade in time but it has not faded at all; it is still red and ugly, even when I cover it with powder. I hate looking at it in the glass. But I can hardly speak too highly of Mr. Sherren, who is one of the best surgeons in London, if not the very best; of all the doctors I have ever met, he is the one in whom I feel most confidence. As soon as I saw him I felt more confident. He examined my neck with so much care and spoke to me so kindly. He has a very soft, warm voice and gentle hands. I noticed how long and delicate his fingers were, the fingers not of a surgeon but a pianist. His finger-nails were perfect. I said to him, 'I always knew it was cancerous, but no one ever seemed to believe me,' and he said, 'Mrs. Hardy, you have come to the right place.'

When he visited me after the operation we had a long talk in which he told me that as a young man he had been to sea as a ship's surgeon, which he had loved, and in return I mentioned the years I spent as a school-mistress, and how fulfilling that had been. I said to him (something I strongly believe) that there is nothing more important than education. 'Sometimes,' I said, 'I think I might still be teaching now, but for my wretched health. Good health is such a blessing.'

He was very sympathetic. He said that good health was as important as good education, and that people who have a naturally strong constitution often find it so hard to understand what life is like for those who do not. In my experience that is true, very true.

Mr. Sherren then asked whether my husband was writing any more novels, and I said that he had given novels up completely and wrote nothing but poetry. I went on to mention that I too was a writer, and that I had written several books for children. He was interested and wanted to know more, and of course I had to admit that they had been published a long while ago and that I had written scarcely anything in the past few years except for one or two magazine articles. My days (I said) are so taken up with domestic duties that I have very little time for writing on my own account, and even when I do have time, no energy. I have not written on my own account for a long time, except in my head. Nonetheless, once I have recovered my health, once I have truly recovered, I shall be able to write again. That is what I constantly tell myself, and what I told Mr. Sherren, who said he would be very interested indeed to read anything I wrote. He was certain that I would be able to write again. 'If there is one thing that I have learnt about life,' he said, 'it is that it is never too late.' There was something about the confidence with which he uttered those words that I found quite inspiring.

I did not tell Mr. Sherren that my husband does not like me to write, although that also is true. When we first met he encouraged me, but soon after we were married this came to an end, or so it seems to me. Indeed I have come to suspect that he despises my writing. He has never said as much, not in so many words, but I have not forgotten what happened over my 'Book of Baby Beasts'. It was a book for young children, describing the characteristics and behaviour of a large number of infant creatures found in the English countryside, and at the start of each chapter there was a little poem, for all children love the sound of a poem as I know so well from my days as a school-mistress. I always did my best to encourage a love of poetry in my pupils, and every morning after saying prayers and taking the roll I used to read them a few verses. Even now I remember the hush in the class-room and their eager faces, listening intently, drinking in the words.

Many of the poems in the book were written by my husband, but there were five that I had written myself, among them one poem in particular I was very proud of, of which I was very proud (grammar is so important). It was about a hedgehog, Master Prickleback.

> My name is Master Prickleback,
> And when alarmed I have a knack
> Of rolling in a ball
> Quite snug and tight, my spines without,
> And so if I am pushed about
> I suffer not at all.

As I say I was very proud of this poem, which I thought and still think is as good as any of his poems in the book, and I remember that he said that it was very good. However, a year or more after we were married there was a very strange incident when I awoke in the night and heard what I believed to be a baby crying in the garden beneath the window. When the cry came again, I instantly jumped to the conclusion that some servant girl must have left a baby that I should be able to take in and bring up as my own. I had never had this idea before, but now it grew upon me with tremendous force, and I ran through to Thomas, who was asleep, and he rose promptly and together we went to the window. The night was still and warm, with half a moon, but the ground around the trees was all in dark shadow. 'It is a pleasant night,' he said, after a time. – 'I heard it clearly,' I said, for I thought that he did not believe me; 'I promise you; I know I heard it. We must search the garden. I am going down. Thomas, I beg you, let us search the garden. I am not imagining it, I assure you. I am sure that there is a baby.' He hesitated for a moment, and then perceiving my state of anxiety he turned and put on his dressing gown and slippers. Together we went down the stairs. The bolts on the back door sounded very loud as he pulled them back, and Wessie began to bark. I was afraid that he would wake the maids who would think that the house was being burgled and I rushed to let him out. We proceeded into the garden. I was barefoot. The dew was very heavy and silvery blue in the moonlight, and Wessie who was very excited to be out at such an hour raced to and fro. Dogs can smell so well in the dark. I heard the cry again near the vegetable garden; it now had a piteous, mewing quality. 'There!' I said. We walked towards it, and found two hedgehogs in the act of congress. Their journey towards each other could be traced by the paths in the dew. Wessie sniffed at them, whereupon they recoiled and curled into their defensive postures. I felt very foolish to have mistaken the cry of a hedgehog for that of a baby, and apologised very much, but he very kindly said that it was an easy enough mistake to make, that the sounds were not that dissimilar and that he might well have made the same mistake himself. Even so, I was so very distressed that it took me hours to get to sleep.

In the morning when we were getting dressed I could see the funnier side of it, and I reminded him of my Master Prickleback poem. 'We saw Master and Mistress Prickleback,' I said. To my surprise he claimed not to remember the poem, so I recited it to him. 'O, yes,' he said, 'very good,' but in a tone that could not have been less complimentary.

'Thomas,' I said, 'it is only a poem for children, you know. It is not pretending to be great literature. Do you think it so very bad? It was meant for children, you know. Children love it.'

He was bending over, tying the laces of one of his shoes. In those days he was still capable of tying his shoe-laces. He said nothing at all, not a word.

'Please,' I said, 'tell me the truth! Do you think it is a bad poem? Is that what you think?'

'I said that it was very good, if I remember correctly. Did I not?'

'You did, but your tone seemed to me to indicate the opposite.'

He began to tie the laces of the other shoe. 'You misinterpret my tone. My opinion is that it serves its purpose admirably.'

He added, as though to soften the blow, that he was sure that children appreciated it, although that was not what I had said, I had said that children love it. There is such a difference between loving something and appreciating it. All the difference in the world! It was clear that he despised the poem, and also that he despised me for writing it. When I say that my entire being felt crushed I am not exaggerating, not at all.

Thus I lost heart. Lacking encouragement, I wrote no more on my own account, and instead I act as his secretary, answering letters, making copies, filing. In addition, I labour ('labour' is the word; it is one of the labours of Hercules as I once said to Cockerell) on his biography, using his old notes to piece together the story of his life. I am glad to do so, I do not complain, it is a very sensible arrangement. Who else could do it? All the same, when, as usually happens, he takes my sentences – the sentences over which I have taken so much care – and writes them over in his own creaking style, it is a little galling. It galls me. It is as if he cannot bear to hear the sound of my true voice. After all, I am supposed to be the author of this biography! Is it so surprising that I am a little galled at the way he rewrites my sentences?

I do not complain. Nor do I point out his deficiencies of style. If I dared to do so, I know what would happen: he would not argue or seek to defend himself, but would withdraw into his own fortress. Yet I am not alone: others have commented on his antique vocabulary and his convoluted, Teutonic sentence constructions. Sometimes I think it is as if my husband was a great tree and I stunted from living in his shadow.

Of this much I am sure: that it is not possible for me to write well on my own account until I have recovered my health, and it is not possible for me truly to recover my health until the trees have been cut back. Once they are cut back, I shall feel such a weight lifted off me. But unless and until the trees are attended to I cannot begin to write for myself.

Here I should like to mention my strong belief that the growth on my neck may have been caused, at least in part, by the close proximity of the trees. I believe it is very probable, or if not very probable then at least highly possible, that the invisible spores shed by the trees, countless numbers of which I must inhale each day, play an as yet unknown but significant part in the formation of cancerous growths. Some time ago I asked Dr. Gowring for his opinion on the matter, but Dr. Gowring is next to useless, a country doctor with an inflated reputation, and all he would say, with a supercilious air, and in a decidedly offhand manner which made me feel that I, as a mere woman, should not have dared to give utterance to such a thought, was that there was no scientific evidence to support my thesis about spores. I could barely control my anger. 'But Dr. Gowring,' I said, 'it is possible, is it not?' With some reluctance, he agreed that it could not be discounted as a possibility.

I naturally put the same question to Mr. Sherren when he came to see me after my operation, and he said that it was a most interesting and original idea. Sensing that he was strongly sympathetic to my thesis, I said that I wished someone would investigate it thoroughly. 'For,' I said, 'if it were true, it would be so valuable.' He agreed, and said that he would certainly mention it to his colleagues in the medical profession. 'If only,' he said, with a sigh, 'we knew the true causes of things.' I said to him: 'I dare say I should persuade my husband to have our trees cut back. We have so many trees crowding round the house, we live in a half-darkness, it is quite sepulchral.' He smiled. 'Some day,' he said, 'I am sure, we shall have a better understanding of these things.'

In a small way, therefore, I hope that I may have contributed something towards the saving of lives, even if my life in itself counts for so very little.

*

Unlike my husband, I have no study of my own; I use a corner of the drawing room, where I have a little walnut writing-desk. Entering the room now, with the day's post – a clutch of letters, and a small parcel, wrapped in string and brown paper – I am frustrated to see wet soot covering not only the hearth but also part of the rug. This is not the first time. The chimneys have not been swept for three years, and the drawing room flue is probably blocked by a jackdaws' nest, a mess of twigs and straw. One watches the jackdaws carrying twigs into it in the breeding season. The fire never seems to draw well. When I speak to my husband about getting in the sweep, he always prevaricates. 'Later,' he says – how often have I heard that word! 'Later' should be inscribed on my tombstone, I sometimes think! I have told him that, if we do not have the chimneys swept soon, it will be too late, there will be a fire, and we will all burn alive. I have told him this, but it makes no difference. It is another instance of his obstinacy.

Let me give another instance: the motor-car. Motor-cars exist, they have existed for a number of years, they are very convenient and useful machines, for that reason I have attempted to persuade him to buy one. A motor-car would be more than convenient, I say to him, it would be liberating; we could drive round the countryside and look at some scenery, or we could visit the sea. The sea is not that far away and on the spur of the moment we could visit the sea. Would that not be lovely? On a day like this, with a little sun, to walk along the beach and smell the sea-air? To breathe the sea-air? We could take Wessie, too! Would it be so hard to unchain yourself from your desk for one day, for a single day, to visit the sea? But it doesn't have to be the sea; if you prefer, we could visit a church or some prehistoric earth-work, or we could even go to Stonehenge! How easy it would be, and how good for us both! We could easily afford a car, after all you are the wealthiest writer in the country according to Cockerell. And, I hurry on, for I have thought about this a great deal, I have waited my moment, I have the arguments at my finger-tips, we would not need to employ a driver because I should learn to drive. A motor-car is not like a horse and carriage; it is as easy for women to drive as men, or so people say, and it would make all the difference to me, it would give me such confidence, I who have always lacked confidence, it might even give me the sense that I was in control of my own destiny, whatever my destiny is. Of course I have never managed to say all this to him, most of it is merely what I imagine I might say. The truth is that we do not have our own motor-car and therefore whenever we wish to go anywhere we have to plan well in advance, employing Mr. Voss, who works for a taxi company in the town, and I have to sit in the back as women always do, and Thomas who insists on sitting in the front never hears a word when I speak, or if he does hear he does not reply, or if he does reply I cannot hear him. Conversation between the front and the back of a motor-car is all but impossible. I do not understand why we cannot have a motor-car. Is it that they did not exist in his youth, that he regards them as in some way contrary to nature, that they are too noisy? Or that he cannot bear the thought of being driven by me? Or that I might drive to the sea by myself, leaving him alone? My suspicion is that he does not want us to have a motor-car because, while he may not realise it, part of him wants to keep me here, looking after him, day after day, night after night.

Elsie and Nellie are both in the scullery, pretending to polish the silver. I know what goes on here. Every day they put out the silver as if they are about to polish it, and then they sit and gossip. This happens every single day!

They look at me in a resentful manner.

'I am afraid there has been another fall of soot in the drawing room. Did neither of you see it when you drew the curtains?'

'No, ma'am.' It is Nellie who speaks; Elsie is a mouse of a girl.

'Well; there it is. I don't care which of you does it, but please get it done.'

'Yes, ma'am.'

[43]

They do not like me, I am convinced of it. I cannot tell why, but I have never known how to talk to servants. It is just the same with Mr. Caddy and Mrs. Simmons. I never manage to strike the right note, I always sound so severe. Did his first wife manage any better?

While they set to work I take Wessie outside and give him his usual brush. We both enjoy this. Dear little Wessie! I don't know what I would do without Wessie, truly I don't.

Five minutes later, I am back in the drawing room (which still smells of soot). Settled at my desk, I examine the post. More than half of the letters bear London post-marks, which is usual; the majority of my husband's readers are city-dwellers who dream of living in the country. For them the country is a perpetual summer. O, what I could tell them of country life in the winter!

Carefully I slit the envelopes with my paper knife. First, a letter from the President of the Wimbledon Literary and Scientific Society, inviting Thomas to attend one of its monthly meetings. 'I am confident that you will have a warm and appreciative audience, for many of our members are avid readers of your novels and will be gratified by your presence.' The answer is no: honoured as he is by the invitation, his health is not good enough nowadays for him to travel up to London, but he wishes the Society well.

Secondly, a letter from a female journalist, who is preparing an article for a newly established women's magazine, 'The Modern Woman'. She claims to be a lifelong devotee of his work (as do most journalists), and asks whether she may call here in order to carry out an interview. The magazine is illustrated, and she hopes that it is acceptable for a photographer to accompany her. She suggests two dates in the middle of December or, failing those, one in early January (any later and she will miss what she calls her 'dead-line'). She and the photographer will catch the London train and arrive about noon, if that is convenient. The answer, again, and emphatically, is no, it is not convenient: he is too busy to give interviews, but wishes her well with her article.

A letter from The National Society for the Prevention of

Cruelty to Children asks for support. I reply to this on my own behalf, sending a cheque for five pounds. I can ill afford it, but the way that children are treated in the slums of the East End horrifies me.

What next? Two letters requesting his autograph. These autograph-hunters are so persistent. Many of them employ cunning ruses, pretending to be young children, writing in misshapen capitals; but I am not fooled.

Next, a letter from a Miss Eleanor Pope of Islington, who declares that she loves his novels more than those of any other writer, and praises his profound understanding of the female mind; even George Eliot, she writes, does not come close. O! Miss Pope! Sit down, let me tell you the truth –

Another letter: this one from a Mr. Edward Bowles of East Grinstead who has apparently expended much time and energy on the task of identifying the locations of the places mentioned (though with fictional names) in the novels. He attaches a list of such identifications which he is 'pretty well certain' are correct, but if there are any errors he would like to know of them. Several places, despite much research (last spring he undertook an extensive cycling tour of Wessex), he has been unable to identify. He lists them. Mr. Bowles appears to be entirely unaware that: a) a book has been written on this very subject and b) several prefaces to the novels make it clear that certain locations are impossible to identify because they do not correspond to real locations!

Now to the parcel, which turns out to hold a manuscript collection of poems by a gentleman of St. Albans, one Harold Blacker. Mr. Blacker has written before, it seems, for his accompanying letter, in a florid hand, begins thus:

My dear Sir,

Thank you for the exceptionally kind letter which you sent me last year about 'The Rains of Paradise'. I am pleased to say that I have now completed another volume, 'The Rowan Tree

– An Odyssey in Twenty Poems', which I enclose with great admiration for a man who as all acknowledge stands preeminent in the world of modern letters.

Why am I spending my life on this drudgery? Am I not worth more? I am a writer too! Jumping up, so suddenly that my chair topples to the floor, I rush up the stairs to his study. I fling open the door and brandish the paper knife which I find sprouting in my hand. Why do you never think of me, you who are supposed to know so much about the female mind? Why do you take me for granted? Why do you never write any poems about me? What has happened between us? What about the trees? Why O why will you not accede to this one, small request? Why are you so obstinate?

Of course I do nothing of the sort – just think of my reception! Instead, as his dutiful secretary, I pull up my typewriter, and answer each letter in turn, taking a carbon copy which I put in a file. Already I feel exhausted. Even as I sit here, my entire body seems to be aching and my nerves are strung to snapping point. I cannot breathe!

How ridiculous this is. All round the country there are women whose situations are incomparably worse than mine, women living in the slums, women too poor to eat properly, women married to ne'er-do-wells and drunkards who beat and abuse them. What do I have to complain of, of what do I have to complain? I live a more than comfortable life here, I am lucky to be alive, I have books and clothes and food and a husband who loves me even if it is not in his nature to show it; count your blessings, Florence. You are alive! Think of the hens, pecking and strutting; unconscious creatures, they live for each moment, they do not fret themselves with questions. Think of little Wessie as he scampers hither and thither, his black nose twitching as he investigates some new scent on a blade of grass. These are good thoughts, and yet how hard I find it to hold on to them, how easy to revert to the old way of thinking:

the weight of the trees, the length of the silences, the passage of the years, the sense of my inner self slowly darkening and drying, the sense of myself dry as an old gourd, dark as a shadow, the sense of something having gone wrong without being able precisely to say what it is, the sense of not being as completely alive as I ought to be, the sense of not being alive at all. Perhaps that is it, the sense that life is passing me by, or has already passed me by without my noticing; or perhaps it is the sense that this house is hostile to me because I am not his first wife. Sometimes I convince myself that she lies at the heart of the problem, and that she still lives here, in the air, in the trees, in the empty rooms; she is the true mistress of the house, and this is why I have such difficulties with the servants. No doubt she ordered the servants about without the slightest qualm. Do this! Do that!

I am determined not to mention her name, I am determined not even to think her name, although one of the things I have learnt is that often in trying not to think about a particular individual one ends up thinking of nothing but that individual, and in exactly the same way the more I try not to think about my neck the more vividly it returns and with it the possibility that Mr. Sherren for all his skill failed to remove every last particle of the infected tissue which is consequently growing back at this very moment. My mind is not my own, that is the truth, I cannot control my thoughts.

But, the truth is, the house is like a shrine to her. The calendar on the desk in his study is permanently set to the date upon which they first met, the shawl he insists upon wearing around his shoulders as he writes, and without which, he claims (a ludicrous claim), it is impossible for him to write well, was made by her; and on her death day we have to stand in po-faced solemn ceremony over the grave at Stinsford in which she is buried and in which he himself eventually plans to be buried (an honour from which I am presumably excluded). Let me add that the shrubbery in the drive is in the shape of a heart to signify his love for her, a love which, if it ever existed, did not exist in the last years of their marriage, when they lived in a state of mutual hostility. He has forgotten all that. (Have I forgotten? I have not forgotten.)

He sits there in the gloom and writes I know not what: another melancholy poem, in all probability. If the trees were cut back, is it not possible that he would begin to write poems that were not so very dark and melancholy, but full of light and hope? This is what I often think, that things might be different, be better.

Lying on my bed after lunch I watch the light moving in the sky and the flicker of the pale green veiny undersides of the ivy leaves on the other side of the window. The house is as quiet and peaceful as it should be, and if I did not know the trees were there I might even be able to imagine that they were not. I drift into a lovely sleep and wake unexpectedly full of energy. Downstairs I catch Wessie lolling on the sofa, his eyes half closed. 'Come on, Wessie,' I say, 'you lazy-bones, what are you dreaming about? Walkies! Walkies! Upsticks!' He gives a shiver of anticipation, as if to say: 'Yes, mistress!' and out we go.

Since my operation I have walked very little, I have not felt well enough, but I am determined to force myself out for the sake of my health. There are several short walks from the house. We might walk down to the railway line, we might walk along the cinder path by the railway and come back through the sheep fields, which would make a nice triangular walk; or we might cross the railway line and walk in the meadows by the river. We take the easiest course, the path down the stubble field and up the rise to the new plantation. Rabbits (their scrapes are everywhere) start at our approach, listen with their pink ears and scurry to their burrows in the roots of the hedgerow. We also see a small fox, a very alarming sight to anyone like me who keeps hens. There are not that many foxes round here but they are so ruthless when it comes to hens, yet even foxes have to live, one cannot blame them.

It trots along the edge of the field, its brush streaming. 'Look, Wessie,' I say, 'a fox!' but he is too preoccupied with smells to hear me. At the top of the rise he finds some clods of fresh horse-dung. 'No!' I shout at him, 'Wessie, no, no!' He lifts his head – 'O but, mistress, it smells so delicious!' and takes a quick bite. – 'No!' I shout. 'No! No! You naughty dog!' He bolts a second mouthful, I haul him away. 'You naughty dog! Bad! Bad boy! I am very cross with you, do you hear? You must not eat horse-dung! You should be ashamed of yourself!' In my heart I am not really cross, I could never be really cross with him. He puts back his ears and pretends to be very contrite but within a few seconds he has forgotten and is lifting his leg on a withered thistle.

Evening. He listens in silence, or does not listen, hands laced in his lap, dressing gown tied tight. Half of his face, on the far side of the oil lamp, is in shadow, but I can see enough; his eyes are closed, his breathing steady. He is asleep. At each inbreath the wings of his nose part slightly and at each outbreath his lips purse and open. I pause, and wait to see what happens. Nothing happens.

'Thomas?'

His eyes jerk open.

'You were asleep.'

'I was listening.'

'I promise you, you were asleep. Shall I go on?' Since the operation I have been very conscious of the strain on my throat and I should be glad to stop.

'If you would; thank you. I was awake, I was listening to every word.'

I permit myself a small, knowing smile (taking good care that he sees it), and continue to read Jane Austen's elegant sentences. His eyelids soon droop, his eyes close again, his breathing resumes its regularity. No doubt someone watching this scene would find it comic, yet my life is not a comedy as I am well aware. To what or whom am I reading? To the empty air? To the silent furniture?

At the end of the chapter I wake him up. We wish each other good night and climb into our separate beds, in our separate rooms.

This is where nothing happens again, although what often used to happen, a long time ago, so long that I almost wonder if it ever happened at all, is that he would leave his bed and arrive by mine, breathing heavily in the darkness. I would lift the corner of the sheets and in he would climb, dragging at my night-dress, wrenching it upward, hauling it above my shoulders. To avoid being suffocated I would pull it off my face, at the same moment turning my body and steering my breast towards his mouth. His bristly moustache would scrape the skin. He would nuzzle and mumble while I stroked his head and caressed his ears, all the while asking myself whether I should do more, whether I should stroke his back or spread my legs or take one of his hands and guide it towards my sex, or reach under his night-shirt, or even utter sounds of pleasure in the hope that they would encourage him to push into me, but there I was far too shy. For (I would think to myself), is it not just as likely that sounds of pleasure will put him off? Is it not safer to stay quiet? What do women generally do? What are women supposed to touch? Are there certain acts that are appropriate for a wife to perform as opposed to certain other acts that are not appropriate for a wife to perform? Where do the boundaries lie? How does one find out? But then I would say to myself, what does it matter that he so rarely pushes into me, surely all that matters is that it makes him happy, although would it not make him even happier if he did push into me? As a wife it is one's duty to make one's husband happy. I firmly believe that.

Generally he would doze off with his arms around me and his head on my chest, and once he was sound asleep I would ease out and get into his bed with my body another one of these unanswered questions. The beds here are single beds, far too narrow for two people.

As before there is a certain comedy in all this, if one wants to hunt it out. Here and now, with the advantage of hindsight, I can see that. But how difficult it was at the time! How difficult and complicated! For all her wisdom Jane Austen is no help here, and so far as I know there are no books that begin to address these matters (if such books existed, I would be far too embarrassed to read them even in secret, even if I could be sure that no one knew that I was reading them). In other fields of human activity knowledge accumulates as it is passed from generation to generation, but when it comes to the subject of sexual relations women today are surely as ignorant as they must have been thousands of years ago. In some ways I am glad that he seems too old to bother with these nightly jousts (jousts? Jousts is not the word I want but it will have to do for the moment), very glad, in some ways, although less glad in other ways. I should not mind it if for old times' sake he wanted to climb into my bed now, but probably he is already deep asleep. He always falls asleep in an instant. He sleeps like a baby.

Lying here I wonder what the first wife did. How active was she? Did she stay silent or utter sounds, either voluntary or involuntary? The vision of them rises before me in the darkness, she with her waxy uneven flesh, he with his scrawny legs, exchanging kisses and caresses on this very bed; they writhe (a horrible word) and her fat thighs widen as he pushes into her. A repulsive expression of greedy pleasure spreads over her face. What is this? I am not jealous, I refuse to be even slightly jealous of something that perhaps never happened, a lurid concoction of my imagination. Besides as I haste to remind myself it is perfectly possible that their physical relations were largely non-existent. I also haste to remind myself that love not sexual relations is the true foundation for a successful marriage and that they did not love each other, whereas my husband and I certainly do, do love each other, that there can be no doubt of, of that there can be no doubt.

CHAPTER III

✿ ✿ ✿

As November progressed, fears about the forthcoming dramatic production began to trouble the old man more than a little. Had he been entirely wise to have agreed to its performance? For years, he had carefully fended off requests from theatrical managers near and far to stage the novel. That he had at last given way was to some degree a reflection of his age, for if he was ever to see the play performed, now was the time; but also instrumental in his decision had been his fervent desire to see Gertie as Tess. He had stipulated that the production was possible only if she were involved. 'I do not think anyone else capable of playing the part,' he had told Tilley.

On the night before the first performance he woke and fretted to himself in the darkness. Gertie would be perfect, of that he had not the least doubt, but the acting talents of the other men and women in the cast were greatly inferior. Considering them one by one, his misgivings increased. He was particularly concerned about the part of Alec, who in the absence of anyone more suitable was to be played by a gawky young man called Norman Atkins, who worked behind the counter in one of the town's banks.

Of course – he reminded himself – it was merely an amateur production, one which could not be fairly judged by professional standards. Yet interest in the play had been enormous, and leading newspaper reviewers from London had promised to be at the Corn Exchange.

The old man was not nearly as indifferent to the play's reception as he pretended to be. More than forty years had passed since his first novels, and while he had forgotten all the good reviews the bad ones stuck in his memory like thorns. Ignorant, insensitive, malicious, they still pricked and festered. The very idea that 'Tess', his dearest creation, might be subject to any criticism, even of the mildest kind, kept him awake for hours.

At breakfast, with rain driving against the windows of the dining room, he was in a gloomy frame of mind. 'I am afraid it may be a mistake.'

'Why?'

He gave a shrug.

'I'm sure it'll be a great success. Where is the mistake? I'm sure it will be a success.'

'I have no great expectations.'

'I'm sure it'll go well,' she insisted. 'I just wish Cockerell was coming.'

'Cockerell is coming tomorrow.'

'Who else will be there? Will Lawrence be there?'

'Tonight? He may not be able to get away. But Cockerell is coming tomorrow, to both performances.' He frowned. 'Maybe no one'll come.'

'Thomas, of course they will. All the tickets have been sold. You do say some ridiculous things sometimes.'

There was a silence in which he wondered whether he might sit back-stage. He liked the thought of being out of sight, watching the actors shuffle on and off. Perhaps he would get a chance to talk alone to Gertie, though she would be on stage for almost the entire time.

'All I hope,' said his wife, 'is that it doesn't go on too long afterwards. Poor little Wessie. I hate leaving him alone.'

'The maids'll look after him.'

'They don't even try to understand.'

'He'll be all right,' the old man said dismissively, though he agreed with her.

He departed the breakfast table in an altogether better mood than had been the case when he sat down. Yet, as the morning went on, his disquiet returned.

Although the town was not quite the provincial backwater that it had been half a century earlier, it remained a place somewhat removed from the main currents of thought that flowed through the big cities. Conservative habits of mind prevailed, particularly in relation to moral behaviour. This was where the problem lay with 'Tess'. Conventional morality asserts that, in the conclusion to any work of art, the author should reward the good and punish the bad, and the novel signally failed to adhere to this long-established practice. And rightly so, in the old man's opinion; when one surveyed human affairs there seemed to be no automatic presumption in favour of the triumph of the good. Lives did not always end well, and it seemed dishonest to pretend otherwise. The fate of Tess was to be hanged, despite her essential innocence. In an attempt to soften the blow – and with more than half an eye to the difficulties of staging the scene satisfactorily – he had removed the hanging from the play and made it end at Stonehenge. Still, the story remained a tragic one, and whether it would be to the taste of the town he could not say.

Perhaps as difficult was the fact that the story implicitly criticised the hallowed institution of marriage, on which some authorities claim the stability of society to rest.

The dreariness of the meteorological conditions did nothing to raise his spirits. There are November days that begin with rain, but the wind hurries along the clouds and by noon the sun is shining from a blue sky; and then there are days when the rain sets in early and never lets up, much like a dog attached to a bone. This was one such. The wind stiffened and swung to the north, and the afternoon brought a succession of squally hailstorms, with white stones bombarding the house and bouncing on the green sward of the lawns. It was the first proper taste of winter, and altogether common sense might have said that it was a day to stay at home by the fire, not to venture abroad. Watching the barrage of hail the old man vaguely asked himself whether he might contrive to miss the performance at the Corn Exchange.

Here he was not in the least serious. If someone had come and forbade him from attending the play, he would have been deeply aggrieved. In truth, what he had begun to dread most was not the play itself, but the prospect of meeting so many people before and after the performance. He had always disliked large social gatherings, preferring those of a more intimate kind.

As the evening drew nigh, he went to his bedroom and began to change into the appropriate apparel. Dressing and undressing always took him some time nowadays, not least because his fingers were stiff, but now he found himself in a paroxysm of indecision with regard to the suit. He had three decent suits: one plain dark, the second a pin-stripe, the third a Norfolk tweed. Florence had laid them out on the bed. The tweed would possibly be too hot, the dark suit seemed too funereal, while the pin-stripe was a little worn. Why had he not thought of this before?

The old man had spent much of his life contemplating the great issues of the world, against which matters of dress were utterly trivial. Yet, as the originator of 'Tess', all eyes would be upon him, a prospect he disliked intensely. He stood and dithered in his shirt and socks.

Florence entered the room.

'Voss is here,' she announced.

'Already? What time did you tell him?'

'Six thirty. He's half an hour early.'

'Then he will have to wait. I'm not hurrying. We don't want to get there early.'

'I know, but we mustn't be late.'

'We won't be late.'

She sighed. 'I almost wish we weren't going.'

She spoke in such a heartfelt tone that he turned to regard her. She wore a long evening dress, dark blue in colour; it hung off her like a voluminous curtain; and her face was full of anxiety. It struck him that this would be her first appearance in public since her operation.

'Is something wrong?' She put a hand to her neck. 'What are you looking at?'

'Nothing at all. But, you know,' he said solicitously, 'there is no need for you to come. If you want, you can stay.'

'O, Thomas, I couldn't possibly. What would people think? I have to come.'

'It's not worth exhausting yourself for. Merely a short play – why not stay and keep Wessex company? You can come to the matinée tomorrow with Cockerell,' he added, knowing how well she and Cockerell got on together.

'No, I have to come tonight,' she said in an impassioned voice. 'I have to. I must come.'

He nodded, understanding, and also relieved. Going alone he would have felt even more vulnerable.

He returned his attention to the matter of the suits.

'You could wear the tweed,' she suggested.

The old man chose the pin-stripe. He sat on the bed and pulled the trousers up his legs until the point came when he had to stand in order to pull them to his waist. He allowed Florence to button on the braces, but managed the tie by himself, although as he did so he regarded himself in the glass and was not much pleased by what he saw. He pressed his moustache with a fingertip, a sure sign of internal agitation. Next came the waistcoat, with Florence again doing the buttons.

'Shoes?'

'O yes.'

He stepped into his shoes and she knelt and did the laces.

'I may sit backstage,' he announced.

'What? Why? Where am I to sit?'

'No one will be looking at you,' he said.

'But I'll be alone.'

'O, there'll be plenty of people.'

Down in the hall they put on their coats: his tweed, hers fur. Around her neck she wound her fox stole. Wessex watched them both, his ears flat, his spirits patently lowered at the idea of being left alone.

By ill chance, the weather had taken a sharp turn for the worse, and the rain was tumbling in sheets through the branches of the trees. With the assistance of Mr. Voss's umbrella, the elderly couple hurried over the wet gravel to the taxi-cab.

The journey ahead was a short one, the distance being little above a mile, and after crossing the bridge over the railway line the road descended into the town. The rain beat loudly on the roof of the car, and the windscreen wipers thrashed to and fro in a furious attempt to clear the water pouring over the glass. The streets were all but empty, save for a few unfortunate pedestrians who had been caught in the downpour and who scuttled for cover. It was a miserable evening. Neither the old man nor his wife said a word, but both seemed equally unenthusiastic about what lay ahead.

The motor-car drew up by the steps of the Corn Exchange. With the rain driving almost at the horizontal, Mr. Voss jumped out and struggled to hold his umbrella at the ready.

The old man had been to events of this nature before, and he fastened on his face the expression he generally used, one in which natural wariness and distrust concealed themselves behind a front of alert attention. It was as well he did so, for no sooner had he entered the hall than a newspaper photographer stepped forward with his camera and tripod. Although he had a strong dislike of photographers, there was nothing for it. He bared his teeth, much like the fox round Florence's neck. Florence herself hung heavily on his arm.

A small reception committee, consisting of the Mayor and several other Council officials, also lay in wait. The Mayor was dressed in full rig, including his fur robe and gold chain, and being somewhat corpulent looked remarkably like a provincial version of the elderly Henry the Eighth in the famous portrait by Holbein. Much shaking of hands and many warm words followed, somewhat to the old man's embarrassment, although he also experienced a degree of pleasure. Even at the age of eighty-four, and even though he had received many awards, he was not immune to the power of flattery. However, he did not allow himself to be carried away, and despite the effusive tributes took care to recognise the event for what it undoubtedly was: an unimportant theatrical performance on a wet evening in a small and unimportant country town, and one that, in the scale of things, would be soon forgotten.

The Corn Exchange was situated in the very centre of the town. It was a building that dated back some seventy years, and from an architectural standpoint was of considerable interest and ingenuity, since it fulfilled a variety of purposes. Chief among these was to provide a roof under which farmers, millers and merchants might meet in relative comfort to conduct their business, and on market days the large hall became a bustling, noisy place as men with dark, weather-beaten faces and shrewd expressions bargained over the price of wheat and barley. Shafts of sunlight slanted through the dusty air while the occasional pigeon, ever alert to the possibility of a free meal, flew here and there, alighting on the floor whenever it spied a few spare husks or grains, and retreating to perch on the hall's exposed beams. Such was the main and original reason for the existence of the Exchange, for corn and all matters pertaining to it had long been at the heart of the town's life. Yet the Exchange had its other uses. The town's Corporation had its offices in a set of rooms at the front of the building, and since the turn of the century the hall had frequently been employed for concerts and performances of a theatrical nature. To that end a stage had been erected at the far end of the hall and equipped with a pair of red curtains.

Commerce and art do not easily co-exist, and something of the market-day atmosphere lingered even when all outward traces had disappeared. The farmers had retired to their homesteads and the last pigeon had flown away, but the smell of grain still hung perceptibly in the air. An observer who had visited the famous London playhouses, with their plush seats and sparkling chandeliers, might have wondered whether the Exchange was ideally suited to dramatic activity. The height of the ceiling was such that words uttered on stage, especially by those with lighter voices, often failed to carry to the spectator seated at the back of the hall, and the floor of the hall being entirely flat, that same unfortunate spectator tended to find his view of proceedings impeded by a sea of heads. In short, the Corn Exchange was not all that a theatre would have been in a perfect world. That ideal state never having come into existence, it was the best building on offer. Nowhere else in the town was of sufficient size to accommodate an audience of several hundred.

A goodly number of those with tickets for tonight's performance had already arrived, and were awaiting the right moment to go into the hall itself. Among them were dozens of familiar faces to reassure the old man, and that so many people had bothered to come here on a wet November evening, some travelling all the way from London, touched him a good deal. Yet there was a part of him which would have preferred them to have stayed away, lest the play turned out a failure. 'I am afraid it is a very amateur affair,' he told everyone he met. 'One must not expect too much.' In truth, he was trying to protect himself from the possibility of disaster.

A couple of minutes had elapsed when a young man in army uniform pushed through the crowd. Florence exclaimed at the sight of him: 'O good!'

The old man's heart also lifted. There was scarcely anyone for whom he felt greater affection and admiration. Lawrence was a hero, an explorer, an adventurer, who in his thirty-odd years had already done much more than most men manage in their entire lives.

On one arm he had a muddy motor-cycling suit, having ridden over from the army camp at Bovington, where he was presently stationed.

'Why, I wouldn't have missed it for anything,' he said, smiling. 'A little bit of rain is nothing. It's the world première of "Tess", is it not? People have been waiting years for this.'

It was not the world première; a long time earlier there had been an unauthorised production in the United States. But the old man did his best to disregard that.

'I am not that optimistic,' he asserted.

Lawrence laughed. 'Tom, forgive me but, you know, you are not in general renowned for your optimism!'

He pretended to be wounded. 'I am not a pessimist by nature; when circumstances justify it, I am always optimistic. But this is a very amateur production, I assure you.'

'He has been like this all day,' Florence remarked.

'Of course it is an amateur production,' Lawrence said, 'and everyone knows it. Surely that is the charm of it. To have the play first performed by local men and women, in the very heart of Wessex, in a town that Tess herself knew – what could be more appropriate? It is the perfect setting. Think of it in London; how out of place it would be. This is where "Tess" belongs.' Lawrence's steady blue eyes shone. 'I shouldn't worry if I were you. I anticipate a triumph.'

He was right, thought the old man. Some of his apprehension began to fade. 'I am not worried,' he said stoutly. 'So long as none of them forget their lines.'

'If they do, it is hardly your fault, is it? But I am sure they have been well drilled.'

Florence intervened. 'We are a little worried about Alec. He is not quite – what is the word? He is possibly not quite nasty enough. He is a bank clerk. And there is a problem with Angel Clare. He is rather old, and bald, but he is wearing a wig! One only hopes it doesn't slip!'

The old man blinked. 'One has to work with the available material. But they have had plenty of rehearsals. Whatever else, I don't think you will be too disappointed by Tess herself.'

'I must say,' said Lawrence, 'I'm longing to see her. The famous Gertrude Bugler – I've heard a lot about her. Everyone says she is something rather out of the ordinary.'

'She is a remarkable young woman.'

'She is the wife of a butcher,' said Florence. 'It is rather incongruous, is it not, for Tess? It is hard to get out of one's mind once one knows it! A butcher's wife!'

She was in the gayest mood, her spirits transformed, but then Lawrence was an inspiring chap. Indeed there were moments when the old man felt that, if he had ever had a son, he would have hoped for someone like Lawrence of Arabia.

Other friends soon appeared, among them James Barrie, the playwright, who to the old man's eyes looked as urbane and prosperous as a banker. A lifetime in London had barely left a mark on his large forehead, and his moustache, thick and glossy, always seemed a sign of his inner confidence. He fished a large gold watch from his waistcoat. 'Ten minutes to go,' he announced grandly. 'I love an opening night. What an occasion! This is history!'

The old man stayed as long as was necessary, but he was not in the mood for chitchat. With Florence fully occupied, he slipped into the hall. A good few people had already taken their seats, but many of the rows of interlocking wooden chairs were still empty. Below the stage, several members of a local orchestra were gathering; it had been Tilley's idea that they should play country tunes between the acts, thus covering the time taken for the scene changes. A horn player had his instrument to his lips and was giving a few experimental toots, while the two fiddlers were tuning up. He pushed open a door and walked along a short corridor.

There was almost no room back-stage, and an obstacle course of props and effects confronted him, including bales of straw, milk churns, buckets, a length of wooden fencing, a hay-waggon and also the three pillars which would be used in the final act to represent Stonehenge. As he picked his way around these impediments he came upon Tess's father and mother, with Angel Clare and Alec. Alec was still reading over his lines, a sight which at this late juncture did not inspire the old man with confidence.

A little further on he found the rest of the cast, among them Gertie. Seated on a milk churn, she was talking to Ethel Fare, who played the part of Izz Huett, and since she had her back to him she did not notice him at first. Near her was Harry Tilley, holding the prompt book.

'Tom,' he said, and they shook hands. 'Everything in order. A full house, you'll be glad to know.'

'I was thinking of watching from here, unless I'll be in the way. Are the scribblers here?'

'Dozens of 'em. They're all putting up at the King's Arms.'

' "The Times"?'

'Of course.'

The old man was somewhat relieved. 'The Times' could be relied upon to write something favourable. 'Well, we shall see.' He nodded at the prompt book. 'I am sure we won't need that.'

As he talked to Tilley, Ethel must have said something to Gertie, for she jumped up smiling.

It was not the moment to speak to her alone, and instead he wished the whole cast good luck, adding with more cheerfulness than he felt that he was sure they would not need it. Then he left them, and settled himself on a chair beside one of the pillars of Stonehenge. From here he had a good view of the stage while remaining hidden from the audience. He could hear the quiet murmur of expectation, he could see one of the stage-hands waiting to pull on the rope that drew back the curtains. Already the village girls who appeared in the first act, each one in a white dress and carrying a nosegay of flowers, were taking their places on stage. As the moment approached, the various contradictory emotions that had been vying within him – emotions of longing and desire, and of fear and apprehension – grew ever more intense. Then the stage-hand heaved on his rope, the curtains drew back in a series of jerks, and the play had begun.

Tess herself did not appear on stage for several minutes, but already she was by his side. She gave him a quick, tense smile, which he returned. How alive she was! How easily she became the girl in the water-meadows, vanishing into the morning mist! Then she started – 'O!' and he felt some hard object pressed into his right hand. 'I nearly forgot! Could you keep it for me?'

She stepped on stage.

The old man opened his hand. In the palm lay a gold circle: her wedding ring.

CHAPTER IV

❦ ❦ ❦

After the strain of last night I wake suffering from a small but painful headache, of the kind that has often afflicted me recently. I wait in the hope that it may go of its own accord, although such headaches never do. I never used to have these headaches and I sometimes think they may be connected to a lack of sunlight, and indeed when I visualise my headaches I do so as dark folds of shadow, heavy curtains hiding light.

I struggle down to breakfast and find my husband in his dark suit. He is reading the newspaper reviews. I wish him good morning, and without a word he passes 'The Times' to me. From his expression of extreme displeasure one would conclude that the review must be unfavourable but, on the contrary, it could not be more fulsome. Glancing over it, my eyes alight on the following lines:

'In Mrs. Gertrude Bugler they have a lady who, one might almost say, was born to act the part of Tess. To begin with, she is so like the Tess of the book in appearance, even to the trick of the smile, that, did chronology allow it, she might have sat for the portrait of this imaginary girl, created before she was born. Another good point is her voice, which is unusually sweet and appealing; and yet another, her undoubted possession of some of that mysterious actor-quality, which compels one to be interested in, affected by, every look and movement and word.'

This is astonishing, more than astonishing; it is patently untrue. Gertrude has dark hair, while Tess's hair is the colour of earth. As for her mysterious actor-quality – what nonsense! I would say as much but for the iron look on my husband's face. Biting my tongue, I dutifully read on:

'A performance full of the right sort of simplicity and breadth, and of a most moving sincerity and beauty – more beauty, one imagines, than could have been achieved by one or two of the eminent actresses who have longed to play this character.'

'Goodness – that is kind. Although it seems a little excessive. What do the others say?'

My husband with his iron face (one wonders: what would be his expression if it had been a bad review?) passes me the 'Daily Mail'; it likewise is full of compliments. Then I am passed the 'Chronicle'. A phrase leaps out at me: 'one of the most beautiful women in Dorset'.

'Heavens, look at that! "One of the most beautiful women in Dorset"!'

'What is wrong with that?'

'It's nonsense, Thomas. She is striking, she is undoubtedly striking, no one could argue with that, but she is not beautiful. What else does it say? "Palpitatingly true to life"? "Golden voice"?'

'She has a good voice. She has the accent to perfection.'

'But it doesn't say that, it says she has a golden voice. A golden voice. It is such a cliché. And "palpitatingly true to life" . . . I've never heard the word. "Palpitatingly"? Have you ever heard such a word? What does it mean, "palpitatingly true to life"? It doesn't mean anything at all.'

I sit down, I lift the coffee pot. My husband is now reading the 'Daily Express'. He gives a grunt. I say nothing. I pour myself coffee. O, my head aches!

I should stay silent but my thoughts pour out of me.

'Of course, it depends what one means by beauty. Her hair is very fine, and she has a very clever trick of widening her eyes, but her eyebrows are too thick, and her teeth much too prominent. I agree she is very striking, but she is not a classical beauty. Hundreds of young women in Dorset are I am sure at least as beautiful – more beautiful. In the classical sense she is not beautiful at all.'

How catty of me this must sound; but I am unable to stop myself.

My iron-faced husband hands me the 'Daily Express'. I spot another mistake. In my frustration I burst out: 'Look at that – for heaven's sakes! A farmer's wife! Her husband has a shop, a butcher's shop in Beaminster!'

I am afraid he thinks I am being catty, but newspapers ought to be accurate.

Silence.

He looks up at me. 'It is November the twenty-seventh.'

'I know.'

I have not forgotten. November the twenty-seventh is the death-day of the first wife, and so we have to visit her grave in Stinsford churchyard.

'I may walk,' he says.

'To Stinsford? It is too far, Thomas. It's going to be such a tiring day as it is. And the meadows will probably be flooded. I'll telephone Voss and tell him to come early.'

The breakfast runs its course. My headache eases. I let out the hens and then brush Wessie. White hairs fly off his coat with each stroke of the brush. I am somewhat amazed to hear myself talking to him in a low conspiratorial voice:

'She is really not that beautiful, is she? She may be striking, but beautiful . . . And there is something almost hysterical about her acting, I promise you, Wessie, if only you could see it. It is good that the reviews are good, though I wish they could have been more honest. The trouble is that it encourages him, that is the trouble. Why do the reviewers write such falsehoods? Do they have no sense of shame? It doesn't bother me; after all, what is it to me, I am his wife, if he chooses to believe the reviews what is it to me? But she is not the most beautiful woman in Dorset! She is the wife of a common butcher! She associates with raw meat, hatchets, blood and gore, where is the beauty in that?'

I comfort myself by imagining her husband, a typical butcher, fat and short-legged, red-faced and cheery, chopping joints, hauling carcasses, gutting chickens, sweeping sawdust, mopping blood, the things butchers do. No doubt she helps him string the sausages.

At half past ten Mr. Voss arrives, and drives us to Stinsford. The sky is grey, but at least it is not raining and there is very little wind. We open the gate and walk down the path to her grave, which is located near a large yew tree. Beside it are the graves of his grandfather and grandmother, his uncle and assorted other relatives. He removes his hat (his black hat, reserved for funerals and similar occasions), presses it against his chest and bows his head. With him he has his walking stick (also black), another of these treasured things given him by the first wife.

What he is thinking of I cannot say, but as I stand by his side my own thoughts fly from the bones beneath the stone to the fat, earnest, vain, empty-headed woman with swollen ankles who chattered incessantly about her cats and never listened with attention to anything anyone said. I know this because I visited, I stayed, I saw them together. She was an utter encumbrance to him, she made him unhappy, and yet now she is revered as the woman he always loved. He has written many nostalgic poems to her dead spirit, love poems. You did not love her, Thomas, I would like to tell him, believe me you did not love her and she did not love you, you did not even like each other, do you not remember her mad obsessive railing about the Pope as the enemy of civilisation? Do you not remember that awful certainty in her voice? She was an encumbrance to you and does not deserve this reverence. Of course, if I said as much he would be mortally offended and might never forgive me, or he would say that I do not understand, that I never saw her as she once was, in the old days. Ah, the old days.

Am I conscious that, if she had not died, I would not now be his wife? I am; it is impossible to avoid that thought. Her death and my life are inextricably linked. First and second wives are like sisters.

After a minute or so he clears his throat, but we wait a little longer. The stone lies in considerable shadow. It occurs to me that during the years in which we have been making these dutiful visits the yew tree has grown a good deal, but this is what trees do, they grow, they extend themselves.

He comes to life with another cough. He replaces his hat on his head and touches his moustache.

'Twelve,' he murmurs.

'What's that?'

'Em . . . it was twelve years ago that she died.'

'Of course it was.'

'We were married for thirty-eight years.'

'Shall we go into the church?'

'I don't think so. No. Yes.'

He is very old, I remind myself. He looks old now. He has another brown spot on his left cheek, and his eyes seem rather watery. As we go down the path I feel a sudden rush of love and take his arm. I claim him; I assert my ownership of him, I cast the first wife aside. He is my husband, he does not belong to you any longer. Begone: you are long dead.

The air in the church is its usual pleasant musty self. The light is dim, as if we were submerged. We stand by the font in another silence. At length I grow so bored I wander off and study the monuments, though I know them all very well. There are more monuments to husbands than to wives, of course. Wives live in the shadows cast by their husbands; that is how things are. I walk up to the altar, and then back again.

'Shall we go?'

We are halfway to the car when he announces in an unexpectedly cheerful voice: 'I may never come here again!'

'Why on earth not?'

'I may well not be alive this time next year.'

'I am not even listening,' I protest. 'What a miserable thing to say! Is that what you've been thinking about?'

'My dear, it is entirely possible. I think about it all the time.'

'I won't have you saying such nonsense.'

He gives a smile. Visiting the first wife's grave always seems to put him in such a remarkably good mood, it is a mystery why we don't do it every day.

I do not want to give the wrong impression. I am not bitter about her; we got on very well together. It is merely the two of them who were so utterly ill-suited.

One thing about their life together I have never quite fathomed. When I tried to ask him about it before our marriage he always deflected my inquiries, and it was not until soon after we were married, on a warm summer's afternoon, that I managed to force him into a conversation on the subject. We had gone for a walk with Wessie, who was not much more than a puppy, and as I remember it there were bees humming busily and flitting from flower to flower, and little lambs crying in the distance, and two men scything hay, although maybe I invent these details. Where does the past exist except in one's mind? That is such a frightening thought but is it not so? (And where the present — but that is even more frightening.) But it is not really important when exactly this conversation occurred; a warm summer's afternoon is as good a time as any.

I began cautiously, tentatively, aware that it might be a sensitive subject, by asking him whether there was some particular impediment or obstacle that had prevented her from having children. He answered that there was not: 'It was merely that it never happened, as is the way. Fate decreed otherwise.' I said: 'So it was not a decision to which you and she jointly came . . . ? It was not a principled decision?' – 'No,' said he, but a little vaguely. – 'But did you and she talk much on the subject?' I asked. – 'Of?' – 'Of children.' He indicated not. 'Never?' – 'I cannot recall.' (Here in my memory we drew near the two labourers, scything the pale hay with those lovely easy sweeping movements.)

I knew that he did not wish to continue the conversation, but I was determined not to let the matter slip that easily. I linked my arm in his. 'But Thomas, you would have liked children, surely? You would have been the best of fathers.' He gave what might be called a shrug of the mouth. 'I am not necessarily sure that she would have made a very good mother.' – 'But you must have wanted children, both of you, surely?' – 'It is difficult to recover one's true state of mind so long after the event. I am sure we did; yes; but it was not to be.'

I asked no further questions. However, I could not put it from my mind, and some months later he and I came close to another discussion on the same matter. This was after the War had begun. He was greatly disheartened by the War; he felt it was as if Time had gone into reverse and sent the world back to the Dark Ages, and he did not agree with the prevailing opinion that we should win easily; when people told him that he was being unduly pessimistic, he replied that he was being realistic, for the Germans had always been very good fighters. One night at bedtime I was reading to him when we heard a distant, heavy tremor that we knew to be the sounds of guns from across the Channel. We used to hear the guns often when the wind was blowing from the south, but I think this was the first time that we had heard them, and I stopped reading at once and we listened as the rumbling went on and on, a little like thunder, the sound rolling towards us in waves. It was so like thunder it was hard to believe that we were hearing the firing of guns, and I remember he said how terrible it was to know that only one or two hundred miles away young men from Wessex were losing their lives in a war against Germany, of all countries: Germany, the land of such geniuses as Bach and Beethoven, of Goethe and Schiller and Schopenhauer. Then he heaved a sigh, and said – I remember this distinctly – that it would be a sin to bring a child into such a world as this. I can hear him now. 'To be born,' he said, 'is the primal misfortune . . .' What a thing to say! I had to protest. 'But, Thomas,' I said, 'there must always be hope, must there not? If everyone felt the same, the human race would be extinct in a century. Imagine!' After a long pause, during which the guns fell silent, he answered that he had often imagined it, a world free of the curse of humanity. I said: 'But *your* life has not been one of misfortune, has it?' He did not answer. Although I felt as if I was speaking to a wall, I took his hand and persisted: 'Your life has been a blessed one, has it not? When you think back . . . surely . . . do you not feel that? Your life has been blessed!' We had been married such a short time; how desperate I was for him to make an affirmative reply! There was an even longer silence, and then the guns began again, with renewed force, and he said: 'If only it were thunder!'

As Mr. Voss drives us home I find myself thinking about that night and my nerves start to jangle. Other thoughts intervene: that while it is perfectly true that he may not be alive this time next year, it is equally true that I may not be alive. Then he will have two wives to mourn. I slip a finger under my stole and touch the scar. I ought not to touch but sometimes I catch myself touching without knowing it.

The matinée. I finger the scar under my stole. In front of me the play grinds on, even slower and more ponderous than it was last night. I am not a highly paid reviewer on a national newspaper, but the creakiness of its construction is obvious: what is it but a

few scenes from the novel, strung loosely together with no consideration of the dramatic, without even a shred of artistic cohesion?
If I were a highly paid reviewer, a highly paid reviewer with an
eye to the truth, I would list numerous faults – that the dialogue
is stilted, the atmosphere non-existent, that Alec is wooden and
the sight of him trying to smoke a cigar, dear me! And that Angel
Clare's wig is the colour of flax, and all the time it looks as if it
is in danger of slipping off his head. That is what I would report,
what the reviewers should have reported if they had been truthful.
As for Gertrude I would have to say that she over-acts, of that
there can be no doubt. In the fourth act her performance is frankly
comical.

As the orchestra strikes up before the final act I turn to
Cockerell. 'Are you enjoying it?'

'I am; very much. This music is very jolly.'

'Have you seen the reviews?'

'I read "The Times". Very good. Perfect.'

'Too good, Sydney, I am afraid.'

'Why do you say that?'

'O, I'm never sure if it is always a good idea, turning a novel
into a play. Barrie was saying that last night. One misses so much
of the novel.'

'Did Barrie come down? Good! What? Didn't he like it?'

'He was very charming and polite, but reading between the
lines I think he felt that the play falls rather between two stools.
Neither one thing nor the other. Half a play and half a novel.'

'Well, is that not inevitable, to an extent? Thomas seems happy
enough to me.'

I consider this. Thomas is sitting back-stage again; he is perched
back-stage. I wish he would sit with me; he is my husband, after
all.

'Sydney, I have no idea what Thomas feels about anything! I
never do!'

The orchestra plays on. There are four of them: two

violinists, a horn player and a 'cellist. If I were a highly paid reviewer (but of course I am not, I am a mere woman), I might well mention the length of time these scene changes takes, and how much bumping and crashing there is from the other side of the curtains!

'I am afraid they are putting up Stonehenge,' I inform Cockerell.

'Ah? Good! I understand there is some talk about it going to London. Something about the Haymarket?'

'So we hope.'

'From the Corn Exchange to the Haymarket. From corn to hay!'

In the final act Angel Clare bumps into one of the pillars of Stonehenge and it rocks to and fro. Unable to contain myself I say to Cockerell, *sotto voce*: 'This is what one gets in an amateur production, I am afraid!'

Between the end of the matinée and the start of the evening performance there is a period of some two hours. With the audience having left, three trestle tables are set up on the stage, with light refreshments for the cast. Someone kindly brings Cockerell and me cups of tea – very strong tea, almost orange in colour – and a plate of fish-paste sandwiches. I have no appetite, but Cockerell tucks in as if he is starving. He missed lunch, it seems.

He is wearing a red rose in his button-hole.

'What a lovely rose,' I say. 'It is impossible to grow roses in the garden at Max Gate any longer. They wilt, they become covered in disease.'

'Why?'

'Why? Sydney, it is the trees! There are one hundred and eighty pines planted round the house, and goodness knows how many beeches. But can I get him to have them cut back? He won't even listen to me. When it comes to the trees he doesn't think in a rational way. He seems to believe that it would hurt the trees to be cut back. He thinks it would wound them, the trees. I am not exaggerating! His views are quite outlandish! Every twig is sacred!

Trees have no nervous system. Human beings have a nervous system, but not trees!'

Cockerell is involved with his sandwich. 'My dear Florence, you know it goes back with him a long way, his reverence for trees. Is it not possible he sees them, in some sort, as feminine creatures, in the same way that flowers are commonly regarded as feminine? Trees are essentially large flowers. And they are quiet, peaceable, rather benevolent, passive things, are they not? Might that not explain his reluctance to have them cut down?'

'Trees are not peaceable at all. Their whole purpose is to spread themselves and so to prevent other plants from growing by denying them light. They are aggressive, greedy, selfish, hostile. It is a great mistake to see them as harmless, they are greedy and aggressive!'

'I didn't know you believed so strongly in Evolution.'

'O, the truth is that it is not good for human beings to live too close to trees, medically speaking. Their spores contribute to the spread of illness. I was talking to my surgeon about it.'

'How extraordinary.' He munches away. 'How alarming.'

'I wish you would say something to Thomas. He pays attention to you. He listens to you. You were so successful with the telephone.'

'About the trees? If you like. Though I fancy Tess would have more success.'

I follow his eyes. My husband is chaperoning Gertrude to a chair near one of the tables. She sits down, pats the seat of the chair beside her in a playful way, a flirtatious way. Obediently he sits down, like a dog. She smiles a flirtatious smile, or so it appears to me. Cockerell may or may not see it as flirtatious but to me, as a woman, there can be no doubt; as a woman one is able to detect signs of flirtatious behaviour, one is attuned to such matters. My husband begins to whisper in her ear.

'Mrs. Bugler will play the part of Tess in London, I understand.'

Cockerell's remark surprises me. 'O no! Heavens no. Sybil

Thorndike will be playing Tess. At least, we hope she will play it. It is partly a question of how long she can do it for. She seems very busy, but we hear she is very keen. Why do you ask?'

'Merely that . . . Thomas gave me the impression that Mrs. Bugler would be playing it.'

'No. Gertrude? Not at all.'

'I must have got hold of the wrong end of the stick. I thought he said Gertrude would be Tess. But I see I've got it wrong. So it is to be Sybil Thorndike, is it?'

'Of course! There has never been any serious possibility of Gertrude playing the part! It has never even been discussed! What on earth did Thomas say?'

'O, nothing much. Well, Sybil Thorndike is a big name. That would be quite something, though would she not be a trifle old? Tess is meant to be, what? Eighteen or nineteen? Sybil Thorndike must be twice that. More. Would she not be better cast as Tess's mother?'

'That doesn't matter in the least. The point is that Sybil Thorndike is a professional actress, that is the point. Gertrude is an amateur. The very idea of her playing the part in London . . . is that what Thomas said? How can he have? It has never been discussed, it is quite out of the question. You've seen what she is like on stage, Sydney; she wouldn't be capable of it. She is too mannered, too melodramatic. There is some raw talent there, but the hysterics!'

I am beginning to gabble, I know, and I should have said 'histrionics', but Cockerell speaks before I can correct myself.

'True – though "The Times" was very polite about her.'

'O, all the newspapers were the same. One of them even said she was the most beautiful woman in Dorset. Can you believe it? She may be striking, but beautiful, she is not beautiful. Look at her teeth. She is simply not, not beautiful. Sometimes one feels the whole world has gone mad! I can't see how anyone could say she was beautiful, let alone the most beautiful woman in Dorset!

Do you think she is beautiful, Sydney? It baffles me. I am baffled by it.'

'Well – you know what they say about beauty,' he says.

'But I simply can't understand it. Her teeth – and that simpering manner! The very thought of her playing the part of Tess on the London stage! The thing is, Sydney' – I lower my voice – 'you know what he's like. His ability to idealise' (do I mean idolise?) 'certain individuals is astonishing. He thinks she is a great actress, would you believe? And when there is the chance of Sybil Thorndike playing the part!'

'Florence, I didn't mean to upset you. I see what you mean . . . she does lay it on a bit thick, and if Sybil Thorndike will do it . . . well, you couldn't have anyone better. Sybil Thorndike is top-notch. I saw her in "Saint Joan", back in the spring.'

He bites into a Scotch egg.

A small, measured voice in my head tells me to calm down. Calm yourself, Florence, you have known her for four years, she has been to the house several times for tea, and we have had any number of pleasant conversations. To all intents and purposes she is a perfectly amiable young woman. This idea of her playing the part of Tess at the Haymarket must be a simple misunderstanding on Cockerell's part. But there is another voice, not in the least measured, saying why is she flirting with your husband, why is he flirting with her, what schemes are they hatching behind your back, what has he said to her about the Haymarket, look at them leaning towards each other, leaning together, heads together, touching, he breathing something in her ear, whispering in her ear, his lips touching her ear! She nods and smiles flirtatiously! All this is so transparent, so unfeigned and open, like a pair of love-birds!

'This is an excellent Scotch egg,' Cockerell says blandly. 'I haven't had a good Scotch egg for ages. But I agree with you entirely, Sybil Thorndike would be a much safer bet. She was magnificent as Saint Joan.'

I remember the time when Thomas and I first met, when the

first wife was still very much alive; in those days I was living in London, and I used to carry out occasional research on his behalf in the British Museum. More than once or twice we met in a little eating house near the Museum, and he leant and whispered into my ear. How happy I felt then! I am not merely saying that: to feel that I was helping him, serving him, it made me so happy!

Is history repeating itself? Am I merely the dull echo of the first wife? Why did I say 'hysterics' when I meant 'histrionics'? Why do the wrong words sometimes tumble out of my mouth? What is happening to me?

But I am nothing if not determined. I interrupt them. I smile and interrupt their conversation.

'Gertrude, well done. You were very good.'

'Thank you.'

'It must be so exhausting. How is your little baby?'

'My husband is looking after her. She is very well, thank you.'

'She must miss you so much, night after night, when she is so tiny. And you must miss being with her.'

How thoughtful and friendly this is of me. How devious you are, Florence.

She gazes at me with those big artless eyes that she uses to such effect. I have eyes too, I want to say to her; I am not blind.

My husband as I can tell is mildly irritated, frowning.

The evening performance is interminable. Afterwards my husband and I are driven home in a sepulchral silence, two old mutes, but it is impossible to talk with Mr. Voss listening to every word. As soon as we get out of the car we hear Wessie barking urgently. The front door opens and he races towards us. I scoop him into my arms and let him kiss my ears with his rough tongue. 'O, my little lamb, have you been all right with those nasty maids? Have you been very lonely? I am so sorry to have left you for so long.' I let him go and he tears into the shrubbery.

My husband disappears upstairs. When I join him, several minutes later, he is already half undressed.

'Thomas, what were you saying to Gertrude?'

'When?'

'You did seem to be talking a lot. You must have been talking about something. During the tea.'

Silence.

This is what happens. Has he heard me or not? Am I his wife or am I not?

I persist. 'I thought she acted very well, but she is only an amateur. I very much hope you did not say anything to her about the Haymarket.'

'My dear, in the light of the reviews, it is only fair that she should have first refusal.'

'And? Is that what you told her? What did she say?'

'She is interested.'

'But, Thomas, she has a husband and a baby to look after! How can she possibly go up to London?'

Silence once more.

'And what of Sybil Thorndike?'

'It will probably be a short run at first. If the run is extended, Sybil Thorndike can stand in for her.'

So Sybil Thorndike is to be a second string, a stand-in for the wife of a country butcher. How happy will Sybil Thorndike be about that, I wonder?

'Would it not make better sense if Sybil Thorndike were to play it from the beginning? She is a much more accomplished actress. Gertrude does so over-act. Do you not think so? She over-acts dreadfully. I know Barrie feels that. So does Cockerell.'

'Cockerell told me he thought she was splendid.'

'Really? He said that! Cockerell?'

'Yes.'

'He was being polite. You know Cockerell, he was simply being polite. I know he feels Sybil Thorndike would be very much better as Tess. He saw her in "Saint Joan". He agrees with me, she would be much better than Gertrude.'

'No one could play the part of Tess as well as Gertrude. I do not think it possible for any London actress to understand the part fully, or to hit the right accent. I am very much looking forward to it.'

'You are not intending to go up to London to see it? You can't possibly. You're eighty-four!'

'I am perfectly well enough to visit London for a night,' he answers in a stiff voice, and pulls on his night-shirt.

I am incapable of speech. That he intends to run after her, up to London, at his age, astonishes me. I say it astonishes me but it also wounds me.

'I cannot see how Gertrude can possibly go to London. She is a mother, her responsibility is to her baby. It would be too selfish of her, it would be unforgivable – taking a little baby up to London. If I were in her situation I would not even contemplate it. Mothers should not abandon their babies, whatever the circumstances.'

'My dear, she is going to discuss arrangements with Captain Bugler.'

'Captain Bugler? Who is Captain Bugler?'

'Captain Bugler is her husband.'

'I thought her husband was a butcher.'

'He may be a butcher now, but he was a Captain in the War. He won the Military Cross, out in India, according to Tilley. I thought you knew that. He is a war hero. No doubt he is capable of looking after a baby for a few days.'

I am now utterly disconcerted; why, I cannot say, but my image of a fat, sanguinary butcher has been ousted by that of a handsome dark-haired man in army uniform, a medal pinned to his breast.

He and Gertrude stand side by side, she holding her baby, as in some photograph. I am not inclined to be jealous, I do not want to be jealous, but it is impossible for me not to feel a certain pang of something or other.

My nerves are trembling like leaves and I have no expectation of sleep. Everything is falling on top of me. I am forty-five years old and my life is in tatters. This is where I am now, this is what my life is like.

CHAPTER V

❦ ❦ ❦

'Tess' was an episode in my life from so long ago. Years on end slip by without my giving it a thought, and then I read something in the newspapers, or I happen to be cleaning the little silver vase, and the memories come back in a rush. It often happens on those still, foggy mornings, but there are other times too. A few months ago a woman came to our local W.I. to speak about Mr. Hardy. The title of her talk was 'The Pessimism of Thomas Hardy' and I sat there in the drill hall and listened. I was told that she had been to W.I.s all around the country, delivering the same talk on Thomas Hardy and his pessimism, and, my, did she make him out to be pessimistic! And cold, and unfeeling, and heartless, too. One thing she said really annoyed me. She said: 'He was a great writer, but no one could really describe him as a great man.' I meant to keep quiet, but when I heard that I decided I had to say something. So, at the end of her talk, when she was taking questions, I stood up and said that whenever I had met him he had been warm and amusing and full of life. 'The Thomas Hardy I remember,' I said, 'was a very great man.' She seemed a little taken aback, and afterwards over coffee she came and asked me how well I had known him. I said that he was my friend, as he was, but I did feel downcast. Once I was home I went straight up to the spare bedroom, and spent the whole afternoon losing myself in the past, nostalgically leafing through my old scrapbooks.

An episode in my life, an episode in a life full of episodes: that's

all it is, in the end. For a long while I tried not to think about it.
I was busy supporting Ernest and bringing up Diana, and it didn't
seem a good idea to look back. What a waste of time! What's the
point? Life is for living, as Ernest used to tell me, and if you walk
along looking back over your shoulder you never see where you're
going. I suppose that, now I'm older, I've come to see things a
little differently; I see that if you never look back, you lose track
of where you are now. It's important. The past stays alive even
though it's past; I think that's what I'm trying to say.

There are three scrapbooks. They contain newspaper cuttings,
tickets, programmes and a number of letters, two from Mr. Hardy
himself. Although I say I felt nostalgia when I was looking at
them, it wasn't only nostalgia. I also felt regret, and some bitterness if I'm honest. It's not nearly as sharp as it once was, but it's
always been there, like a scar on the heart. I should have come to
terms with it by now – enough time has passed, after all – but I
haven't. I still don't know why things happened quite as they did.
The first two scrapbooks are full. With the third, you turn over
five pages and the rest are a blank.

I shouldn't want to forget it, or for it to be forgotten entirely.
'Tess' is part of how I am and always will be, I expect, and some
day I should tell Diana – sit down and tell her the whole story,
just so that she knows, if only because there's nothing about me
in the official biography, the one written by Mrs. Hardy. Not one
word. To judge from the biography, I might never have met him,
I might never have visited the house and sat and talked to him, I
might never have existed. I don't think I shall ever forgive her.

The first time I knew that we would be putting on 'Tess' was
when Mr. Tilley brought me the news. Harry Tilley was the
driving force behind the plays; without him I doubt the Hardy
Players would have kept going as long as they did. He was a
lovely man, full of energy and enthusiasm. He must have been

in his early sixties. I had known him since I was a child, when for one year he had been town mayor and had worn the ceremonial fur-trimmed robe and gold chain of office. His profession was that of a monumental mason; chiefly he made a living by carving tombstones, which he did with great skill and precision – the graveyards of the town and the surrounding villages contain hundreds of stones carved by Mr. Tilley, and by his father before him – but sometimes he undertook other church projects, such as making a new font, or a capital. Here he probably found common ground with Mr. Hardy, who as a young man had trained as an architect, and had helped restore churches that were falling into a state of disrepair.

Anyway, one day he turned up in Beaminster, and said that he had been talking to Mr. Hardy, and Mr. Hardy had agreed to us putting on 'Tess' that winter, but only on condition that I played the title role. Mr. Tilley was worried that I wouldn't be able to, because Diana was about three or four months old at the time, but I said yes at once, and he was very relieved. I knew it would put a great deal of weight on Ernest's shoulders, because I couldn't drive and so he would have to drive me to Dorchester and kick his heels for hours while we rehearsed, when he was busy enough as it was. Some people felt I shouldn't have done it when Diana was so tiny. But acting meant such a lot to me, especially the thought of acting Tess. I had been dreaming of being Tess for such a long time and I was very excited. It was flattering that Mr. Hardy wanted me to be Tess, though I dare say I'd have been very upset if he'd wanted someone else.

I do remember Mr. Tilley saying that it might be a good idea to have someone understudy the part, just in case. That was what he said: 'just in case'. Ernest and I laughed about that. What Mr. Tilley meant was, in case I became pregnant again. Having Tess with a big bump would have looked very odd!

I had known Mr. Hardy for years, of course, from other productions. He and Mrs. Hardy occasionally came to rehearsals, especially when the opening night drew near. He rarely interrupted, but after the rehearsal he would have a quiet word with Mr. Tilley, and then Mr. Tilley would tell one or other of us that he would like such and such a line delivered in a certain fashion, with more or less emotion, or more or less emphasis on a particular word. Whenever he spoke directly to me, he was always very warm and complimentary.

He must have been about eighty years old then. He was quite short, his face was heavily lined, his eyes were a light, watery blue, and the shape of almonds, and he had a pronounced nose and a thin white moustache. At rehearsals, he usually wore a dark blue pin-stripe suit and a waistcoat. Mrs. Hardy had dark brown hair worn up in a bun, and a floury complexion. Some of the members of the cast didn't like them there. They said that it was like being watched by two ghosts, and that he never looked pleased. I don't know. It's true that a sombre expression sometimes seemed to settle on his features, and that looked like displeasure, but I don't think it was. I didn't mind him watching; in fact I felt that it was his right to be there, if he wanted to be. I was never put off. Maybe by her, but not by him.

I recall an evening when we were rehearsing "The Return of the Native". I was playing the part of Eustacia, who is meant to have a London accent, and I wasn't sure if I had it right. So, at the end, I went up and asked him whether I was speaking as he wanted me to. He assured me that I was doing very well and should continue as I was.

After that rehearsal I was invited up to his house for tea, on a Sunday afternoon, an occasion that I remember very well. The other Players were a little jealous, and Dr. Smerdon said that Mr. Hardy had 'taken a shine to me'; I think those were his words. 'Watch out,' he said, 'next thing you know he'll put you in one of his novels.' Everyone laughed at that. Mr. Tilley warned me to beware of Wessex, Mr. and Mrs. Hardy's dog, who had a long history of biting strangers.

People did have divided opinions of Mr. Hardy. He was the town's most famous resident, and most of us were very proud of him, but there was always a bit of gossip. One story, and I remember hearing this long before I came to know him, was that he had been very cruel to his first wife and had even, in some unspecific way, driven her to her death, and that, within a few days of her funeral, if not before the funeral, the Mrs. Hardy I knew had moved into the house as his mistress and he had tried to pass her off as his secretary. I don't think there was ever any evidence for it. Perhaps it was true that the marriage had not been a success, but the same could be said of many marriages. My view was that no one who had written such novels as he had could possibly have committed the cruelties that he was accused of committing, and I think the problem is people hadn't bothered to read his novels and were unable to see what he was truly like. There were other stories, too, other bits of tittle-tattle, all based on ignorance. I am afraid that you always have gossip in a small country town. People like to peer and pry into other people's affairs, and spread stories for which there is not a grain of evidence.

Anyway, that Sunday afternoon, I was quite nervous, and I set off much too early from the town. I dawdled the last part of the walk up the hill and as I did so it began to rain, at first lightly and then more heavily. I had a scarf to cover my hair, but I much regretted that I had not brought an umbrella. When I came to the house, I stopped outside, by the gate, and changed out of my walking shoes, which were muddy, into my best pair, with heels, which I had brought with me in a bag, and I hid the shoes to the side of the wall, in the roots of one of the pine trees. I also got out my compact and checked my lipstick; I did hope to make a good impression. I went up to the porch and pulled the bell, and as soon as it rang a ferocious burst of barking erupted from within, and then the door opened and Wessex tore outside, barking furiously and growling. The maid screamed at him and stamped her foot, but he ignored her entirely. On Mr. Tilley's advice I stood quite still with my arms folded and let him sniff round my legs and ankles, and once he had completed his inspection he lost interest and I was allowed to go into the house and out of the rain. I was relieved about that! I should say that I came to find him quite a sweet little dog. The maids hated him with a passion, but in time he and I got on very well.

It was a slightly curious house, and it surprised me at first. I don't know what I was expecting, but it looked like a big suburban villa, rather than a house in the countryside. What I mean is that it wasn't at all grand, not like a mansion; it felt very ordinary and domestic and old-fashioned. It could be dark, because there was no electricity, and the hall was especially dark. There was a grand-father clock in it, and a barometer on the wall, and it smelt of polish. Tea was always taken in the drawing room, which was much lighter. It had a lovely bow window, and a wooden floor covered in rugs, and near the fire was a tapestry screen depicting three Oriental storks. It was full of things that interested me – pictures, drawings, ornaments. Above the fireplace there were pictures of the poets Keats and Shelley, whom Mr. Hardy admired very much. He once said that if there was a single man in history whom he would most have liked to meet, it would have been Shelley, and when I asked him what he would have said to Shelley he said that he would probably have asked Shelley to tea, but that Shelley would have refused. I asked why and he said that he didn't think tea was Shelley's favourite meal, but he said it with a certain smile, and I remember that he also said that if I were there Shelley would have been certain to come. He was good at that kind of flattery.

When you went to tea, there was always a big plate of cucumber sandwiches, cut very small and without crusts, and since neither Mr. nor Mrs. Hardy touched them they would end up being eaten by Wessex. He was persistent and quite relentless when it came to sandwiches. He would sit under the table and whine and whimper, and both Mr. and Mrs. Hardy always gave way to him.

Wessex was really the master of the house, and I don't remember him ever being told off for anything except jumping on the sofa, and even then he wasn't really told off. He did what he liked. Mrs. Hardy used to cuddle him on her lap and kiss him on the top of his head and when he barked she would try to stop him by stroking his throat and telling him not to be so wicked, which made not a blind bit of difference.

On that first occasion, Mr. Hardy asked me about my surname, Bugler, which is a common surname in Dorset, and whether one of my forebears had been a bugler in the army. I didn't know, of course. He then said – he must have found this out from Mr. Tilley – that my mother's maiden name was Way, and that he remembered her from years ago, when she had worked as a dairymaid on a farm in Stinsford. As you can imagine, my mother was astonished when she heard that. 'Thirty years ago. Why should he remember me? How could he possibly know it was me? There were lots of us dairymaids! He never spoke to me, or not to my knowledge!'

I remember two other things from that first visit. One is that it was the first time I had ever drunk Chinese tea, and the other is that Mr. Hardy said something about the weather being 'inclement'. As I say, it was raining, and he made some remark to the effect that the weather was very inclement. 'Inclement' wasn't a word ever used by ordinary people, and it has stayed in my mind for that reason.

I went to tea on several other occasions over the next year, and usually I was the only guest. We talked about books, and about acting, of course, and things generally, especially things relating to the past. Mr. Hardy lived a great deal in the past, imaginatively, and he liked to talk about the changes that had taken place in rural life. Once he mentioned walking across the heath at night when he was quite young, and how he had frightened himself silly with the thought of ghosts. Sometimes he came up with old sayings that he remembered from his childhood but that were dying out. One was 'A green Christmas makes for a fat churchyard.'

He never put on any airs. He was very famous but you wouldn't have thought it from his manner, and he always did his best to put me at my ease. Mrs. Hardy seemed friendly too, at least at first.

At tea he always wore a tweed suit and a tie; men were never seen open-necked in those days, unless they were workmen. Mrs. Hardy wore dark, heavy dresses with high necklines, and I often thought how mournful they made her look. After she had cuddled Wessex his white hairs would be left all over her lap and she would pick them off, one by one.

There was such a big gap in their ages that it felt surprising that they should have been man and wife. She must have been half his age, while he was old enough to be her father. But what people don't realise is that he had a quite youthful manner, whereas the reverse was true of her. She seemed much older than she was. Even so, the gap in age did make you wonder. Mr. Tilley, who had known them before they were married, said that the two of them would have been lost without each other; in his view it must have been a privilege for Florence to be married to him, to have been privy to his closest thoughts. I am sure that is true, but my experience of them was different to that of Mr. Tilley and at times I did sense a certain friction. To give an example: one Christmastime I was up there for tea and there were mince pies instead of cucumber sandwiches, and Mr. Hardy kept on feeding Wessex mince pies, and Mrs. Hardy told him off. 'You will make him sick,' she said. In fact if I remember rightly what she said was 'You will make him sick again,' so obviously this had happened before. Mr. Hardy calmly replied that it was Christmas: 'Christmas is Christmas,' he said, and she then said, in a very reproving tone, 'You spoil him, Thomas. It is very naughty of you.' It sounded as if Mr. Hardy, far from being a world-famous writer, was a small boy being chided by his mother. As I recall it, he was completely unperturbed. He said, 'The old deserve their pleasures,' and immediately gave Wessex another mince pie. Mrs. Hardy tried to laugh, but I felt she was quite upset.

When it came to Wessex, there was a degree of competition between them, if only because they both doted on him so much. When Mr. Hardy was giving him the mince pies, Mrs. Hardy felt jealous. Whether the dog should have been fed the mince pies wasn't the issue, the issue was whether the dog liked him more than her. The fact that I was there was what made it awkward; if I hadn't been there the conversation would have been different. At least that is how I saw things, but I may have been mistaken.

I did feel honoured to be invited. Some of the other Players used to say that when he came to rehearsals it was chiefly to watch me, and that he was under my spell, and it's true that I often felt his eyes following me around, but as I was playing the part of the heroine that was only to be expected. I think that maybe it would be truer to say that I was under his spell, as were we all.

As I say, Mrs. Hardy could be very friendly, and one afternoon in summer when she and I seemed to be getting on well together we went for a stroll round the garden, and she talked to me about teaching in a school. As a young woman she had been a school-mistress in London, and she said how rewarding it had been. She told me about one of her pupils, an orphaned boy. She had taken him under her wing and befriended him, and she said it was one of the best things she had done in her life. 'I would love to have adopted him, if I could have done,' she said. I asked what had happened to him, and she said he had gone to Birmingham to live with his uncle, and she often wondered if he now remembered her at all. 'I am sure he does,' I said, 'how could he not remember you?' because I could see that he mattered a great deal to her.

I hadn't been sure why she was telling me about all this, but after we had strolled on a little further we stopped by one of the flower-beds, and she said: 'You would make an excellent school-mistress, you know, Gertrude.' Since I had never been very good at school-work, I said something to the effect that my spelling would let me down, whereupon she exclaimed: 'Oh, but there is nothing more worthwhile than teaching. But what am I thinking of? You are an actress. You should go on the stage.'

There was nothing I should have liked more than to go on the stage as a professional actress, but I felt embarrassed to say so, and I replied that I felt very lucky to be able to act in Dorchester. 'Oh, but acting there is not in the least like acting on the professional stage in London,' she said, 'the difference is so great it is hardly possible to describe. I love our little productions as much as anyone, but the general standard of acting is not very good, as you know. You are head and shoulders above everyone else. Are you very nervous when you go on stage?' I answered that I was often nervous before I went on stage, but that once I was actually there, in front of an audience, I felt completely at home, and Mrs. Hardy said that was a sure sign of a born actress. She said: 'You are so talented, I am sure it is your destiny to be on the stage.'

Can you imagine? That it was my destiny! I had already had some very favourable notices from London reviewers for my performances in 'The Return of the Native', but Mrs. Hardy's remarks that afternoon did set me thinking. I didn't talk to anyone else about it, if only because it seemed an impossible idea – you know, my parents ran a little hotel, and we didn't have any connections in London who could have helped me, but I knew that was what I wanted to do more than anything else in the world. I used to think about it at night when trains were coming into the station. I'd hear the screech of brakes, an occasional hoot, the clanking of a long procession of goods vans, and if I stood up and went to the window I'd often be able to make out a faint flurry of red sparks as a train went over the points. What I mean is that the sound of the trains made me think how easy it would be to get to London, and then in a jump I'd be on stage, acting, in some beautiful theatre with huge red curtains. I am sure all this sounds as if I was very naïve, which I was.

Not knowing what to do I decided – after much thought, I may say – that I would ask Mr. and Mrs. Hardy for their advice. I didn't want to mention it when any of the other Players were nearby, in case they thought me big-headed, and so I waited until I was next invited to tea, and then cautiously brought the conversation round to my question. Mrs. Hardy immediately exclaimed, 'What a lovely idea!', but Mr. Hardy said nothing for a moment. When he was thinking hard about something his eyes took on a particular expression, and I could see him turning the idea in his mind. Eventually he said that, while he wouldn't advise anyone to go on the stage when acting was such an uncertain way of life, nor would he advise anyone against it. If everyone were discouraged by the difficulties, there would be no actors or actresses and all the theatres would have to close down. He also pointed out that it would involve me living in London, and he wondered what I would feel about that. I replied that if I were able to act, I could live anywhere, which was what I did feel – the idea of acting was so important to me. Mrs. Hardy was much more enthusiastic, and immediately said that I needed some famous playwright to write a part for me in his next play, to launch me on the stage. I remember her word 'launch' – as if I was a ship. 'What about Barrie?' she said. 'He could do it.' – 'Barrie?' said Mr. Hardy, plainly surprised. – 'Yes,' Mrs. Hardy said, 'I am sure he would, if you were to ask him.'

The conversation didn't go any further, and it wasn't until later I realised they were talking about Sir James Barrie, the author of 'Peter Pan', but I did feel very encouraged, and very grateful to Mrs. Hardy. She instigated the whole thing; that's what makes later events so inexplicable.

The idea of my pursuing a stage career was complicated by the fact of Ernest, if I can put it like that. He was my cousin. We met by chance one market day in Dorchester when it was pelting with rain and I was sheltering in the doorway of a jewellery shop. The road was like a river, and people were running for cover, and he dived into the doorway. I hadn't seen him for years. When I was a little girl I used to meet him occasionally at family gatherings, but he was nine years older than I was and always seemed very grown-up. During the War he had been away with the Dorset Regiment, and then in the Indian Army, and he had only lately come back to England. He was very handsome, or at least I thought so. He had dark hair and warm eyes, and his complexion was still slightly sunburnt. We talked and got on very well, and soon after that we began courting. He worked with his father, who ran a butcher's shop in the middle of Beaminster, but sometimes he could get away late on a Saturday, and then we either went to the pictures, or to a dance. Ernest wasn't a very good dancer – he trod on my feet more than once or twice, and I had to do most of the steering, which earned us a few black looks from some of the other couples – but he learnt quickly. On Sundays, if the weather was kind, we used to go on walks. We would stroll along the river towards the great house at Kingston; this is the most gentle walk, and very lovely in spring and early summer. We also explored further afield. Ernest would borrow my father's bicycle, and we would cycle out of the town, and sometimes our route took us up the hill and past the Hardys' house, and I used to ride slowly in the hope that I might see them out for a walk. One day we stopped by the brick wall that runs round the house, and Ernest lifted me up so that I could look over the wall, and I saw someone walking across one of the lawns, but it may have been the gardener. I ducked down very quickly. It would have been so embarrassing if either Mr. or Mrs. Hardy had seen me peering in!

I have to confess that, at the start, I was fairly sure that I didn't want to marry Ernest! Maybe that's wrong; he was very handsome, as I say, and I did like him very much, but liking someone isn't the same as loving them, and I was frightened by the thought of marrying the wrong man. Here I know I was very strongly influenced by Mr. Hardy's novels, which are full of misconceived alliances, you know, the husband and wife fall out of love, if they were in love in the first place (which they often are not, even when they think they are), and are condemned to live in domestic misery for the rest of their lives. To marry the wrong person, to marry without love, I thought, would be a terrible fate; better not to marry at all.

The character in my head that summer, the first summer we were courting, was Eustacia from 'The Return of the Native' – I had long dark hair like her, and I too was emotional and impetuous, and I am sure that I began to read my own life as a version of her life. Eustacia's great mistake, given her restless character, is that she chooses a man who has come back to settle in the countryside after living in Paris, and I couldn't avoid thinking that Ernest, too, had come back to settle in Dorset after years away. I remember asking myself whether I really wanted to marry a local man, a cousin. Did I want to spend my life in Beaminster? Beaminster is such a small gossipy place. Although it calls itself a town it's not really much more than a large village. I've come to like it, as one does – one makes the best of things – but at that time the thought of spending the rest of my life there horrified me.

I also knew that if I went to live there it would be very difficult to do any acting, even in Dorchester, never mind London. But my mother and father were very keen on Ernest. During the War he had won the Military Cross, which was quite something, and they liked the fact that he was my cousin; if he and I married, they thought, it would help bring the Beaminster and Dorchester sides of the Bugler family closer together. We'd only been courting for a few weeks when my mother started trying to find out whether he had proposed, and telling me that I didn't want to be left on the shelf. She said that it wasn't fair of me to string Ernest along if I wasn't serious. In hindsight it seems funny but at the time as you can imagine it drove me mad, not least because he hadn't proposed! So I could hardly be accused of stringing him along.

I remember when I thought he was about to propose. We were in a café in the middle of Dorchester when he pulled a little box from his pocket, and more or less chucked it at me across the table. I was convinced it was going to be an engagement ring and then I opened it and it turned out to contain his medal! It had a purple and white ribbon attached to it. Heaven knows what my face looked like, and what I'd have said if it had been a ring I have no idea.

Still, that was when I finally managed to get him to tell me why he'd been awarded the MC. He'd always put me off before. 'You don't want to know, Gertie,' he'd say, 'it's just a bit of tin, it doesn't mean anything. I didn't do anything that much. It's in the past, it's finished with, forget it.' That was what Ernest always felt; the past was past.

He'd been out on the North West Frontier, on the border with Afghanistan. He and his company had been sent there to safeguard the border, and they were ordered to take control of a particular mountain ridge. It was called Stonehenge Ridge, oddly enough. I asked Ernest if it looked like Stonehenge and he said, not at all, except that it was covered in boulders. As there was no proper cover, trying to capture the ridge from the Afghans was a fairly hopeless idea, and all of them knew that, and nobody wanted to fight. However, they set off before dawn; in his company there were about three hundred Sikh soldiers and twenty-five officers, half of them British, the rest Sikhs. As soon as they came within range of the Afghans they started taking casualties, Ernest said – the Afghans weren't very heavily armed, but they knew how to shoot straight. He was awarded the medal because, under heavy fire, he had helped rescue a number of men who'd been wounded. Two of his fellow British officers – one a good friend – had died, and he felt the whole affair had been a waste of time. That was why he was so reluctant to tell me about it. He felt it was best if he kept it to himself.

'So you could have been killed?' I said. – 'I might have been,' he said with a smile, 'but I wasn't.'

By then I'd realised that Ernest was quite shy and not that certain over what to do next. When he'd been in India, he said, he'd always pictured Beaminster as home, he'd longed to be back, but now he was there, it was like being a child again. Beaminster was full of Buglers – aunts, uncles, grandparents, first cousins, second cousins. I remember saying to him: 'I'm your cousin!' and he said, 'Oh, you're different!' and we both laughed. But half the time he felt that he hadn't grown up. He was thirty-two, after all – much older than I was.

What he hated, dear old Ernest, was being a butcher. He used to say that he liked animals when they were alive but not when they were dead. So it was difficult for him, and one Sunday afternoon he was really down in the dumps. It ought to have been spring, or nearly spring, but the weather was miserable, cold and wet; all weekend it had rained non-stop. There were daffodils out round the town but they were spattered with mud. We'd tried going for a walk and had given up, and now we were standing on the station platform, waiting for the train, waiting to say good-bye to each other for the week, and he began to talk about his relations with his father. 'We get on well enough, but working in the shop with him, day in day out, it's a strain,' he said. 'He can't help it, it's not his fault. He still thinks I'm eighteen. He's in charge. I had enough of being ordered around in the Army.' I put my arm through his and tightened it. 'What's brought this on?' I said, and he said he knew he didn't want to be a butcher for the rest of his life, but he couldn't think how else to earn a living, and so we began to talk about the future, and I realised we were talking not only about his future but also mine. 'Would you go back in the Army?' I said. – 'God, no,' he said. 'No, I was thinking I might have a go at farming.' I asked him where and he said Devon. Land was relatively cheap, and if he borrowed from the bank, he might be able to buy a small farm; fifty acres would be enough to start with. The trouble was, this was the nineteen twenties, a very bad time for agriculture, when almost all farmers seemed to be doing very badly. I knew that he wanted my opinion, and I said that I thought things were bound to get better eventually, but, if he wanted to be prudent, he could rent some land, and see how things went, and in time he could get a proper farm. That was how we left it, because we could hear the train on its way. You could always hear the chugging of the train before you saw the train itself.

The idea of being a farmer's wife was very attractive to me, and when he proposed, a few weeks later, I accepted him at once. By this time I was very busy again with the Hardy Players. We were doing 'Far from the Madding Crowd', and as I'd hoped, I was playing the part of Bathsheba, the heroine, and I loved it. I found her a very sympathetic character. She is emotional like Eustacia, but less of a schemer, and she also happens to end up happily married to Gabriel Oak, who is a farmer! I don't know how important that really was but, as I say, I did have a habit of reading my own life through novels and it did cross my mind that I was almost exactly the same age as Bathsheba. Ernest timed it nicely: he finally got round to proposing about half an hour after the end of the last performance, back-stage, when I was still dressed as Bathsheba. He did it very romantically (I'm not saying how). It felt as if there was some sort of Fate about it all.

The wedding was in September, at Stinsford Church. Several people have asked if we chose to be married there because of Mr. Hardy, but it wasn't that; it was simply that we liked the church so much. Neither of us realised that he had so many associations with it. However, some weeks before the service, when the banns were published, we walked round the churchyard and found ourselves by a big old yew tree, staring not only at his first wife's grave, but also at the graves of his mother and father, and his grandparents; and I did wonder if we should invite him and Mrs. Hardy to the wedding. All the Hardy Players had been invited. However, there were already a lot of guests, and Ernest was a bit doubtful, and so we decided not to invite them. I regret it now: I should have liked him there. Whether he would have come if we'd invited him, I can't say.

When it came to the marriage form, Ernest insisted on putting down his occupation not as 'butcher' but as 'farmer', which was a statement of intentions as much as anything. 'I'm not a butcher – it's just temporary,' he said. 'I'm already a farmer; that's how I feel.' The Reverend Cowley, who married us, didn't say anything to object. After the wedding we had a lovely week on the Isle of Wight, and then moved into a little cottage in Beaminster, on Prout Hill. That was a big change for me. A big change! There was no electricity supply, so we had to use oil lamps and candles. It was like living back in the middle of the nineteenth century! And it always seemed to rain a lot. Beaminster is a very rainy place, much more than Dorchester; I don't know why that should be the case, but it is. Other people have remarked on it. And, of course, I was living away from my family. It was a big change. We didn't have much money and I had no help with housework, and I felt quite isolated. I couldn't drive – I've never learned to drive – and in those days there was no direct bus service between the two towns, so to get from Beaminster to Dorchester by public transport one first of all had to catch a bus to Bridport and then a train to Maiden Newton, and then wait half an hour for the connecting train to Dorchester. The journey took nearly two and a half hours!

In getting married I hadn't given up my acting ambitions, or not entirely. Ernest and I had talked about it and he was all for me continuing to act with the Players. As things turned out, the year after we were married I became pregnant, and of course, that meant I couldn't possibly do any acting. I remember writing to Mr. Tilley to say as much, and I had a lovely letter back, in which he congratulated me and said that there was nothing more important than having a baby. In his letter he did also say that he knew Mr. Hardy would very much like to see me if I happened to be in Dorchester, and that was the start of all the difficulties that I had with Mrs. Hardy.

It was a summer's day – late summer, I think. I'd left home early so that I should be back in good time to make Ernest's tea, and all the connections worked well, so I was in Dorchester by eleven o'clock, and I walked up the hill to the house. By the time I got there I was feeling quite tired, and I was very much looking forward to sitting down. I rang the bell, and the maid answered, and I said I had come to see Mr. Hardy – she asked me if I had an appointment and I said I had been asked to call, and then she went indoors, and then Mrs. Hardy appeared. I was immediately struck by how unwell she looked; that is to say, she always looked less than well, but now she seemed quite ill. Her face was very pale, and she had dark patches under her eyes. She reminded me of a lemur. She was very cold and hostile. She told me that Mr. Hardy always worked in the mornings, and could not possibly be disturbed. Well, obviously I didn't want to disturb him at his work, but I had come all the way from Beaminster, and so I asked whether it would be more convenient if I came back in the afternoon. She then said – I remember this very clearly – that it would not be more convenient, that he could not receive uninvited visitors, and anyone wishing to see him had to make an appointment with her.

It was her tone that shocked me more than anything else; I felt as if she was treating me as a complete stranger. And she must have been able to see that I was pregnant; that was obvious to anyone, because my stomach was a big bump! I was completely thrown. I think I asked her to tell Mr. Hardy that I had called – because I didn't want to seem discourteous to him – and on that note I left, wondering how on earth I had offended her. I could think of nothing that I might have done. A letter arrived the next day, in a cream envelope. She must have written it almost as soon as I'd left. It was written on headed notepaper, and it was very long and unpleasant. It accused me of not knowing how to behave properly. Several sentences stick in my mind, even now; one was that 'all invitations naturally come from me, as is the custom' and that it was 'not usual in our station of life for any lady to call upon a gentleman'. She also accused me, in so many words, of making up the story that Mr. Hardy had asked me to call. I showed it to Ernest, and when he read that phrase 'our station in life' he said that it showed what a snob she was. 'You've rubbed her up the wrong way, the old witch,' he said. I am afraid we often called her 'the old witch' after that.

Ernest's advice was that I should forget about it, but the more I read the letter, the nastier it seemed. The tone was so unpleasant, and the idea that I might have lied to her made me angry, so I wrote back, and a few days later she wrote back again, another, even longer letter, in which she now tried to make out that there had been some misunderstanding, and offered various excuses for dismissing me as she had. She blamed her nerves, and some piece of news she had had. However, she still refused to accept that I had been asked to call on Mr. Hardy – instead of saying that I had made it up, she now suggested that I had remembered incorrectly!

To be honest, the whole affair left a bad taste in my mouth. It did make me feel very wary of her. And it came in the middle of all sorts of other things. I had a very difficult pregnancy, I became anaemic, and then something else happened. As a sideline Ernest had started renting three small fields on the edge of Beaminster, which he stocked with some cattle that he had bought at market, and during the day I would walk up to the fields to check that they were doing all right. One afternoon a big bullock barged into me and knocked me over, knocked me down in the mud, and I was very shaken by that. I wasn't trampled or anything, but I fell awkwardly. I felt very sick. Not long after, I went back to live with my parents in Dorchester, thinking that it would be better to have the baby there with my mother at hand, and the baby was still-born. He was a boy. The nurses tried to take him away before I could see him, but I made them give him to me, and everything about him looked so perfect: his head, his hands and feet and toes and ears. It was very hard. It upsets me even now, after all these years. Whether losing him had anything to do with being knocked over I don't know; everyone said that couldn't have made any difference, but I've always wondered.

Tess loses her baby too. I thought of that later. Tess isn't allowed to give her baby a proper Christian burial, and I wasn't either. The nurses took him away. There's this idea that the soul doesn't enter the body until the moment of birth – such nonsense! Afterwards, back home, I was very low for a long time; I lay in bed or sat in an armchair like an old woman. It sounds illogical, but I felt I'd let Ernest down. My mother fussed round me, and baked and tidied, and tried to cheer me up by being very bright and positive, saying that I was young and that Ernest and I would have many more chances to start a family, but I remember thinking, what if we don't? What if that was our one and only chance? Oh and the skies were grey, the fields were muddy, winter was coming on. But then, one day, a car pulled up outside the cottage and there was a small man in a brown raincoat at the front door, and he gave me a bunch of red carnations, in a silver vase, and with them was a little envelope, and inside it a card which I still have. It reads, 'My dear Gertrude, with best wishes for your speedy recovery, yours truly, T.H.' I was so touched by that; I thought how good it was of him. He must have heard via Mr. Tilley. The card was written in his own hand, too.

It cheered me up no end, and I pulled myself together and got on with things, and by late summer I was pregnant again. The March after that I gave birth to Diana, which made me very happy.

I didn't meet Mrs. Hardy again for a long while. Not until we were rehearsing for 'Tess', which was more than a year after our – whatever you call it. Our misunderstanding, to use her word. And she behaved as if nothing had ever happened. She was a little distant, but very polite. It was odd. I tried talking about the misunderstanding to Mr. Tilley, but he never liked being critical of anyone. 'Mrs. Hardy means well, but she's under a good deal of strain with her health,' he said. 'She's not a robust woman. I wouldn't pay too much attention if I were you.' Ernest took a different line – he thought she was a bit doolally, which was one of his favourite words, and in the end I came to agree with him; there was an underlying instability in her makeup, I think.

As I remember it, she and Mr. Hardy only attended one or two rehearsals, and it's true that she didn't look well. She'd had an operation on her neck which she tried to hide with a fur stole, a dead fox, not that it fooled anyone; it drew attention to her neck rather than the reverse. Somehow the stole made her look even more lemur-like. I did my best to avoid her, but a while before 'Tess' opened I had an invitation from her to tea, which surprised me a great deal. Half of me didn't want to go, but Ernest saw it as an olive branch and said that it was her way of trying to apologise; if I didn't go it would be rude. So I went. But, and this struck me as very strange, I never saw her. She never appeared. Mr. Hardy told me she was unwell but I thought she had had cold feet and couldn't face meeting me. Whatever the reason, I have to confess that I was very relieved! There was just Mr. Hardy and me and Wessex, and Wessex knew me by then, I was accepted, and he allowed me to feed him lots of sandwiches.

When there were other people around, or when he wrote to me, Mr. Hardy always addressed me as either Gertrude or Miss Bugler, or Mrs. Bugler after I was married. But when we were alone together it was always Gertie. He called me Gertie that day, and it was a very important day, because he told me about the possibility of putting on a professional production of 'Tess' at the Haymarket Theatre in London. As soon as he broached the subject I saw what was coming – I knew he was going to ask me if I wanted to play the part – and my heart began to beat a little faster. Dear me! It was a bit like being proposed to! He went on to say that nothing was settled, and it all depended on how well 'Tess' went in Dorchester and what the reviewers said, but I was very excited. When I left, I felt as if I was walking on air. I did worry a little about what Ernest would say when I broke the news to him, because I knew what a strain it would be for him looking after Diana when I was up in London, but he was good about it. He knew how much it meant to me, a chance to act on the professional stage.

'Tess' did go well in Dorchester, although in one performance – I think it may even have been the opening night – I nearly forgot to take off my wedding ring. At the last moment I remembered, and I gave it to Mr. Hardy for safe keeping, and he put it back on my hand just before the scene where I was married. The newspaper reviews were very nice, though the one in the 'Daily Express' made us all laugh. I still have it in my scrapbook. 'No one could be more like Hardy's heroine; she was attending to her manifold duties at her farm a few hours before she became Tess on the stage.' Well, we had three fields and a herd of bullocks – not really a farm! But really that was my fault, because whenever I was asked what Ernest did, I always said he was a farmer.

The best moment, I think, was after the play had ended on the Saturday evening – we went into the Council Chamber and there were speeches, and a poem was recited in my honour. I felt very proud, but embarrassed, really. By then it was common knowledge about the Haymarket, though my parents still refused to believe it; to them it was a bit of a joke, I think. It's hard to describe, but London used to occupy a strange place in the mentality of most people in Dorchester; if you even mentioned it they would recoil in horror, or they would say something like: 'Well, it may be all right to visit for a day or two, but I couldn't ever live there, not in all that smoke! I couldn't breathe!' No one country born and bred could be happy in London, was the general view. My mother had never been to London in her entire life, even though it was only two and a half hours on the train, and she couldn't believe in the Haymarket. Even a good deal later, after I'd gone back to the Hardys' and met the manager of the theatre, Mr. Harrison, she didn't think it could be true.

I remember that day so well, even better than the first time I went to the house. Several of my visits there for tea have blurred in my memory, but this was lunch. Ernest drove me, and it was one of those horrible foggy days and I got there late and in quite a panic in case I was thought very rude. But everyone was so kind. We drank champagne, and Mr. Harrison told me that I'd be paid for playing Tess – twenty pounds a week! That was such a surprise, when I'd've done it for nothing! To be paid for acting! But staying in London was going to be expensive, so I was very pleased about that. We talked about all sorts of things – hotels and trains, and what the other members of the cast were like. Professor Sydney Cockerell was there – I'd met him before, because he'd come to see 'Tess' at the Corn Exchange – and we had a fascinating conversation about ghosts! Mr. Hardy was on very good form, too.

The only difficult moment came as I was leaving. I'd told a small lie, a white lie – I'd said that I had a taxi-cab waiting for me at the end of the drive, which I felt sounded better than to say it was Ernest in our old car, and then Mr. Hardy decided to walk me down the drive. He'd never walked me down the drive before, and I was quite taken aback because I thought I'd be found out, but the fog saved me. It was so foggy you couldn't see very much at all. But, as we stood by the gate, just before I got into the car, he did say something very touching, the most touching thing he ever said to me. He said that I should always think of him as my friend. It was such a generous thing to say, and I felt very moved. To say it to someone like me! I shall never forget it. When I heard that speaker at the W.I. telling everyone that his character was cold and withdrawn, I went straight back to that moment in the fog and thought how she didn't really know what he was like at all.

As I drove home with Ernest I was in a daze of happiness. I really believed it was the start of a big acting career, and that we would be able to escape Beaminster and live in London and – oh, everything would change. We would start a new life together, I would become famous. Ernest told me to steady on – 'don't count your chickens', but I was already counting. For weeks I pushed little Diana in her pram up and down the steep Beaminster hills and dreamed about it all. It was very hard not to be carried away.

PART TWO

꙰ ꙰ ꙰

CHAPTER VI

✻ ✻ ✻

One tranquil January morning, at a time not far removed from the present, the inhabitants of a certain region of the west of England awoke to find themselves submerged in a fog of such density that the entire world of meadows, fields, woods, rivers, towns and villages was reduced to a few yards of visibility. Such fogs, developing during the night and pouring their spongy masses over the land, vary greatly in their persistence; some clear rapidly, especially when assisted by a sufficiently strong breeze, while others take hours to disperse. To judge from the stillness of the air, it seemed likely that this particular miasma would last for the whole day.

In the midst of the fog, on a hill-top about a mile from a well-known county town, stood a handsome brick house enclosed by a belt of trees, from the branches and twigs of which droplets of water fell and made an irregular patter on the dead leaves. There were few other sounds, one characteristic of such vaporous weather being its muffling quality. Birds declined to sing, preferring to wait for better times, noises from any traffic on the nearby road were muted, and while the railway line was not that far away, even the whistle of a steam train was scarcely audible.

Such conditions create in the minds of those who experience them a powerful disorientation. Lacking familiar landmarks, travellers often lose not only their way but also their sense of time. Gazing towards the house, its slate roof receding into white obscurity, an innocent observer might easily imagine himself into some other age, not the early part of the twentieth century.

A door of the house opened, and out stepped an old man, who stood motionless on the gravel drive. From a distance, he seemed less a living human being than a spectre who had temporarily chosen to haunt the spot where he had once lived. The textures of the fog drained the substance from him so thoroughly that it might not have been surprising had he faded entirely from view. With him, and equally ghostly, was a dog, a white terrier.

The old man wore a long dark coat and a hat, and in one hand he carried a walking stick. His age was probably somewhere upwards of four score, and his face, with its pronounced nose and white moustache, as wrinkled as a prune. It was the face of one who had spent much of his life thinking and observing; in it were lineaments of shrewd wisdom, good humour, and grim resolve, yet it also held more than a little doubt. The sceptical expression that it bore at this moment perhaps owed something to his sentiments concerning fog, but also seemed to bespeak more generally his relation to the world.

Anyone seeing him there would have drawn the reasonable and entirely accurate conclusion that he was the owner of the house, who had come out in order to take the morning air and to give the dog a run in the garden.

He began to walk slowly down the drive, which was somewhat overgrown by trees, the low branches extending overhead to form a tunnel. The dog dawdled to inspect a particularly interesting stick and then trotted into a shrubbery.

After less than a hundred yards the old man reached the white barred gate which marked the edge of the property. Here the fog seemed even thicker than it was by the house, and nothing could be seen beyond the tufts of grass shining on the far side of the road. The road itself was one of some importance, but at this early hour few people were abroad; it lay still and empty, its surface covered in needles and cones, along with a liberal scattering of beech leaves which, despite the monochrome light, registered on the eye in glowing shades of gold and russet.

Presently there came the very faint sound of wheels, made by some waggon as it left the town and ascended the hill. The sound grew louder by degrees, and when the steady clop of a horse's hooves could also be discerned the old man moved away and called the dog's name several times. 'Wessex. Wessex.' His voice was not at all peremptory, and indeed there was something in the tone which suggested that he had no great expectation of being heard. When the dog did finally reappear, wagging his stumpy tail, he did so from a completely different direction to that which his master had anticipated. 'Where have you been?' the old man asked him. 'Eh? Wessex?'

The waggon passed; silence prevailed once more. The old man took a thin path that threaded under the trees and led to a stretch of worm-cast lawn bordered by flower-beds. On it a fat rabbit was feeding. It vanished into the fog, but the dew on the grass was heavy, and its trail could be followed as far as the edge of the vegetable garden, an area of ground stocked with sprouts and other winter greens. The leaves of the sprouts had a blueish tinge in the fog, and fat pearls of water, condensed from the air, lay in the crinkled folds of the cabbage leaves. Snails with glistening horns oozed over the damp soil, smoothly negotiating its uneven surfaces.

The old man tapped the dog's hind-quarters with his stick. 'Go on,' he urged. 'Rabbit. Rabbit!'

The vocabulary of the dog was an extensive one, in which the word 'rabbit' occupied a prominent place, and in times gone by he would have chased the thief from its dinner without more ado. Wessex was, however, now eleven years old – an age, in canine terms, perhaps not much less than that of his human master. He gave a start, sprang eagerly forward and rushed towards the looming form of a man bearing a spade.

'Mornin', sir,' he said in a rich local accent. 'Mornin', Wessex.' In a desire to be respectful he raised the handle of the spade to touch what would have been his forelock, had he possessed any hair, which he did not: his head was bald as an egg.

'Good morning, Mr. Caddy,' the old man replied. 'A foggy morning.'

''Tis, sir, 'tis, the worst this year. In the town it be even thicker. Down there you can't see your hand in front o' your face, it be like a night without a moon.'

'Will it clear, do you think?'

The gardener looked about him with a scientific air, as if to assess the peculiar quality of the fog. 'It may do, possibly it may. Then again, it may not. If you asks me, sir, it don't seem like it has a mind to clear, but then you never knows with fog. An hour from now it might have all gone, but I wouldn't say so.'

When it came to matters meteorological, Mr. Caddy, like many a true countryman, was evidently unwilling to venture too decisively one way or the other. At his assessment of probabilities the old man seemed mildly amused. 'There is a rabbit in the garden.'

'Yes, sir, I seed it yesterday and I've been all around the walls a-lookin' for where it might have got in. I can set a snare if you want, sir. Or I can borrow a gun. My wife's brother has a gun, sir, I could borrow that.'

The old man shook his head. 'No shooting, no. It may leave of its own accord. So long as there is only one of them.'

'Yes, sir.'

They parted, the old man walking further round the shrouded garden. Again they came upon the rabbit, and this time Wessex gave pursuit, though never with any prospect of success. The old man patted him, however. 'Well done. Well done, Wessex.'

Shortly afterwards both had returned into his house, while Mr. Caddy had also disappeared from view. The house was then as still as a photograph, the fog having closed over the scene so completely that it might never have taken place.

*

The morning continued. Far above, the sun doubtless shone with its customary brilliance from a sky as blue as those in the paintings of Raphael, but its rays penetrated the vapour only enough to diffuse a general whiteness. The old man, now seated at his desk, and with a woollen shawl around his shoulders, did not greatly mind, such fogs, like frost, ice and snow, being a familiar part of winter in the English countryside, and infinitely preferable to the acrid sepia versions of the same phenomenon found in the city. Indeed, he was grateful to the fog for hiding the distractions of the exterior world, leaving him free to concentrate on his writing.

The poem on which he was working was one he had begun some months earlier, when his wife, Florence, had been in London for an operation on her neck. It was an expression of Wessex's love for his absent mistress, expressed in the dog's own voice. Will she ever return, the lady of my heart, or is she gone for ever? Will I again hear the call of her soft voice? Will I again run toward her as she stands at the field's edge? Composition on such a theme should have been easy – the time was when he could have thrown it off in a trice – but the words had not come, and he had put it aside. Regarding it now he found it a clumsy affair, with the opening verse especially weak. Still, the idea was an appealing one and he was reluctant to abandon it, not least because Florence had been nagging him for years to write something about Wessex.

It was an unwritten rule that when he was in his study he should not be disturbed, but as he set to work she knocked on the door. Three guests were coming to luncheon, and she wanted to know whether champagne should be served. 'After all,' she said, 'it is an important day.'

'Yes,' he said, turning slightly in his chair. (He liked champagne. It was his one luxury.)

There was a short silence in which her stiff face stared at him. She seemed badly out of sorts, he could tell; at breakfast she had said barely a word.

'I've asked Mrs. Simmons to do a cherry cake for tea. And Thomas I hope you don't mind, but I've told the maids to light the fires early. The drawing room is so damp in this weather, and the fires never seem to draw well. We must get the chimneys swept soon. We simply must. All the chimneys.'

He wondered why she needed to bother him with this information. One day it was the trees, the next the chimneys. And when he was working!

'I am writing a poem about Wessex,' he announced.

If he had entertained the hope that she would be pleased, he must have been disappointed, for her expression remained quite fixed and rigid. 'Is it going well?'

'I am not sure. Probably not.'

'Well, I shall leave you to it. But we do need the chimneys swept. There is no point in having one or two swept. We must have them all swept, including this chimney.'

She withdrew, and he returned to the poem, shifting lines here and there, changing words and making other improvements. Outside the fog lightened and thinned, but showed no inclination to remove itself in its entirety.

The old man's study was located in a part of the house above the kitchen, and as the morning advanced he was aware of occasional noises emanating from that quarter, among them the clanking of pans, the bang of the oven door and the shrill whistle of the kettle, denoting considerable activity in the cause of luncheon. Mrs. Simmons was the latest in a series of cooks, none staying for very long, possibly out of an aversion to the house's isolated situation. The old man had only ever spoken to her a few times; as convention decreed, the business of managing domestic affairs was primarily his wife's concern.

A different sound, that of Wessex's loud barks, eventually penetrated his ears, and no more than a minute later one of the maids knocked on the door. 'Mr. Harrison and Professor Cockerell have arrived, sir.' – 'Mrs. Bugler?' – 'No, sir, not yet, sir.' – 'Thank you, Nellie,' he said, only to recall, after she had gone, that it might have been Elsie.

He descended the stairs slowly. A suitcase stood on the hall's wooden floor, and the air smelt agreeably of roast lamb. The grandfather clock gave the time as nearly half past one, somewhat later than he had expected.

A gust of laughter blew out of the drawing room, where Harrison and Cockerell were in excellent spirits. Their train journey from London had been delayed on account of the fog, but they had been greatly diverted by something that had happened within their compartment. They had already told Florence, but it was such a good story that both wanted to tell it again. An elderly lady, wrapped in furs – 'a veritable dragon!' declared Cockerell, flinging out an arm in a theatrical manner – had fallen asleep and begun to snore, with her mouth wide open. As the snores grew louder and more hoarse, her husband nudged her awake and told her that she was snoring. She had denied it, vehemently. 'I was not snoring!' she said. 'I do not snore!' – 'My dear, you were snoring,' said the husband. – 'I was not snoring,' she retorted. 'I have never snored in my life!' The husband did not persist but exchanged covert glances with Harrison and Cockerell, who in order to conceal their amusement had been obliged to retreat behind their newspapers.

The old man was amused, too, more at their amusement than at the story itself. Cockerell was always good company, full of lively anecdotes like this.

Florence, who was seated on the sofa, told the two men in a severe voice that it had been very ungentlemanly of them to take pleasure in someone else's misfortune. Cockerell replied that it was perfectly right for her to defend her sex. But for the presence of the husband, he would have been very much tempted to have put a peppermint on her tongue.

'One wonders what their marriage is like,' he remarked. 'What do they say to each other when they are alone in each other's company?'

Harrison replied that they were probably at each other's throats all the time. 'If we hadn't been in the compartment, they would have argued on and on.'

'How old were they?' the old man inquired.

'Fifty or sixty.'

'Thirty years ago, I am sure they were deep in love.'

'I very much doubt it!' Cockerell retorted. 'Impossible! In love! If you had only seen them —' and he gave an imitation snore.

Florence, who was in a miraculously good mood, said: 'Sydney, that's a pig grunting!'

'Well, that's exactly what she sounded like!' Cockerell replied; at which moment the laughter was interrupted by the front door-bell.

Florence, as the hostess, went out of the room and came back with Gertie. She was wearing a gold cardigan over a black dress, with a long string of doubled pearls. Her cheeks were flushed, and droplets of mist speckled the strands of her hair. What a fine creature she was, the old man thought.

She shook hands with them all. 'I am so sorry; the fog is terrible. It has taken such a long time to get here. I hate being late. I have kept you all waiting.'

Cockerell reassured her. 'Not in the least. We were late too, Harrison and I; we've only just arrived. The train crawled along. We didn't think we'd ever arrive!'

A bottle of champagne stood on a side table, and at Florence's request Harrison dealt with it efficiently. Cockerell took round the tray of glasses. 'Well,' he said, 'now we are gathered together, a toast seems to be in order. To London, and to "Tess"!'

Echoing these sentiments, they raised their glasses and drank.

It had been already agreed that rehearsals at the Haymarket should begin on March the eighth, with the first performance to be a month later on April the eighth. The run would be a month long and would consist entirely of matinée performances, on Wednesday and Friday afternoons. The old man had been less than pleased by this arrangement, because he suspected that the critics would pay less heed to a matinée production, but Harrison took the view that it was best to begin cautiously.

'One knows fairly soon, with experience, how a play is likely to do,' he said. 'After a couple of performances, one can sense it. If the reviews are favourable, and if there is sufficient demand for seats – as I am sure there will be, with proper publicity – the run can be extended. There is no problem there.'

The old man was only partly mollified. 'And evening performances?'

'Without a doubt. If it is sufficiently successful, as I am sure it will be.'

'Why, everyone knows that it will be a great success,' Cockerell declared. 'Mrs. Bugler, you will be the talk of the town, and it is only what you deserve – is that not so, Thomas?'

The old man muttered his agreement.

Gertie smiled. 'I only hope that I don't suffer from stage-fright!'

Harrison said: 'Believe me, Mrs. Bugler; I am an expert in these matters; you are not the nervous type. You have never suffered from stage-fright before, have you?'

'I have never played on a London stage before.'

'You'll be perfect,' said the old man, very sincerely. 'And don't let anyone tell you otherwise. I very much intend to be there to see it.'

'O!' she exclaimed. 'But not too near the front row, please. You will put me off my lines!'

He promised to sit near the back, or to hide behind a pillar, or to go in disguise, wearing a false beard and a broad-brimmed black hat, a remark which seemed to amuse everyone a little, although Cockerell said that if he did so he would be instantly recognisable and probably arrested as a Bolshevik revolutionary.

The maid – Elsie or Nellie, one or the other – came in to say that luncheon was served, and the party moved across the hall to the dining room, where a saddle of lamb with roast potatoes and mint sauce awaited. The old man sat at the head of the table, with Gertie by his right hand and Wessex at his feet.

Cockerell carved energetically. 'So you live at Beaminster?' he asked Gertie, pronouncing it as it was written.

'Sydney, you know, it is supposed to be Bemster,' Florence corrected him from the other end of the table.

'Bemster?'

'Yes. Bemster.'

'Not Bemsturrr?' he asked, putting on a comic Wessex brogue.

'No, plain Bemster.'

Cockerell laughed. 'Well,' he said, 'whatever it is called, do you like living there?'

She said that she did, yet there was a certain catch in her voice.

'O?'

'It is very quiet,' she said with a gentle smile. 'Not a great deal happens in Beaminster.'

Her pronunciation of the town's name was subtly different to Florence's. Cockerell was delighted. 'Bemister!' he proclaimed. 'Is that right?'

'Nearly.'

'But not quite – Mrs. Bugler, where am I wrong? Bemisster?'

'Very nearly. But I am not a native – I am not really qualified.'

The old man listened attentively. William Barnes, that great Wessex poet, had rendered the vocalisation of the town as 'Sweet Be'mi'ster!' – but Barnes, too, had not come from the west of the county. 'There are several ways in which it may be pronounced, none of them worse or better than the other,' he said, 'but sometimes it is perhaps more like Bemestur.'

'Yes,' she said, 'that is how my husband pronounces it,' and she turned her eyes on him in such a way that made him feel – what? Merely that he should like to kiss her. To put an arm round her waist, and kiss those soft lips . . . the thought made his mind swoon.

'I always think it is such a shame that the town has no railway connection,' Florence complained.

'Why is that?' Harrison politely wondered.

'Frederick, I have no idea. They have been talking about extending the line for years and years, but they never seem to get any further!'

From Florence's tone, one might have concluded that no one knew why Beaminster lacked a railway line, but the reason was obvious to anyone with an understanding of local topography. Being surrounded by steep hills, the town was situated in a kind of basin, and the costs of constructing a railway line were prohibitive. Economics, as so often, had the final word on the matter. The old man did not bother to say this, and instead chose to point out that, while Beaminster might have no railway line, it did possess a fifteenth-century church, in honey-coloured ham-stone, with a magnificent tower – perhaps the most magnificent church tower in the entire county.

He spoke to Gertie. 'Is your cottage near the church?'

'Not far away,' she said. 'A little way down the hill.'

He wondered what her cottage was like. The postal address, Riverside Cottage, helped but little, if only because Beaminster's river, the Brit, was not much more substantial than a large stream. As for cottages, they varied greatly. Since the War there had been a considerable fashion among urban dwellers for cottage living, albeit on a weekend or holiday basis, and many such cottages had been modernised to provide comfortable accommodation. Others remained as they had been for centuries, dank and cramped, with mud floors, rotten plaster and mouldy thatch.

Once they had settled to eat, the conversation turned to the subject of where Gertie should stay in London. Some actresses stayed in diggings, but Harrison recommended several very good, respectable hotels, close enough to the Haymarket, which he said were not too expensive. To the old man's irritation, Florence then started to say what a lonely place London could be if one was by oneself, and how hard it would be for Gertie to leave her baby: 'I would find it impossible, I think.'

Sometimes he wished that Florence could hold her tongue. He shot a look of sharp disapproval down the table, but she seemed not to notice.

Gertie said that she hoped she would not be lonely; her sister would be staying with her in London, and she would be able to go back home at weekends to see Diana: 'It will give my husband the chance to get to know her so much better. Fathers so often are remote figures nowadays. And it is only for a month.'

'But what if the run is extended?'

'Everything will work out well,' the old man told her, and he passed a small piece of lamb to Wessex, who had been whining in a polite manner. 'Gently, gently. Where are your manners? Now, now.'

Florence reproached him. 'Thomas, he will get fat.'

'Nonsense – he is too old to get fat' – and he defiantly lifted the dog to the level of the table and allowed him to lick the side of the plate.

'He even likes mint sauce,' said Gertie.

'He likes everything. There; spotless.'

An excellent apple pie, thick-crusted, spiced with cinnamon, and eaten with cream – as was his wont, his hand holding the cream jug shook and allowed him to pour an excessive quantity into his bowl – completed the luncheon; after which, they again went to the drawing room. The fire was smouldering, and while Cockerell jabbed the poker into the coals the old man seated himself in a low chair beside Gertrude.

A conversation about the history of the Haymarket had begun, with Harrison warning Gertrude to keep an eye open for the resident ghost. This was supposedly the ghost of John Baldwin Buckstone, one of Harrison's eminent predecessors as theatre manager. Harrison maintained that it had been sighted by dozens of actors and actresses, often during the course of a performance, though he had never seen it himself. 'It's slightly disappointing,' he said. 'Why should ghosts appear to some people and not to others?'

Cockerell said: 'I once saw a cat, which I believed was a ghost. It was on the back stairs, in Cambridge. It ran up and disappeared. We searched for it, but never found it.'

'It was probably just an ordinary cat,' Harrison suggested.

'I'm sure it wasn't!' Florence declared. 'I'm certain that ghosts exist – I've seen one! Two Christmases ago, I woke in the night and it was by my bed.'

'How frightening!' Cockerell was entertained. 'My dear Florence! Was it Scrooge?'

'It was shaking its head at me.'

'Was it? Hmmm! What – like Hamlet's father? And then what?'

'Nothing. It vanished. You remember, Thomas? I told you about it. It was very frightening. I couldn't sleep for hours.'

The old man nodded, though in truth he did not remember at all. 'The trouble with ghosts is that they always vanish,' he remarked.

'Did it have a long white beard?' asked Cockerell.

'No, it was a young man, or fairly young.'

'Ah! An old flame! Did you recognise him?'

'No, but you are right, Sydney, he was extremely handsome!'

The merriment continued. Harrison said that, when his time was up, he fully intended to do a little amateur ghosting; he would join forces with Buckstone and haunt the Haymarket. Cockerell said that the best course of action, when encountering a ghost, was to run it through with a rapier, and if he met Harrison's ghost he would do just that. Florence said, but surely, since a ghost had no substance, to run it through with a rapier would be entirely useless. Cockerell cheerfully conceded that this was probably true: 'I may have misunderstood something. But, you know, it may be not Harrison's ghost but Harrison pretending to be a ghost. By stabbing it with a rapier, at least I would know that I'd got the real thing.'

Gertie spoke here. She said that very near where she lived in Beaminster there was a big stone house, dating from the Elizabethan period, which contained a ghostly lady in a blue dress. At night her shoes could be heard tapping on the stone floors as she walked round the house, and one particular room always felt chilly, even in high summer.

'This entire house feels chilly,' said Florence.

Cockerell made protesting noises.

'I assure you, Sydney, it is one of the coldest houses anywhere! The only truly warm room is the kitchen, and I am not allowed to go in it! The servants stay warm, and we perish! I am cold here now! Do we know who this mysterious lady in blue was?'

'No,' said Gertie, 'although she has been photographed.'

'How extraordinary! That is extraordinary! Is it a good photograph?'

'I haven't seen it, but those who have say that you can see her quite distinctly, and that she looks very unhappy.'

'It must be a trick,' said Cockerell. 'It must be. Ghosts do not exist. One may as well believe in fairies and elves.'

The phenomenon of ghosts interested the old man greatly, and when Gertie turned to ask him if he had ever seen a ghost he was ready with an answer: that he saw one each morning, upon looking in the glass. It was perhaps the dry tone with which he gave this answer, as much as the answer itself, that provoked such laughter; whatever the cause, it particularly pleased him that Gertie laughed so freely, and that, as she laughed, she was looking at him. It was as if he and she were the only two people in the room. Her eyes were bright, the curving string of pearls around her neck shone with a faintly pink light against the translucence of her skin, and her right hand, with its flawless nails and slender wrist, was a mere three feet away. In a single movement he could have reached out and taken it in his own.

Her physical presence dazed him so much that he lost track of the subsequent conversation, although vaguely he began to ponder whether he might contrive some pretext that would allow him to be alone with her. None sprang to mind. Had it been spring or summer, he might have given her a tour of the garden – but it was a cold winter's afternoon, already turning to dusk. Soon the curtains would need to be drawn against the dark.

A jet of blue flame issued hissing from one of the coals on the fire.

'Ah!' Cockerell exclaimed. 'Isn't that meant to signify something? I've read about it! A stranger!'

This was true; it was an old country superstition that such irruptions foretold the approach of a stranger. The old man explained it to Harrison, who smiled.

'How quaint. People still believe that?'

'O, we are still in the Dark Ages down here,' Florence told him. 'Sometimes we hear wolves!'

'Any moment now the door-bell will ring,' predicted Cockerell. 'Hark! Hist!'

They listened. The flare continued to burn with its fierce blue light, while the hiss developed into a loud sibilance.

He sat mute, scarcely daring to look in her direction, but entirely taken up with her nearness. She seemed so fond of him – she was fond of him, he was sure of it. When he glanced up and caught the flash of her eyes – those eloquent, dark eyes, shining in the fire-light – he felt that he knew her thoughts as well as his own. How easy it should have been to take her hand, and how impossible! Would that he and she were alone!

Within a short space of time he heard her say that she had to leave. A taxi-cab was picking her up at half past three, at the bottom of the drive.

The significance of her words at first failed to penetrate his consciousness. He roused himself. 'What? But you must stay for tea. The cook has made a cherry cake.'

'I should love to, but my husband will be waiting for me.'

So saying she picked up her hand-bag, and rose decisively to her feet. Cockerell and Harrison stood up too. 'A woman's work is never done,' Cockerell sententiously remarked.

Harrison struck the right note, however. 'It has been a great pleasure, Mrs. Bugler,' he said. 'I shall send you a list of hotels. The next time we meet, it will be in London town.'

She smiled, thanked him and turned to the old man, but he was not yet ready to say good-bye. He accompanied her to the hall, and when one of the maids brought her coat he took it and held it out. As she turned to push her hand through the second sleeve he caught a drift of perfume.

'I'll walk you down,' he said gruffly.

'You'll catch a cold,' objected Florence, who had also come into the hall.

'No, no. Do me good.' To his own ears he sounded like some aged colonel, staggering from his London club. 'Drowsy in there. Too stuffy. Only take a minute.'

He opened the porch door. The same fog which had been present that morning had returned in dense quantities to smother the closing day; after the heat of the drawing room, the raw, clammy air was like a slap in the face.

The distance from the house to the gate was a short one, too short. Would it had been longer, would it could have stretched to the world's end! Their footsteps – his, perforce heavier than hers – crunched on the soft gravel, out of time with each other. He walked as slowly as he could past the shrubbery; slower than he needed, if truth be told. The trees dripped. No birds sang. 'The sedge has withered from the lake, and no birds sing' – Keats's fine lines entered his mind. That was a wintry poem. But Shelley, his hero of old, was more in his thoughts than Keats.

The moment of parting, the moment marked by destiny as the one when he ought to declare himself, was approaching fast. No better moment was ever likely to arrive, and yet he found himself at a loss. What should he say? All? A part? Nothing? Everyone agrees that, in matters of love, 'faint heart never won fair maiden', yet he shrank from too rash a declaration. Inbred caution and distrust inhibited him; and he was old, and would soon be gone

— be nothing but dust. The long years ahead, the years in which he would play no part save as a memory, stretched before him like a procession of lamps leading into a dark nebulousness.

When the pale bars of the gate loomed he had still not broken his silence. The taxi-cab was parked under the trees by the road's edge, waiting to carry her away. What if he were to clasp her waist, to kiss her? So would Shelley have done; so might he. But it was all in his head; there was never a possibility that he would do any such thing.

He cleared his throat. 'Mrs. Hardy would like the pine trees cut down. She feels they make the house too shady.'

'I like them,' she said.

'So do I. They are Austrian pines.'

'O! In the novel — at Alec d'Urberville's house — aren't they Austrian pines?'

'They are, you are right. It was after I planted them that I began to write Tess's story.'

'Then you must not have them cut down,' she said fiercely. 'You must not. Not unless you want them cut down.'

'No,' he said. 'I do not. They are fine trees.'

The trees rose above them, their crowns veiled in vapour, their limbs outstretched. All around there was a continual musical pattering as drops of water fell upon the dry leaves.

'Well,' she said. 'Thank you. I am so grateful to you.'

She was on the point of leaving; if he failed to speak now, it would be too late. Desperate as a youngster out courting for the first time, he put a hand on the arm of her coat.

'Gertie.' He stopped. 'If, in after-years, anyone should ask you — if anyone should ever ask you if you knew me, you must say, you were my friend.' And then, unsure as to whether she understood his true meaning, which was more to do with love than friendship, he tried again: 'If anyone asks, in times to come, what you knew of old Thomas Hardy — you were his friend. Remember that.'

Absorbed into the fog-bound dusk, her expression was too dim to discern in its fullest clarity, but her eyes were enormous. 'I will,' she said.

He tightened his grip on her arm. 'Safe journey,' and then he let her go.

The car came to life. Fog swirled and poured through the beams of the headlamps.

The old man watched as the lights were swallowed by the darkness of the fog. With some effort, he swung the gate to its latch. As he shuffled back to the house, he was affected by a profound and unaccountable foreboding that his life was drawing to a close, and that he would never see her again.

Harrison left soon after tea, catching the last London train, while Cockerell, who was to stay the night, settled by the fire with a book and almost immediately dozed off, his spectacles hanging from one ear. Wessex snored at his feet, and Florence, also in need of sleep, retired to her bedroom. Sleeping by day was one of her errors; as a result, she often found it impossible to sleep at night.

The old man, wide awake, felt himself strangely at a loss. He was not in the mood to sit at his desk, and although he did open the latest issue of the proceedings of the Dorset Natural History and Antiquarian Field Club, of which he was an honorary member, he found little in it to stir his interest. As he turned its pages, his mind anxiously pursued Gertie home through the fog. The road to Beaminster was an up-and-down affair, ending with an exceptionally steep descent. When the grandfather clock struck five, he thought: 'She must be nearly back by now'; when it struck the next half hour, he thought: 'She will certainly be back by now, unless the fog has been very bad.'

Time ticked on, the fire burnt lower, and his mind turned to the ghost she had mentioned. A long while ago, soon after Emma had died, he had written a poem in which he had visualised her as a ghostly figure calling to him. She had worn – he had written these words – 'an air-blue gown'. How strange that this lady in Beaminster should likewise wear a blue dress! There could be no significance in such a detail, and yet as soon as Gertie had mentioned it he had made the connection. Emma and Gertie: the two women merged and became one, standing and waiting for him on a station platform, or in some lonely upland spot. The line of thought went no further, for the while.

He prowled the house. Animated chatter came from the kitchen and scullery; about what, he could not tell, and it was beneath him to eavesdrop, though he would have enjoyed doing so. The word 'eavesdrop' appealed to him. To 'eavesdrop', to stand unnoticed beneath the eaves of a cottage, listening to secrets; such, in a manner of speaking, had been one of the great pleasures of his life.

Shortly before dinner Florence emerged from her bedroom. He was in the hall, tapping the glass of the barometer, when she appeared at the head of the stairs.

'Thomas,' she said. 'Are you aware what date it is?'

He looked interrogatively.

'It is the twelfth of January.'

There was a pause.

'It is my birthday, Thomas.'

Her voice shook.

The old man had not been aware that it was her birthday. It was a bad mistake on his part, but he could not be expected to remember everything. Did a birthday really matter so much? Birthdays were for children. Besides, the whole business about the Haymarket had put it clean out of his mind.

She came down the stairs. She stood before him. Her face looked haunted. 'All you think of is her. I am no one, no one, no one.'

'Who do you mean? Emma?'

'Don't pretend, please. What fool do you take me for? You know perfectly well who I mean.'

'I have no idea.'

'You know very well. I am not deceived. I am not having this, Thomas.'

'Get out of my way,' he said roughly, and pushing past he walked into the drawing room, where Cockerell was blearily rubbing his eyes.

The evening passed in an awkward fashion. He talked to Cockerell, she talked to Cockerell, but not once he did talk to her, or she to him. Soon after supper, she said that she had a headache and returned to her bed.

Clearly he was meant to feel responsible, but why had she waited so long to remind him about her birthday? All day she must have been brooding on his failure to remember. He now comprehended her chilly manner at breakfast, but why had she not said anything then? Why wait? The answer seemed clear: whether consciously or not, she wanted to be able to blame him. It suited her to have him put in the wrong.

Sometimes he felt that there were two Florences, one who helped him and understood him, the other who hindered him greatly and failed to understand him at all. One was this angry, distressed being, preoccupied with her health, patently unhappy; the other was the soft-spoken, sensitive, brown-haired creature with doe-like eyes whom he had met long ago and who, after expressing admiration for his work, had eagerly offered to help in any way she could. (He had craftily invented some historical research for her to carry out on his behalf at the British Museum.) He could picture that woman now; he had not forgotten how absorbing he had found her. She must have been in her mid twenties; about the same age that Gertie was now. He was dimly aware of the existence of a third Florence, which must have had something to do with his burgeoning feelings towards her. In some subtle associative way, it seemed as if the spirit of the Italian city, with its gentle magic, lay within her inner self, or as if she herself was the flower of the city's soul. Florence was where Civilisation had arguably reached its highest point; it was the city of Dante, who had written the Divine Comedy, in which his spirit had been guided through Hell by Virgil, and through Heaven by Beatrice, his ideal.

However, if he had once thought of Florence as his Beatrice, he no longer did so. Either she had changed, or he had changed, or both of them had changed.

She had changed, certainly. Had he changed? He did not feel he had – not one jot. But, whatever the truth, it was impossible not to feel yet again that there was something terribly amiss with an institution that yoked two individuals for the rest of their lives. Monogamy was not a natural state for the human species, was his considered opinion. Love was a migratory phenomenon, not to be controlled by human laws, any more than a migratory bird might be controlled by borders and customs. Shelley, who had also lived in Florence, and had worshipped Dante, had much to say on this score.

Since Florence was in bed, it fell to him to take Wessex out last thing at night (the maids could not be expected or trusted to do it). While the dog trotted into the cold fog he waited by the porch, holding a lantern. Less than six hours had passed since he had walked Gertie to the hidden gate. Was it impossible, even now, that they should go away together? It was. Shelley would have gone – Shelley, who had eloped not once but twice in his short life, would have kissed her, and sprung into the cab without a thought to the consequences – but Shelley had been young, a free spirit. He was old, too old. The rays of the lantern sparkled but were constrained within a short circle by the fog's dancing droplets. Would I were young again, he said to himself. Would I were young again.

The morning was colder but clearer than its predecessor, a brisk breeze having dispersed the vaporous air, and Cockerell and Florence walked into the town. The old man settled at his desk. After the troubles of the preceding day he was a little tired, and it disappointed him to find that the poem about Wessex was as bad as ever. Sometimes he would look at a poem that he had put aside, having thought it useless, and discover that it was in fact a good piece of work. This poem still lacked something; it did not entirely believe in itself. If he could have brought it into a satisfactory condition he would have given it to Florence, and thus, in some measure, atoned for his failure to remember her birthday. Her coldness of manner at breakfast made it clear that he was still being punished on that score.

The time was not entirely wasted, for he wrote a letter to Harrison, in which he said how much he was looking forward to the production at the Haymarket. He took it to the post-box, which was set in the outside of the wall by the gate. As he posted the letter he became aware of a small showering of vegetable fragments, and looked up to see a squirrel which, having ventured from its winter refuge, was nibbling on a pine cone held in its paws.

In the afternoon he went for a stroll with Cockerell. The sun, though not visible, betrayed its presence by a certain watery brightening in the sky's southern quarter.

'Is it true, that when you were born, you were cast aside for dead?'

'So I was always told. There was some impediment in my breathing.'

'Who saved you?'

'The nurse, apparently. Whether "cast aside" is exactly the right phrase, I am not sure. There was some discussion as to whether the vicar should be sent for.'

'So you could be baptised?'

'Yes.'

Cockerell was interested at this and asked him whether it had inspired a scene in 'Tess of the d'Urbervilles', in which Tess gives birth to a baby which dies before it can be baptised properly by a priest, and is therefore denied a proper Christian burial.

'Perhaps.'

The track on which they were walking was one that led south of the house, passing a field which some years earlier had been converted to allotments for townsfolk. On such a wintry day no one was at work, which relieved him; he had no wish to meet anyone. When these allotments had been originally proposed, fears were voiced that the horticultural produce would be stolen by gipsies or children, but the only thieves had been rabbits and birds, both attracted in great numbers by the cabbages and cauliflowers. Shooting kept the numbers down, and in an attempt to discourage the birds, three scarecrows, composed of sacking, rags, sticks and the remnants of old clothes, and tied together with string, now stood among the vegetables like some modern version of the Crucifixion. The birds were far too intelligent to be deceived, however. Several pigeons, even now, were waddling among the cabbages.

Whether Cockerell noticed the scarecrows was not apparent. He was one of those men for whom a walk is a conversation on legs, and he tended to keep his eyes firmly fixed on the ground.

'But you had a regular nurse?' he inquired.

'She was the local woman who helped with births. That is the story, at least.'

'A very good story, too. I hope you have put it in your biography.'

'I expect so, yes; Florence will know. I expect it's there,' he said, affecting a certain vagueness, for while he knew very well it was there he liked to pretend that he was entirely ignorant of the content of his biography, or even of its existence.

The notion that he should write his biography had, in fact, come from Cockerell, years earlier. At first the old man had been unconvinced. He did not like biographies, and as a private person saw no reason why anyone should take any interest in what had been, when all was said and done, a fairly dull sort of life, largely spent seated at a desk. Cockerell argued the opposing case: that people were always intrigued by the lives of famous men, and that if he did not write it, someone else would, a journalist, a hack, who would no doubt include many inaccuracies and inventions that would then become established as truths. It was, he suggested, a matter of ownership. Whose life was it?

He had not been persuaded; not for a long while. But Cockerell was a persuasive chap with a great deal of tenacity, and he had eventually been won over to the principle of the scheme. The practical work involved – the collation of material, the checking of dates and deciphering of notes, not to mention the transcription of trunk-loads of yellowing letters – had been far too onerous for him to undertake, but he had kindly delegated it to Florence, in order to give her something to occupy her time and to distract her from herself. Over a number of years she had worked on the biography, writing loose chapter drafts which he had then written in his own style, incorporating anecdotes as he thought appropriate and deleting material that seemed irrelevant.

It did not please him, particularly. Fiction had been a generous mistress, allowing him to shape and adapt and invent as he thought fit; a biography, in contrast, was a tyrant master, obliging him to stay much closer to the truth in such matters as time and place. Of course, he was able to deviate here and there, and it had helped him to use the third person, as if the biography had been written by Florence, but the result lacked tension and coherence. Truth does not have the tightly ordered quality of art. Still, there it was; after his death, people could make of it whatever they liked.

'The early history of great artists is always interesting,' Cockerell observed. 'So many seem to have had difficult childhoods, in one way or another. One often begins to feel that, from an artistic point of view, it is important not to have been too happy, in a way. Or is it rather that those of an artistic temperament seek out and explore the difficulties, which other men ignore?'

He considered this remark. 'Mine was not altogether a difficult childhood,' he said, 'or not especially so, given what some people have to endure. I was not unhappy. I had loving parents. My mother, especially, was a very fine woman.' He considered further. 'On the other hand, perhaps it is in the nature of things that childhood should be difficult.'

'Why?'

He shrugged. 'The world does not seem designed for the well-being of the human race. Or designed at all, unfortunately. If there were a designer, he would appear to have been entirely indifferent to the happiness of humankind.'

Cockerell, a confirmed atheist who felt that organised religion did more harm than good, did not dissent from this view.

'Where were you baptised, in the end?'

'In Stinsford.'

'And now you are living less than two miles away. I envy you that sort of continuity. You have had a more rooted life than I, here in Wessex. I was brought up in various parts of Kent – Sydenham, Beckenham – and when I was ten or eleven we moved to Margate. But there was no sense of tradition. We never felt rooted.'

'I have never been to Margate.'

'You wouldn't like it much. Everyone's a stranger, and no one ever stays for long. People come, people go. I was sent to boarding school.'

The track rising slowly, they reached the top of the hill. Here the old man paused to catch his breath, and to study the view; by training he was something of a connoisseur of scenery, just as other men are connoisseurs of art. The landscape, drab and feature-less enough to the untutored eye, contained much to catch his scrutiny. The fields, left to rest until they were sufficiently dry for the spring ploughing, were a haphazard assembly of rain-washed hues, light and dark greys, muted browns and sepias, with occasional pieces of charred ground black from September's stubble-burning. The silver line of a winterbourne threaded through a green pasture grazed by sheep, while a widening scarf of smoke stretched from a farmhouse chimney.

This prospect was one that he knew intimately, for he had been up here on countless occasions and had seen it in all weathers and seasons. Although it was never the same, from one day or hour or minute to the next – even now, as the clouds thinned and thickened, the light came and went on a momentary basis – its essential character had scarcely altered over the course of his lifetime. Indeed, the contours of the land, the swell and fall of hill and valley, were as they had been for thousands of years. As an example of what Cockerell called continuity it ought to have elated him, and sometimes he did experience a little of the old elation, though in an etiolated form. Looking now, however, he felt – whatever he felt, it was not elation, but some much more subdued, uneasy emotion.

Behind his unease, no doubt, lay his fundamental apprehension of Nature as an indifferent force, rather than a benevolent one; as he had written in 'Tess', the planet was a blighted one, the lives of its inhabitants always subject to the whims of fortune. The view before him was a beautiful one in which all appeared to be well, but who was to say that it was indeed well? Agriculture was not presently in good health; a number of farms had been repossessed; a local farmer, apparently prosperous, had hanged himself the previous winter. In truth, the problem was wider; it was one of knowledge. If he and Cockerell had walked in another direction, they might have looked towards the town, which was rapidly spreading beyond its former boundaries, or they might have stood by the railway line and watched truck-loads of Portland stone trundling by on their way to the metropolis. Other views intruded; it was no longer possible to live in blinkers. He knew too much.

Not far from where he and Cockerell stood was a thicket of trees hiding the circular ditches of an ancient fort. It was one of dozens of such encampments in the country hereabouts; the land had once been owned and tilled by agriculturalists of the Iron and

Bronze Ages. Often, on misty autumn afternoons, he had pictured them in their coarse clothes, chopping with their rudimentary axes, steering their muddy beasts through the dead woods. The scattered fires still burned and glowed in his imagination. He was not fool enough to make this world into some kind of primitive paradise; life had been hard, no doubt; yet it was life blessed by an ignorance of the true nature of existence. Who was to say, despite all the claims made on behalf of Civilisation, that those men and women had been less content with their lot than people now? If they had possessed the gift of sight into the complications of this present troubled age, and had been invited to choose between it and their own time, they would surely have remained where they were. Privately, the old man doubted the direction of much of what passed for progress, and indeed doubted that, given the intractability of human nature, progress of any lasting kind was possible. To be an optimist after the senseless blood-letting of the War (a war in which more than eighty young men from the town had lost their lives) flew in the face of experience.

He stared, with his characteristic expression of scepticism. A mixed party of thrushes – fieldfare, with smoky-blue capes and grey rumps, and redwing, which were smaller and more delicate – made off with a dipping flight in the direction of a leafless hedgerow. A crow on a clod of earth cawed repeatedly at some unknown enemy.

Cockerell's mind was elsewhere.

'I was a fat boy,' he announced. 'Exceptionally fat.'

'Were you teased at your boarding school?'

'Relentlessly. It did permanent damage to my self-esteem. Privately, I assure you, I am a bag of nerves.'

The old man was amused. No one less fitting that description could be easily imagined.

They walked on a little further, surprising a pair of snipe that had been feeding in a watery trench. They burst upward, uttering quick hoarse calls, zigzagging into a pallid sky.

Cockerell was staring at his feet. The track was growing muddier and more slippery, and his shoes were ill-suited to such conditions. They edged past the trench, but upon meeting a puddle which stretched from one side of the track to another, and into which Wessex plunged with alacrity, the two men retraced their steps.

Cockerell talked without a break. He was made uneasy by silence.

'You know,' he remarked in a casual tone, throwing out an arm, once they were past the allotments, 'far be it from me, but you really ought to have a few of those pines attended to. It would give you so much more light, more air. I can see it must be good with regard to privacy, but as things stand, the house is almost engulfed.'

'Florence has been badgering you, I see.'

'Well, you know, it's none of my business, but she does have a case. They have become rather overwhelming, have they not? Every time I visit, they seem larger. When one thinks back . . . when was it I first came here? Nineteen eleven? They were half the height then. Extraordinary how fast they've grown. Thirteen years! Is it the soil? One wouldn't need to do anything too drastic.'

'When trees are cut back, they invariably look disfigured and unnatural. They are tortured out of their natural shapes.'

'I am sure you're right, but no one is suggesting that they should be cut right down. A little minor surgery would suffice. A branch here and there, if only for safety's sake. Florence was saying how tragic it would be if a branch were to fall on your head. Imagine the newspapers.'

The old man grimaced inwardly, for he felt a paternal sense of responsibility towards the trees. They had been planted around the perimeter of the garden, the pines as a wind-break, the beeches for the colour of their foliage, and he himself had helped with the business of planting them, carefully spreading the delicate roots with his fingers to give them the best chances in life, and, in accordance with an old country superstition (in which he did not believe but which, nonetheless, perversely, he chose to observe) tossing a farthing in each hole. Perhaps, after all, the superstition did have something in it, for they had grown – at first slowly and uncertainly, and then with greater confidence, pushing their branches upwards and outwards. Trees live to varying ages. The pines were now nearing their middle term, the beeches were in the last stages of youth. To cut them back now, in the midst of their leafy lives, to prevent them from achieving their biological destiny, seemed an unnecessary act of barbarism, and one from which he recoiled.

'None of the trees is in the least dangerous,' he said. 'Florence has the notion that they make her ill.'

'Not true?'

'It is all in her mind.'

Cockerell nodded. 'I am not a medical man, but if she feels that the trees affect her health, then one might argue that they do. You know – *mens sana* . . . And she does seem a bit down in the mouth at the moment . . . her system a bit run down. That operation has rather taken it out of her.'

These easy formulations – 'down in the mouth', 'a bit run down' – implied that Florence's poor health was a temporary matter, like a foggy day. Whether that was so, the old man wondered; in some fashion or other she had been unwell for years, even if the symptoms varied. He wished she could have prevented herself from confiding in Cockerell.

'Naturally she is anxious about you,' Cockerell continued, 'and of course she has a tendency to dwell on things, as women do. Common enough . . . the female of the species –'

'No reason for her to be anxious on my behalf.'

'I'm sure. It is merely that she loves you.'

This remark hung with considerable awkwardness between them. The old man could think of nothing to say by way of response, though he profoundly disliked the turn that the conversation had taken.

Cockerell continued: 'If a tree or two could be given a hair-cut, it might perk her up, give her a little fillip. You would still keep your privacy.'

He gave a stiff reply: 'It is not a question of privacy.'

'I thought that's what it was all about?'

'Not entirely. To a degree, but not entirely.'

'Well, as I say, it's none of my business. Forgive me for raising the matter.'

The matter had been raised, however; some further explanation seemed necessary.

'When I was a boy, I met a woodman who told me of certain ancient oak trees that shivered at the very sight of an axe.'

'The idea being that the trees were afraid?'

'The woodman thought as much, certainly. As soon as he and his fellows walked towards them, carrying axes, they began to shake their branches and rustle their leaves.'

'It sounds very Polynesian to me,' said Cockerell. 'How can a tree feel fear? Or even see an axe? Trees don't have eyes. Scientifically speaking, it must be bunkum, mustn't it?'

'Who knows?'

Cockerell was silent for a moment. 'So is that your opinion?' he asked in a voice of some incredulity. 'You believe trees can feel? Do you think they are also conscious?'

'It is not entirely impossible.'

'Really! I've always thought of you as thoroughly rationalist!'

At this the old man's mind went back to a letter he had received, four or five years earlier, asking whether he would be prepared to join a campaign on behalf of rationalism, the purpose being to prevent future wars. He had declined, largely out of a strong disinclination to commit himself publicly to any particular philosophical position which he might later change, but also out of a suspicion that the world itself was fundamentally irrational, and that wars were therefore not inexplicable outbursts of irrationality in a rational universe, but volcanic expressions of an underlying chaos. The conclusion which necessarily followed was that a campaign to prevent war by the promotion of rationalism would be as effective as an attempt to prevent an eruption by tossing a cork into a smoking volcano.

In reply to Cockerell's remark, he might have asked what it meant to be 'thoroughly rationalist', or he might have suggested that consciousness was not quite as easy to define as it might seem. Or he might have pointed out that trees were not so different from human beings, physiologically – that trees breathed, inhaling carbon dioxide and exhaling oxygen.

He said mildly, 'My old mother brought us up to believe that it was ill luck to cut down a holly.'

'Surely that is paganism? How can it possibly be ill luck to cut down a holly?'

'It is hard to know, but my mother's advice was generally sound. For better or worse, I never have had one cut down.'

'Did her advice apply only to hollies?'

'It applied especially to holly. However, she did not approve of cutting down any tree unless it was necessary.'

'I see,' said Cockerell, and he laughed merrily. 'Well, I promised Florence I would try my best, and I understand that I am bound to fail, since I am now arguing against your mother! But, you know, the time will come when you will be obliged to have the trees seen to, or the postman will be unable to get up the drive.'

'I shall be dead and buried long before then.'

'Nonsense. You'll live to a hundred. I'm willing to put a bet on it.'

The old man gave a snort. 'I very much hope not,' he said, although in truth he relished the idea of living that long. As long as possible, surely. To die was the end of everything.

Aspects of this conversation resonated in his mind for days. Did he truly believe that trees could feel? An animistic world? Or was it merely that, for reasons of sentiment, he liked the notion of trees as human? Walking down the Max Gate drive early one morning, wrapped in hat, coat and gloves against the cold, he paused to study the pines and was struck by the sheer physicality of their bodies rising into the pale winter sky. How powerful and strong they were! With their reddish trunks and stiff branches, they were as straight as sentries. Yet it was impossible not also to notice how much they varied among themselves. No two were alike, although all had been planted at the same time. Some had grown tall and thin, some were short and stocky; some had branches much lower than others; a few were stunted.

The same was true for the beeches. These differences were not only down to heredity, but also to experience, for it was in response to the wind, rain, sun and storm that the trees had developed into the beings they were. Their trunks, pocked, scarred, were tablets of memory. In all this he saw resemblances to members of the human race.

A dozen or more rooks had settled in the pines above his head and were cawing loudly. Enjoying their company, he pottered about for a time. The needles of the pine trees were slightly twisted, and the cones, which a few weeks earlier had been tightly packed, were now beginning to open their plates like the wings of birds. As for the beeches, their seed cases were covered in bristles, each one of which was equipped with a small hook like those on a hog's back.

Considered alongside humans, he thought, these trees had lived quiet and admirable lives. Resolute, determined, they had remained rooted to the same ground, much like the man whose entire existence is spent in the same village. There was a distinct virtue in this loyal commitment. If humans were to be judged morally, why not trees? The philosopher's answer that trees did not have the power of moral choice, and therefore could not be considered moral beings, was a specious one; after all, trees and human beings were fellow inhabitants of the planet. The influence of the former was entirely benign; of the latter, largely malign.

To Cockerell, who took a narrowly humanist view of existence, none of this would have made sense; but Cockerell had not been born in the country and had no instinctual feeling for the natural world. Indeed it seemed to him that Cockerell in the country was half blind, unable to see more than a small part of what was to be seen. He was deaf, too, in that to him the sounds of trees were merely sounds, whereas to the countryman they were a form of expressive language, and the soft flutterings of a beech, the ecstatic whisperings of a birch and the languid sighs of a pine so close to conversation that they could be nothing else. It was at night, when other senses were attenuated, that he himself was most conscious of the voices of trees, but even now, in a wintry dawn with a light wind, the squeal of two branches chafing each other seemed to speak of irritation.

Of what, he wondered, might the trees talk, between themselves? An idea sprang in his mind. 'The old man planted us here,' one murmured to another, 'a long time back; he dug the holes and set us here. Then he was younger, then he was stronger, and taller than us, even; look at him now, bent and bowed, stick in hand!' – 'Yes,' said the second, 'how often we have watched him, in dawn light, on his walk down the drive. He has aged and grown weary, as men do – their lives are not as long as those of trees – he will not be with us much longer. See how unsteady he is. The day of his death is approaching.' – 'Sometimes he seems to be listening,' said the first, 'do you think that he hears us?' – 'We cannot tell,' came the reply of the second tree, 'but he has been our friend. He gave us life, and has protected us from the sharp teeth of the axe and saw.' – 'Why do men hate us so?' asked the first. – 'They have always been like that, and always will be,' said the second. 'They are creatures who might live in peace, if they would only try, but ineluctably they are drawn to violence. The spilling of blood lies ingrained in their natures.' – 'Is he the same, the old man?' – 'No,' said the second tree, 'we may be sure, he will protect us, as much as he can, as long as he can.' The two trees murmured thus and then, with the ebb of the wind, fell silent.

That morning he began to turn the conversation into a poem. It proved unsatisfactory – almost as soon as it was finished he screwed up the paper and threw it on the fire, which was the fate of much he wrote. But trees were much on his mind, and after lunch he managed to compose several quick verses about the unknown tree whose boards were destined to enclose his body. Though strangers now, the tree and the man, each rocked and blown, would come to rest in deep ground and there lie safe from the convulsions of the world. It was only after he had written the poem that he recognised its inspiration to be one of Wordsworth's 'Lucy' poems:

> No motion has she now, no force;
> She neither hears nor sees,
> Roll'd round in earth's diurnal course
> With rocks, and stones, and trees.

A storm blew up in late afternoon. Seated at his desk, he watched as the trees heaved and tossed, their branches swaying and shaking. Groups of rooks whirled past, riding the crests and troughs of the gale, uttering their strange cackles and yaps. Did these trees not belong to the birds as much as to him? Who owned what? What right did he have to cut them down?

More than ever, he thought of the trees as a community of beings, akin, perhaps, to an Attic chorus, and, of course, Ancient Greece also had its dryads and hamadryads – a hamadryad being a nymph who died upon the death of the tree that she inhabited. He remembered Eurydice, the wood nymph who had fatally pursued her lover, Orpheus, into the underworld, and also Keats's invocation to the nightingale: 'light-winged dryad of the trees'. Perhaps dryads were birds. Or might birds be angels? But, whether he did or did not believe that trees were capable of feeling, he was quite certain that he did not believe in angels.

This entire train of thought was enough to make him open his

copy of James Frazer's 'The Golden Bough', where there was a
long account of individual trees which had a special affinity or
relationship with particular humans, the tree being dependent on
the man, and vice-versa; thus, when the man died, the tree sympa-
thetically withered away, and likewise, when the tree perished, the
man fell into a mortal decline. A passage in the same chapter
concerned the rituals employed by primitive peoples to propitiate
tree spirits, and made him ponder the Mayday customs practised
in the English countryside, in which young women fetched
branches laden with white blossom from the woods and copses
and paraded around the parish. In the opening pages of his novel
'Tess of the d'Urbervilles', he had described such a village procession – each woman clad in a white frock, holding a bunch of white
flowers in her left hand, and a peeled willow wand in her right.
Thus Tess herself, with her mobile mouth and innocent eyes, had
been introduced to the reader. Had that immemorial custom – now,
sadly, dying out – once been about the propitiation of tree spirits?

Frazer also wrote of trees as the temporary resting places of
wandering spirits. Such, apparently, was the belief of 'the inhabitants of Siaoo, an East Indian Island', and of 'the people of Nias'.
The spirits moved around at will, taking up residence within individual trees ('on the Tanga coast of East Africa', mischievous
spirits particularly liked to live in giant baobab trees). 'Instead of
regarding each tree as a living and conscious being,' wrote Frazer,
'man now sees in it merely a lifeless, inert mass, tenanted for a
longer or shorter time by a supernatural being . . .' The idea, at
least in his own mind, readily connected itself to a somewhat
different but related notion, one which he had originally found in
Shelley: that for each man there is an ideal though unattainable
female spirit, a restless creature that does not reside permanently
in any one shape, but moves freely from one woman to another.

It was in the form of Gertie Bugler that his own ideal spirit
currently seemed to have taken up residence. Often, in this change-
able winter weather, he became abstracted in thoughts of where

she was at a particular moment. He saw her in a small, low-ceilinged bedroom; saw her slowly undressing, one foot resting on the seat of a willow chair; saw her in a white petticoat and bodice, in the languid act of unclipping a stocking, rolling it down the sculptured curve of her leg, while sending a quick, sidelong glance in his direction. Her breasts rose and fell, and her hair, lush and heavy, shone like varnish in the candlelight. Several times he contemplated paying her a visit in Beaminster, but could think of no good excuse for doing so.

PART THREE

✿ ✿ ✿

CHAPTER VII

✹ ✹ ✹

I wake with frozen feet. The room is cold, and the prospect of the day ahead, a day like every other day, a day of filing papers, answering correspondence, fighting to stay warm and longing to be elsewhere, daunts me. Immediately I begin to talk to myself. Look at the insides of the window panes, covered in frost flakes! Please, feel the tip of my nose!

One of the maids knocks on Thomas's bedroom door and Wessie, who sleeps by Thomas's bed, or on it, begins to bark; whereupon the other maid hurries into my bedroom with the tea, sets it down and leaves in a fearful rush. They are such foolish things; we have this game every morning. It is quite unnecessary for them to be frightened of little Wessie, who is only saying good morning in his doggy way.

I put on my dressing gown, light a lamp, and pour out two cups of tea. I carry one through to Thomas and ask him whether he has slept well. He nods, but does not ask me whether I slept well. He always sleeps well while I, even when I seem to sleep, do not sleep well. It is far too cold to sleep well; even if I were to sleep, I should wake up exhausted. I used to sleep well, so well, as well as a child, I would sleep all night and wake fresh as a daisy, but now I never do. I wake exhausted, hauled from a pit, haunted by the shadows of dreams I can no longer remember. Is anyone listening to my complaint? This is not a comedy. The sentences come and go, and repeat themselves.

I hurry to dress. I put on a thick vest, which feels damp and smells of mould, followed by a blouse, three jumpers, woollen stockings and a heavy tweed skirt, which also smells mouldy. Downstairs I add a coat, fur-lined boots and my fur stole, and in this swaddled fashion I venture outside. It is the dead of winter, the air is alive with cold, the ground blue with frost, the wind blowing from the north; I give the hens twice as much grain as I did in the autumn.

I watch my husband walk down the drive with Wessie. Once he is safely out of sight, I hurry indoors and up the stairs. I push open the door of his study.

Six mornings ago, I slipped in here and glanced over his desk. I was looking for a poem about Wessie that he told me he had been writing: a slipshod piece of work, he said, not a success, not worth keeping. I thought to myself, it cannot be so very bad, I shall encourage him to finish it. Instead my eyes lit upon verses that he had written to Gertrude Bugler. She was not mentioned by name but they described her bewitching eyes, her coral lips, her raven hair. (I should like to cut off her raven hair.)

It was a love poem. It put forward the idea of his love for her and her love for him as that of two fiery stars linked by magnetic force, spinning for eternity through the darkness of space. Ridiculous! But this was a fair copy, beneath it I found earlier drafts. He must have worked on the poem for hours and hours.

Since then I have found four other love poems, and it is possible that in the heaps of scattered papers there are many more that I have not found. Four is quite enough, however. In one, he writes of eloping with her. He! Eloping? At his age? He is eighty-four! It would be comic if it were not so sad, so undignified, so unpleasant, so unworthy.

This morning another neat poem awaits me, without any attempt at concealment (has he left it out on purpose?). He is a spirit impatiently waiting for her to die so that they may sink together into the gloom of the underworld. What of her husband, may I ask? What part does the mysterious Captain Bugler play in this charade? And what of me? But this is how he must have spent the whole of yesterday, this is how I am rewarded for so many years of devotion and love. It is all I can do not to tear the poem to shreds. No doubt even now, as he wanders in the garden, he is meditating more poetic effusions to his dark lady.

It is an open betrayal. No, it is more than that. Each moment spent composing these poems, allowing his mind to move around her person, allowing her person to fill his mind, is a humiliating betrayal of our marriage. Does he dream of her? I have had enough trying to contend with his first wife and now there is this infatuation. O, Thomas! Can you not see what you are doing to me? Can you – you who are supposed to be such a keen reader of the human heart – not see how the heart of your own wife is breaking?

Once upon a time I might have been able to confront him, but years of living here have left me so short of confidence that I hardly know how I would manage. No doubt if I were to say anything, he would tell me that I should not have been looking at his papers. Yet I am his wife!

Silence is my answer. I shall fight fire with fire. Through the medium of silence, not speech, I am resolved to communicate my feelings.

Thus at breakfast I refuse to utter a word. I do not even give him good morning. I drink my coffee and eat a piece of toast, though in my mouth it tastes like dust, and wait for him to speak. To my astonishment, he eventually clears his throat.

'Do we have any visitors today?'

'No.'

'Good.'

'We have had no visitors for twelve days.'

'It is winter. People never want to visit in winter.'

'Thomas, we never invite them. That is why they never visit! If we invited them, they would visit! Why don't we invite Barrie?'

'Barrie hardly ever leaves London. I know he came to "Tess", but he hates leaving London in winter. He wouldn't come.'

'How do we know unless we invite him? He might like to be invited, at least.'

'We should invite Mrs. Bugler here sometime.'

'I see no reason to invite her,' I reply, but my voice is barely audible and he does not hear. He inclines his head. In my irritation I fairly bellow at him: 'I see no reason to invite her!'

'I merely thought you would like the company,' is his response. What deviousness! How cunning! How shameful! How dare he!

And then he leaves, as he always leaves.

The silence remains. I rise and open the kitchen door, whereupon a hot fug of marmalade steam hits me in the face. Standing by the black range, and with a long wooden jam paddle in one hand, Mrs. Simmons turns her heavy face on me. She does not like me coming in the kitchen; it is her province, according to etiquette.

'O, Mrs. Simmons,' I say, awkwardly (why is everything so difficult for me?), 'I am very sorry to disturb you. I am looking for Nellie or Elsie.'

She shakes her head. 'Not here, ma'am. They may be in the laundry room.'

I leave her, and search the laundry room. Neither of the maids is there. Nor are they in the scullery. I climb the stairs to the attic and come upon them in their room, hastily smoothing down the beds on which they have no doubt been lying and gossiping and talking about me.

'When I was up in London, at the end of September, did Mr. Hardy have many visitors?'

'No, ma'am.'

'Did he have any visitors?'

'I think Colonel Lawrence may have visited. And Mr. Tilley, ma'am.'

'No one else? Did anyone stay?'

'No ma'am. Not that I recall, ma'am.'

I look at Elsie.

'No, ma'am,' she manages.

'You don't remember either?'

'No, ma'am.'

'Do either of you remember whether Mrs. Bugler called?'

'I don't remember, ma'am. She may have done.'

'May have done': Nellie's words, uttered in a casual tone, are another wound in my tired heart. Does she not understand how important this is?

'Was it for tea, or another time of day?'

'I don't know, ma'am.'

'But it was when I was in London?'

'I think so, ma'am.'

'Did she call more than once?'

'I don't know, ma'am.'

'Well,' I say. 'Thank you, Nellie. O, and Nellie –'

'Yes, ma'am?'

But for some reason I am unable to remember what I was going to say.

'Nothing,' I say. 'Thank you.'

I go down the stairs. Is it my imagination, or do I hear stifled giggles behind me? I know they think me half mad.

She is not beautiful. She is not even very handsome. Her bewitching eyes – what nonsense! She simpers and makes her eyes bigger for effect, but to say that they are bewitching is simply wrong. As for her hair, her long raven hair, I should like to wait until she was deep asleep and then steal up with a pair of garden-shears. Behold the mad witch-woman, shears in hand, tip-toeing towards her unsuspecting victim! Behold her as she slides a blade under the famous hair! A single chop should do the job. If she were shorn she would not look in the least handsome.

In the silence of this winter morning I stand in the hall and attempt to preserve the sense of my own existence. The clock ticks slowly, too slowly; the spaces stretch between each of the ticks, the glass shines and the furniture seems to watch me as if I were a stranger. It would not surprise me if the first wife, fat and haughty, hair piled in clods, were to waddle down the stairs and order me to leave, nor would it surprise me if Gertrude Bugler were to drift past with her baby on her breast. Such visions I ought to be able to kill at a stroke. I ought to be able to assert myself as mistress of the house, a person of some importance and influence in the world, a person in charge of my own destiny, and if it were not for the cold I truly think that I might succeed in doing so; after all, I am a woman who breathes and has blood in her veins, not like these spectres. Yet my connection to the present moment feels so utterly slender and tenuous that were I to scream at the very top of my voice it would make no difference; the sound would be akin to a stone thrown into a deep lake, a few silky ripples before the surface recomposed itself. What could change this? There are warm, loose silences, easy, comforting silences, even musical (I think of the hush of summer afternoons) silences that liberate the mind and allow it to take wing. This is not one of them; it has a taut, strained, chilling quality. It needs to be broken by some external force, say, the ring of the telephone. If someone were to ring, if someone were to ring for me, I should begin to live again, but no one ever seems to ring. People say that if one sufficiently desires something, if one directs one's mind to a single end, one can force one's desire into being. Ring, I tell the instrument; ring, please, I implore you. Is there no one in the whole world who would like to speak to me on any matter, however trifling?

I might stand here in the darkness all day and all night, glaring at the telephone and turning slowly to black stone like some woman in a fairy-tale under the spell of an evil enchantment, but I force myself into action. 'Wessie! Wessie!' I march round the house. As usual he is asleep in the drawing room. 'Wessie! Off! Off! It is time for your brush. Come along, look sharp! Brush time!' Reluctantly he obeys, toppling himself from the sofa and following me through the conservatory to the frosted side lawn. I brush him vigorously, and comb through the knots and tangles of his fur. 'What's this? What a mess! Where have you been, you naughty boy? You are in a state! O Wessie, what shall I do? Help me, please! What can I do?'

Were it not for Wessie, I should have no one to talk to. He is my true confidant. 'Wessie,' I say, 'I am sure she visited. They sat together. They may have kissed. She may have allowed him to touch her, to fondle her, to stroke her hair, to unbutton her blouse, to run his dry hands up her leg. How disgusting, how reprehensible!' (Even the word 'fondle' nauseates me). 'He is an old man. Did you see them together? Did you? What did they do together? Did you hear them planning their elopement? Do you think he loves me at all? If he loved me, how could he possibly write like this?' His sorrowful brown eyes gaze into mine. 'O, Mistress,' he seems to say, 'I am so very sorry for you, I wish I could help, but, you know, I am only a little dog.' – 'O, Wessie,' I reply, 'you do help, you do, you do, you do,' and I smother him in kisses.

Were it not for Wessie, I do believe, I should have died here. And yet sometimes, in spite of him, I feel as if I were dead already. Am I alive? Am I dead? Who am I speaking to like this? Will no one answer?

What is certain is that he would miss me if I were dead. On the day after my funeral, finding that there was no one to run the house, deal with the servants, lay out his clothes, help him dress, answer the post, read to him at night, cut his ancient toe-nails and soothe his worries, he would realise how much he has taken me for granted. Consumed by the ache of loneliness, he would take to his study and pour his grief and regret into a series of elegiac poems lingering on the time when he and I first met, dwelling on such details as the softness of my voice, the quality of my smile, the touch of my hand and the scent of my hair. Poems of true love, not of some paltry infatuation, they would be hailed by critics as his greatest achievement. In this way I should triumphantly displace both Gertrude and the first wife, although since I would be dead it is not a triumph that would afford me any satisfaction. O Florence, these are bitter thoughts and you are not a bitter person; you must not give yourself up to bitterness.

I return to the telephone. I speak to the woman at the exchange, giving Cockerell's number in Cambridge, and to my utter relief, for I am desperate to unburden myself, he answers at once. 'Sydney,' I say, 'Sydney, is that you? It is Florence here, I am so sorry to ring you so early.'

'O?' There is a catch in his voice. 'Is something wrong? Is Thomas well?'

'He is as he always is. I thought I should telephone to find out how you were.'

'I am very well. How are you?'

'It is freezing here. I can hardly breathe for the cold.'

'You sound upset.'

'O – Sydney,' I say. 'I am so sorry to ring, but you have no idea what is happening. Things are even worse than they were. He is thinking of eloping with Mrs. Bugler!'

'What! Great Heavens!'

'I know, I know. It is terrible.' For fear that the maids may overhear, I cup a hand to my mouth, turn to the wall, speak in a conspiratorial whisper. 'He has written a poem about it! I'm sorry, I know I shouldn't have bothered you, but I had to speak to someone. I feel so utterly crushed!'

'Are you sure? With Mrs. Bugler! Where are they planning to elope to?'

'I told you that he was infatuated, but I never expected this. He is eighty-four! Sydney? Are you there?'

'Yes.' Cockerell sounds rather remote. 'How curious.'

'What do you mean?'

'It doesn't strike me as eloping weather at the moment. Winter is not an ideal time to elope. The eloping season is generally late spring or early summer. He hasn't packed a suitcase or anything, has he? Where are they thinking of going?'

Is he laughing at me? Is he amused? There is a definite undertone of amusement in his voice. Or is it that he doesn't believe me?

'Sydney, I am not making this up. He has written dozens of love poems to her! I have no idea what to do. It is beyond me. They are planning to meet at a place called Toller Down Gate.'

'That exists, does it? It's a real place.'

'Yes! Of course it exists! It's in the middle of Dorset.'

'Does the poem say how he proposes to get there?'

There is a substantial silence. He does not believe me.

'Hallo? Florence? Has he done anything about the trees?'

'No. Of course not. Of course he hasn't!'

Another silence.

'Florence, you know what I think you should do? I think you should get away for a good holiday. That would shake him up and make him appreciate you. The south of France – there's the place! Two or three weeks there would do you the power of good. Change of scene, change of air . . . I am serious. You could do with a break. And it's quite simple, and very civilised – you take the boat train from Waterloo, pick up the sleeper at Calais and wake up by the Mediterranean. Nice or Menton would be rather better than Cannes. There are some excellent hotels.'

'Sydney, you know I couldn't possibly leave him.'

'Or you might consider a cruise. Last winter I went on a cruise, in the Mediterranean; it was beautiful. Everything is looked after. You don't have to lift a finger. It's not as expensive as one might think.'

'I couldn't possibly.'

'Two weeks. A week.'

'Not even for two days. He would be helpless.'

'He managed perfectly well in the autumn, didn't he? How long were you away then?'

My operation, he means. I was away in London for eleven days. 'I couldn't.'

'But you say he is planning to leave you.'

'Yes. O, I don't know if it is imminent. I really don't know, Sydney. I don't know where I am any longer!'

What is so strange is that all the while I seem to be watching myself. Who is this hysterical creature whispering into the telephone? Yet sometimes I think that if I could only give myself up to hysteria, if I could tear my clothes and scream, and smash a plate or vase, I should feel better, but I have to hold my feelings in check.

'It'll pass,' says Cockerell, in a voice which attempts to reassure me, but which fails to reassure me at all. 'It'll pass. You mustn't worry, Florence; that is the most important thing, believe me. He does love you, you know.'

I hold the ear-piece in my hand and listen to its empty sound, like the end of a breath. Cockerell's words hang in the air and the whole house seems to be listening. The grandfather clock ticks, the floor shines dully. Do not listen to me! What are you looking at? Get back to work! Go on!

I take to my desk in the drawing room. The maids have lit a fire but the heat seems to be swallowed by the cold and it is difficult to think in such a temperature, just as it is difficult to type when my fingers are frozen. This is the twentieth century! I continue to wear my coat – am I also expected to wear milkman's mittens?

The day's correspondence awaits. First, a letter from France: a writer of biography, M. Rollin, requests an interview with him on the subject of his early life. There is not the slightest chance that he would be willing to give such an interview. Another overseas letter, from the United States (clearly written by someone who does not know how old he is, and has no inkling of his views) invites him to give a series of four lectures this coming summer in New York, proposing the following subjects: *1. The future of Christianity in the modern age. 2. The direction of Literature, with particular reference to the 'new school of poetry' as represented by T.S. Eliot. 3. Relations between the sexes, specifically relating to the marriage contract. 4. Prospects for world peace.* One would have thought, from this, that he was some great seer. What, living here, and never going anywhere, can he possibly know about the prospects for world peace?

An envelope postmarked London contains a typewritten letter, as follows:

My dear Sir,

I hope that you may be able to assist us in clearing up a puzzle which arises out of your excellent novel 'The Return of the Native'. It concerns a passage in Book IV, Chapter II, in which Clym Yeobright is working as a furze-cutter on Egdon Heath. Therein you write how:

'The strange amber-coloured butterflies which Egdon produced, and which were never seen elsewhere, quivered in the breath of his lips, alighted upon his bowed back, and sported with the glittering point of his hook as he flourished it up and down.'

None of the lepidopterists of my acquaintance has been able to identify the species concerned. Some of us believe it must be the Small Copper, others favour the Lulworth Skipper, or the male of the Fox Moth. I myself explored Egdon last summer in the hope of finding the butterfly in question, but without success. Is it, perhaps, some species once found on the Wessex heaths, but no longer present?

If you would settle a matter which has aroused much keen debate, I should be most grateful.

I remain, my dear Sir,

Etc. etc.

Does it matter so much? I feel like saying. Does it matter at all? Children in the slums, children with pinched grey faces, children dressed in rags, huddled, crouched, shivering, children whose parents have died and who in their entire lives have never known the soft touch of a mother's hand, are at this very moment begging in the streets of our capital city. (Such children haunt and reproach me with their pleading eyes. How I have always longed to help them! How I have longed to sweep them into my arms and to carry them off to some place of safety, a refuge from the storms of life!) Against their plight, what possible excuse can there be for dwelling on the identity of a fictional butterfly? What excuse for a life spent writing novels and poems about the dead?

According to Cockerell, he loves me. Seated at my cold desk, I consider this proposition as calmly as I can. He loves me, he loves me not, he loves me. A child's game. What is certain is that love is more important than anything. I remember so many years ago when I taught in a school and the children with their bright innocent faces eager for knowledge used to flock around me and hang on my every word, and after the lesson had finished I would dismiss them from the class-room and away they would run, so excited. A tousled-haired little boy was a favourite of mine, and one morning I saw him with such a sad face, standing alone in a corner of the playground and I went up to him and asked him what the matter was and why he wasn't playing with the other boys and girls; and he told me that his mother had died. 'O, Tommy,' I said, 'I am so sorry,' and I took him in my arms. My heart bled for him. He came from a very poor family, and he always looked half starved, and after lessons ended I asked him if he might not like to walk home with me for tea. He took my hand and we walked home together, like mother and son, and I made him some scones and opened a pot of strawberry jam, and he ate and ate. Perhaps he had never eaten strawberry jam. He was starved of food, but he was (I know) also starved of love, which I should have given him had I been allowed to, but of course it was not possible. Within me there is so much love still waiting to be expressed, I do sincerely believe that.

Some thoughts on the future.

1. I sit at the breakfast table, buttering a piece of toast, and sipping a cup of coffee. The front door-bell rings urgently. I wait, and it rings again. The maids are so slow! Where are they? Do I have to answer it myself? What are servants for? I rise from the table, go into the hall, but Nellie is hurrying down the stairs – 'I'll get it, ma'am' – and she opens the door on the coal delivery man, his face smudged with coal dust, his hands black. 'Is the missus in?' he blurts in a hoarse voice, 'I need to see the missus. It's urgent. It's the master. I needs to see her.' I step forward. 'Hallo? Is there something the matter?' whereupon he delivers his news: 'Very sorry, ma'am, but it's the master, ma'am; 'e's 'ad an accident, ma'am, down the drive, I don't know ma'am, but I'm greatly a'feard, ma'am –' – 'Show me,' I say, and we run down the drive. The coal-man's cart and horse, attended by his boy, are waiting by the gate. Nearer them, beneath an enormous branch that must have fallen from one of the pine trees, lies the body of my husband. The main thing, however, is that Wessie is with him, safe, untouched, unhurt. What a relief, what joy! He springs towards me, wagging his tail; I kneel and cuddle him. 'O, my little boy,' I say, 'thank goodness, thank goodness, you have escaped. Don't be too upset.' My husband is face down under the pine, with one arm sticking out at an odd angle. I look up at the coal-man. 'Can you not lift it, please?' – 'No, ma'am. It be far too heavy. Unless you have any ropes or chains?' I send Nellie for Mr. Caddy, who finds some chains, and the horses are then able to drag the great

weight of the branch off my husband's body. I turn him over. How very dead he looks; his face is blue, and covered in little dents from lying on the gravel. The irony of it – that he should have been killed by one of the trees – does not entirely escape me. His hand holds a letter; he must have been on the way to the post. I put it in my pocket. I know what it is: a letter to her, a love letter. I cradle Wessie indoors. 'Now it is just you and me, alone together,' I tell him. 'Your poor master is dead. Do you understand?'

2. Night. He gets up to answer a call of nature. Shuffling along the corridor, he becomes confused, stumbles, trips and falls headlong. Disturbed by the noise, I light a candle. His body lies crumpled and still at the foot of the stairs.

3. Another night. A fire breaks out in the drawing room chimney; it takes hold and spreads along the rafters, the flames curling around each rafter, filling the roof-space. Smoke drifts through the house. Pops and bangs go off like a firework display. We are asleep, however. Look at us, sound asleep, sleeping like babies, he in his bed, I in mine, with the blankets pulled to the chin! Finally the roar of the fire wakes me, but by now my bedroom is thick with smoke. I fumble to the stairs, colliding with the maids, and we flee (as does Wessie) into the cool clear air of the garden. He does not escape. The fire engine with its hose and buckets races up the drive, but far too late; he dies in the inferno and all his papers, including his last poems, his poems to her, are consumed.

4. I am doing the post in the drawing room when Nellie bursts in – 'Mrs. Hardy! Ma'am! Come quick!' – and I follow her up the stairs to the study. He is slumped in his chair, his head to one side, the pen dangling from his fingers. The long-awaited event has at last occurred. 'Nellie,' I say, very decisively (I know my lines off pat, having rehearsed them in my head so many times), 'we must call a doctor. We must telephone Dr. Gowring.' – 'O, ma'am!' she gives a wail, 'is

he —?' — 'Yes,' I say. 'I am afraid so. Go and telephone, would you please?' and she runs for the telephone. (It occurs to me that this is the true purpose of the telephone, one which we have all known from the very beginning, this moment for which the telephone, in its long silences, has been waiting: to notify the world of his death.) In her absence, I gather together every one of the shameful poems that he has written to Gertrude Bugler, and in front of his dull eyes I tear them up, over and over and over. Yes, I have destroyed them; they are no more! I scatter them like confetti, and an extraordinary wave of elation begins to rise within me. He is dead at last! I want to crow in triumph. Such elation inevitably brings into being a contrary wave, one of guilt and sorrow, but it remains true that my life can now begin again. (Will it be like that, I wonder? A sudden collapse, without warning? Or will it rather be a slow decline, lasting for many more years? How long do I have to wait?)

5. In all the years that I have lived here we have had the same gardener, Mr. Caddy, good old faithful Mr. Caddy. Where is he now, this winter's day? Hard at work? I think not. Red-faced, breathing heavily, trousers around his boots, in the small lean-to privy which he has erected beside his wood-shed? Possibly. But no: Mr. Caddy is where he spends half his time, in the wood-shed itself — I push open the door and catch him by a paraffin stove, smoking a pipe and studying the newspaper. 'Mr. Caddy!' He starts to his feet and takes the pipe from his mouth. 'Ma'am.' — 'Mr. Caddy, are you very busy?' (An ironical question: look at him! Pipe! Newspaper! And a mug of tea! Is this what we pay him for? To sit and smoke tobacco and read?) He tells me that he is about to sharpen the knives. When, I wonder to myself, in an hour or so? He drinks; I am sure of it; you can smell it on his breath, above the waft of the pipe and the paraffin. It would not surprise me if the tea were laced

with something stronger. But as I talk to him I am not paying that much attention; I am looking, rather, at the array of tools on the wood-shed wall. The rake and fork, the spade and saw, the hoe and hatchet, hanging side by side. The big axe, its wooden handle leaning at an angle. They are what I am looking at; yes. 'Thank you, Mr. Caddy,' I say in a satisfied tone, and I leave him no doubt somewhat mystified as to the reason for my little visit.

Night comes. I steal from my bedroom. With a coat pulled over my night-dress, I inch open the back door and creep into the moonlit garden. The key gleams in my hand. I slide it into the lock and it turns easily, with the faintest scratching sound. Once inside the wood-shed, I lift the axe. The handle may be four feet long and the head heavy as a rock, but I am strong as a man, strong as Hercules. Watch now in the moonlight as I carry the axe towards the black trees. In the muddle of moonlight and grey shadow I select the tallest of all the pines and, with perfect balance, lift the axe, and swing through the dark air. Despite its weight it feels as light as a dream, but the thud of the blade striking the wood is real enough. Birds, roosting in the branches, clatter into the night. I swing and swing again, in whirling movements. How easily the blade sinks into the flesh! He says that trees feel pain, that trees suffer; I beg to differ. This tree, I say as I swing, this pine tree, this tree is an inanimate object which does not possess a central nervous system and therefore is unable to experience sensation in any form whatever. This tree (and I swing once more, with the ease of a practised wood-man, and without the slightest moral qualm) is a member of the vegetable kingdom; this tree cannot feel. I, on the other hand, am a human being: I feel! I speak! I cry! I suffer! Do not ignore me! This is how I feel! Hear my anguish: I am a human being! The tree sways, hanging by a sinew; I give a last chop and stand back to watch it fall. As it does so, blood erupts from the inside of its trunk and sprays me in a crimson cloud. I do not care. I rejoice in this tree's death.

The night has gone; an angry dawn is breaking in the eastern sky. I look up; he is at his bedroom window, staring at the fallen tree, blood dripping from its stump. I hold up my crimson hands. 'Heartless man!' I shout. 'Look what I have done! Behold! It is you who have driven me to this, with your poems to her! Do you understand now?'

Thus the morning passes, which is a comfort, for imagine what it would be like if time were to stop like an unwound clock and we were all trapped in a morning without an end, repeating the same meaningless gestures. I know this is not so since the hands on the grandfather clock continue to move, but the impression of paralysis remains. Something must happen to change things, which is why I again lift the receiver and place a call to my sister Eva in London. I am not optimistic that this will help; never before have I tried confiding in Eva on such a personal matter, and I am sure that, like Cockerell, she will jump to the conclusion that my nerves are behind it all. She asks me what is wrong. O, my sister! Where should I begin? I begin with a succinct summary of the situation. I am forty-six years old. I am not in good health. I live in a dark house with an old man, my husband, who is planning to betray me by eloping with a married woman one third his age. All this I deliver in a strained whisper. I cannot talk too loudly because of the servants.

'Florrie, aren't you making a mountain out of a molehill? It's not as if he and she could . . . without being indelicate, he is too old, surely, to manage anything in the bedroom department. He could not actually be unfaithful to you.' I do not reply. 'Or am I wrong?' I do not reply. 'And when she is only twenty-odd years old – you know Florrie – it is just a fancy – a speculation! Maybe he thinks he would like to elope with her, but I promise you, she's never going to elope with him. Not in a month of Sundays.'

Into my mind there comes a picture of them together on the sofa, his hand like a reptile's claw on her bare leg. Grotesque! Loathsome! My legs begin to buckle; I slide my head against the wall. Eva does not understand, just as Cockerell did not understand. We are talking about love, my sister! We are talking about the heart, and there he is unfaithful to me, for in his heart he is eloping with her, that is the only truth that matters! I begin to hiss into the mouth-piece.

'My life here is intolerable. It is miserable. I live in silence. I am going mad.'

'If it is so intolerable, Florrie, there is the obvious solution. You should leave him.'

I gasp. 'Eva! Don't talk like that!'

'Why? It's true!'

'The operator may be listening!'

'You are ridiculous, Florrie. No one is listening. You don't need to divorce him, although lots of people are divorced nowadays. You can simply leave him. Pack your bags, catch a train. Come and stay here, at least for a while, until you feel better.'

'Eva, I can't leave him,' I say quickly. 'I can't! If I leave, she will move into the house. The next day! I know she will!'

'She has a husband! She has a baby! O, Florrie, Florrie.'

Both of us draw breath.

'I am sorry,' I say quietly. 'I don't know what to do.'

'I'm sorry too. You shouldn't have married him. What on earth did you think it would be like? An old man? What did you expect?'

'That is no help. Eva, that is no help at all. What is the use of asking me that? You know why I married him.'

'Florrie, I have never known why you married him. But he is old; he can't live much longer.'

Everywhere in this house there are presences. The walls seem to close in, shrinking the space inside my head. I feel as small as a hazel-nut. I go up to bed. I lie with hands by my side, ankles together, unable to move, like an Egyptian mummy in the British Museum, a dried-up cocoon swinging in dead air, beyond the reach of time.

*

There is no sound, but ten feet away, through the study door, he is thinking only of her. I know this. His mind is occupied with her; like a genie it is shaping itself to her voluptuous shape, leaving no room for me. I survive in a crevice barely able to breathe, I am a rose dying in the shadows of his thoughts. All I ever wanted was to be loved, and indeed that is why I married him, Eva; to answer your question, I loved him, and was in no doubt about it, and yet there are other answers, among them that I did not like the hustle and bustle of London and thought the countryside a green peaceful place, a place in which happiness might be found more easily than in London, and that I was flattered that he asked me, for no one had ever asked me before, and that at the age of thirty-five I was afraid that no one would ever ask me again, and that I was doubly flattered to be asked by such a great writer. I had, in my mind, the romantic image of helping him. Perhaps at this point I should admit that, even when he was so old, I hoped I might bear his child, something the first wife had failed to do. The lack of a child is the true source of his melancholy, I said to myself; it is the gap in his life that I as a young woman will help him fill. I shall help him to be happy, and thereby achieve happiness myself. Our child will be the sign of our love for each other, and so back it comes to love, that most precious of human emotions. Can a tree feel love?

According to Cockerell, he loves me. So Cockerell says. So says Cockerell. Has he said as much to Cockerell? It seems unlikely; Cockerell will say anything. What is certain is that he has never said anything of the sort to me. There have been times when I have thought he might be about to make some declaration of love, but he never has. Not once! Not once in all the years! I used to say to myself, why, of course he loves you, Florence; it is merely that he is no good at expressing his love; that is in his nature, like many men, for men are not good at expressing emotions such as love, they are much better at hiding their emotions than at expressing them. Look at Jane Austen's novels! How inarticulate the men are, how difficult they find it to express their love! However, without a doubt, he does love you – and to convince myself, I would take this or that gesture – a moment when he happened to touch my arm, for instance, or when he smiled at one of my remarks – and build it into a tacit declaration of love.

It was a delusion. He does not love me. He loves a woman a third his age, and writes her love poems. When has he ever written me a poem? Not for a long time. Yet he writes her poems, just as he wrote love poems to the first wife after her death. Does he not understand how much this neglect hurts me? Why has he never said that he loved me? Do I have to die before he writes me another poem? Is it possible that her baby is his? Of course, of course. How else can one explain his blind infatuation? How else explain these disgusting poems? Everything which did not make sense begins to do so. When, how, I do not know, but it must be his child! No, it cannot be his child. Again I am deluding myself. But, in truth, I am not in control of my mind; I am not able to assess whether I am deluding myself or not.

I knock on the door as lightly as possible, so as not to give him a start. There is no reply. I knock again, somewhat harder. My heart is thudding in my breast. I breathe deeply, and try the handle.

CHAPTER VIII

❧ ❧ ❧

The study was not a large one, nor was there anything in it that inclined to the remarkable. A dusty violin hung on one wall, and a somewhat battered 'cello stood in a corner, but the room was dominated by several large bookcases containing hundreds of books, some of a poetical and literary species, others concerning themselves with such matters as natural history, archaeology, geology and local topography. These volumes, to judge from the worn leather of their spines, had been much consulted over the years, probably by the old man who even now, this quiet winter's day, sat at a rectangular desk with a pen in his hand and a blank sheet of paper before him. The desk was drawn to the window and the pale light of the morning fell upon him.

He was, as any onlooker would have discerned, in that late stage of human existence commonly described as old age. His countenance, deeply inscribed by wrinkles, furrows, clefts and corrugations, and reminiscent of a dried-up river bed, seemed to be that of one who, in the course of a life's long journeying, had found much matter upon which to reflect and ponder. His head, although largely bald, retained enough straggling hairs to enable one to reconstruct an image of his youthful self, and to hint that in former times he might have been sufficiently handsome to have caught the eye of a young woman searching for a lover. The arches of his eyebrows were a pale ash-grey, almost the same colour as his moustache, which drooped faintly beneath a strongly curving nose, more Roman than aquiline.

As to the details of his habiliments, he wore the following: a pair of corduroy trousers, ginger in colour but faded in their upper parts, in consequence of much crossing and uncrossing of legs, with several pieces of knotted string acting as a belt; a light brown knitted waistcoat, fraying at the edges, and with one bone button hanging loose; a white shirt; a dark green woollen tie, inaccurately knotted at his neck; and an old, crocheted shawl, beige in colour, which lay over his shoulders. These appeared to suggest an individual who paid but little attention to matters of dress and for whom the vagaries of fashion no longer held any interest, if they had ever done so.

A fire had been lit some time before, and was even now down to its last coals. Dozing before it on a small rug lay an elderly dog of the terrier variety, with brown ears and pale fur, the matted and dirty condition of which inescapably led to the conclusion that it had lately been engaged in some private agricultural activity, possibly involving the pursuit of rats or rabbits or the burial of bones. Its eyes were closed, but every so often it began to whimper in some canine dream; its paws twitched, its muzzle trembled, it uttered a low growl as it encountered some phantasmal enemy.

None of this appeared to breach the meditations of the old man, who had been seated at the desk, in much the same posture, for more than an hour, without stirring, or without paying any heed to the goings-on of the external world. In truth, he was in an interlude – a reverie, of a kind that had become altogether familiar to him over the years. That is to say, although he was not writing, he was waiting to write. The pen was there, the paper there, but the creative moment had not yet arrived. Considerable periods of time might pass in this fashion, especially in the lull of a winter's morn such as now, while his mind moved at its own steady and mysterious pace, like that of a planet revolving round a sun.

He had learnt that it was a mistake to force the issue. Usually, not always but usually, after an extended period of contemplation, a thought would occur and lead to another thought, and thence to a line of verse, and after this first line others would arrive rapidly, of their own volition. He could not have easily accounted for this mysterious process, although at times it seemed akin to dreaming, and indeed the poems often came to him like dreams.

After a little, a phrase began to appear like a sail on a distant horizon. 'The veil of time'. 'The veil of time'? – he considered it as from afar, then closer to. 'When the veils of time are lifted'. Or would this not be better: 'When the veils of the present are lifted'? He contemplated 'When the veils of the present are lifted on the past' – and began to suspect that it was an old line that he had used upon some other occasion, or an echo of a line that some other writer had used in a poem he could no longer remember. Spenser? Shakespeare? Shelley? Fitzgerald? Or was it, as so often turned out to be the case, Biblical in origin? At all events, it seemed too familiar, and too superficially attractive. He was wary of glibness.

Another phrase, 'the bride of time', tried to engage him. 'The veil lifts upon the bride of time' – but no, he did not like that at all. He lost interest.

He gazed at the calendar that stood on his desk, the crimson numerals and letters on its page inaccurately announcing the date to be that of March the seventh. Beside it lay a pair of scissors; beside that a magnifying glass; beside that an ivory paper-knife.

He rose from his chair, the back legs of which gave a slight scrape on the wooden floor, sufficient to disturb the dog, which lifted its head and stared at him with an interrogative look. 'No,' he said, 'nothing. Nothing – go to sleep' – whereupon the dog obediently lowered its head and returned to its uneasy slumbers.

The window of the study faced in an easterly direction, over-looking a part of the vegetable garden, and also one of the lawns. A heavy frost had fallen, and even now, in the shadows untouched by the sun's rays, left a pallor on the grass that would probably remain all day. Late winter was generally the hardest season of the year, much harder than that of early winter; each night the polar air irresistibly tightened its grip on a passive countryside. Here on the hill above the town the fields were drab and bare, with every flinty rut as solid as stone. Trees stood motionless, deep in thought, the sap like old glue within the casing of their thick trunks. Buds slept in a trance, dreaming of the future.

Nothing that could stay in shelter willingly ventured abroad at such a time, but birds are obliged to hunt for sustenance. As the old man watched, a wood pigeon with a rosy breast landed on a slender bough and, shuffling to its further extremity, attempted to pick at a cluster of dark lustrous ivy berries before losing its perch and flying off with a clatter of wings.

As so often, this small and unexpected event was enough to dislodge any mental impedimenta, and to set him going. He took a book of poetry – one bound in green leather – from a shelf, opened it at a particular place and set it on his desk. He was writing freely when the knock came, and he recognised it at once, for the maids always knocked harder. Indeed, it was scarcely a knock, more of a light, interrogative tap which, being so timid, irked him more than somewhat, for it seemed to suggest that the knocker was frightened of the reception she might receive.

He did not answer, though the sound halted the progress of his pen across the page.

At the second tap he sought to expunge from his features any trace of irritation. 'Yes?' he said, and saw the handle turn. The next moment she stood before him, her hands clasped in an attitude of entreaty.

'Thomas,' she said, 'may I speak to you? I am sorry to disturb you. Are you not cold? It is very cold in here.' So saying she glanced at the fire, which had burnt very low. 'I don't know how you can work like this.'

Was he cold? True, it was cold in the study, but not that cold; a certain amount of heat rose from the kitchen below and a certain amount emanated from the embers of the fire. Besides, old habits die hard, and he had long ago taught himself to ignore the cold. Sometimes he felt that he wrote better in cold conditions.

Rather pointedly, he put down his pen. Whatever the purpose of her entry, it was not to discuss the temperature of the room; much more likely, she had come to badger him about the trees. The trees: if that was it, he would refuse to discuss it now. Now was not the moment: he was writing! He had begun – was in mid flow! Did she not understand what that meant?

'There is a letter,' she began, and unclasping her hands she gave him a letter she had been holding. 'I am not sure how you would like me to reply.'

The letter concerned a passage in an old novel of his in which, apparently, he had referred to certain amber butterflies that appeared on Egdon Heath and 'were never seen elsewhere'. What, the writer of the letter demanded to know, was the species in question?

He did not know: that was his first, impatient response. The novel dated from a period so distant in his past that he could no longer recall the twists and turns of the plot, let alone the impulse that had led him to mention a butterfly of amber hue. Looking over the passage quoted in the letter, he had a curious sense that he was reading the work of another man. The inquiry was frankly pedantic, besides. The Fox Moth? The Lulworth Skipper? It did not surprise him to note that the writer came from London, for the urge to identify and classify species was a characteristic example of urban thought. Country folk generally saw beyond the narrowness of scientific nomenclature to the essence of things.

He handed the letter back to Florence. 'I have not the slightest idea. Write anything. I am busy, I am writing.'

'Thomas, I can't write back and say you don't remember. He requires an answer.'

'Thank him for the letter and tell him that such matters are best left to the judgement of the reader.'

'I am not sure that will satisfy him.'

'Well, I am sorry.'

Upon which note he picked up his pen, as a signal for Florence to leave. She did not leave, however. 'What are you writing?' she asked in a tremulous voice.

'Nothing of any great merit. A poem.'

'I see.' She remained where she was, her face suffused with anxiety. 'Thomas, there is something else. I know that this may not be the best moment, but I have to speak. It concerns Gertrude Bugler.'

Gertie! The old man said nothing, though his eyes might well have shifted to the lines that he had just written, or to the open book, on one page of which lay a long black hair.

'I have been thinking of her a great deal, and of her performing on the London stage. I am convinced that it is a mistake, a grave mistake, and that we should discourage her from proceeding any further in the matter. I fear that it will end in disaster for her.'

'We have talked of this before. She is a very talented actress.'

'She is a very limited actress. I am sorry to say such a thing but it is true, even though you are blind to it. She is striking, I grant you, and has many excellent qualities as a person, but she over-acts all the time. She over-elaborates. Her voice at times is painfully affected. I am not alone in this, you know. Others feel the same. The reviewers have been kind thus far, but only because they are judging her as an amateur. Once in London, at the Haymarket, judged by professional standards – you know how cruel they are. They will pitch into her and her illusions will be shattered. They will tear her to shreds.'

The old man put down his pen. 'I understood that you were in favour of her going to London. You encouraged her.'

'I did; but that was before she had a baby.'

'What has that to do with it?'

'Her baby is less than a year old. To be parted from its mother at this age – it cannot be right! It is her duty to stay with it. We must dissuade her.'

'My dear,' he said, doing his best to adopt a reasonable tone, 'Gertrude has told us that she has talked it over with her husband, and that he is more than willing for her to go to London. That should be enough, surely.'

'I fear for her marriage!'

'Neither of us knows anything of the true state of her marriage. How husbands and wives behave towards each other in private is impossible to say. Besides, it is her chance, is it not? She has decided to take it.' He paused. 'I do not agree that she over-acts. She acts the part exactly as I conceived it. As for the newspapers, the same reviewers who praised her here will be judging her at the Haymarket.'

'I am thinking of you and your good name. If she is savaged, you will be touched. Your reputation will be tainted by her failure. It would be so much better if a professional actress were to play the part. If Sybil Thorndike could play the part!'

The old man stared at his desk and said nothing.

She continued: 'I should like you to write to Harrison. Tell him that he must engage a professional actress, if not Sybil Thorndike then someone else. I beg you, Thomas.'

'But I do not want anyone else as Tess. I have every confidence in Gertrude.'

His mind was settled on this; nothing could have shifted it. Gertie's performance of Tess at the Corn Exchange had won universal praise, and he could see no good reason for her not to play the part in London. Indeed, he very much doubted that a professional actress, even the redoubtable Sybil Thorndike, would play it any better. He had seen photographs of Sybil Thorndike: she did not look in the least like Tess, and almost certainly she would mangle the Wessex accent, which Gertie had to perfection.

'Please, Thomas.' She twisted her hands in agitation. 'I beg you, for your own sake.'

'But what would you have me say to Gertrude?'

'She will understand.'

'I disagree; she will not understand. Harrison has her offered the part, and she has accepted his offer. It cannot be withdrawn. The newspaper reviewers may or may not be cruel, but for us to tell her that she cannot play the part, that we have found someone else, would undoubtedly be an act of cruelty.'

'Her marriage will be destroyed.'

'I doubt it very much,' he said in a tone of brutal finality, hoping to end the conversation. 'A month or so away from her husband is scarcely going to destroy her marriage.'

'But where will she live?'

The old man was bemused by the way her mind seemed to jump from one place to another. 'In London? In an hotel, I imagine.'

'And you intend to go up to see her?'

'Certainly. When the time comes, I hope to be there. If I am still alive,' he added dryly. 'One never knows.'

'You are not well enough. You are eighty-four . . . believe me, Thomas. You must not go. It would be most unwise.'

'If I am unwell, then of course I shall not go. But I have every intention of going. I dare say I am capable of judging my own health. One can worry about one's health unnecessarily,' he remarked.

It was perhaps not the kindest of observations, given Florence's state of health, but it was not unjustified. The bump on her neck – what an Icelandic saga that had been! Dr. Gowring's view, throughout, had been that it was merely an inflamed gland, but she had determined from the outset that it should be cancerous and that she needed to visit Harley Street for a second opinion. This had upset her greatly, for the Harley Street doctor had agreed with Gowring that there was no need to do anything about it; whereupon she had insisted on trying for a third opinion, and at last the doctor told her what she wanted to hear by pronouncing the gland to be 'potentially cancerous'. Whether it was cancerous or not remained highly debatable, but finally, this last September, she had gone up to London for an operation to have it removed.

It was this to which her next remark referred.

'You would not go up for me! When I was in London you would not go up – you stayed here! You said you were too old. But now you are ready to rush up to see her!'

The accusation was, he considered, less than just, for he had freely offered to accompany her to town – had been ready to put his work aside, and to reside alone in an hotel for an indeterminate number of days while she recovered. True, the offer had not been made with any great enthusiasm, and he had been greatly relieved when she had agreed that he should remain at home in order to look after Wessex, who would otherwise have been left alone. Nonetheless, he had made the offer.

'My dear, if you remember, I stayed here on account of Wessex –' he began.

She interrupted: 'Did she come here?'

'What do you mean?'

'When I was in London – did she come here?'

Momentarily he was lost for speech. She swept on:

'She did! You had her here!' Her face began to contort, preparatory to tears. 'How could you? How could you?'

I have done nothing, he thought to himself. Why does she carry on so? He sighed: 'I have done nothing, Florence. Mrs. Bugler did not come here.'

'I am sure she did!'

'She did not come here. All the time that you were in London, my thoughts were with you, and nowhere else.'

This too was true, at least to a great extent; he had missed Florence during her stay in the metropolis. He had been unable to work well, he disliked solitary eating, and without her reading to him the evenings had dragged interminably. On the day of her expected return, after asking Mrs. Simmons to prepare a suet jam roll for dinner (this being her favourite), he had spent two hours stationed with Wessex by the drive gate, awaiting her arrival. He hoped that when she saw him thus, devotedly greeting her after her ordeal, she would be impressed and grateful, but the journey back from London had taken longer than expected, and by the time of her return he had abandoned his lonely vigil.

Nor did she seem pleased to see him, he might have added. One of the very first things she had done was to berate the cook for the jam roll.

'You are infatuated by her! You are infatuated! I saw you both! You and she – I – I saw! Everyone saw!'

He was now entirely baffled. 'When?'

'At the Corn Exchange . . . after the matinée. Leaning towards her . . . whispering in her ear . . . holding hands. Do you not care what people think? You will make yourself a laughing-stock.'

He gave her a wintry look. 'As you say, I am eighty-four; I am too old to care what people think. But you mistake: there is nothing for them to think. Mrs. Bugler and I were not holding hands, and the reason why she and I were leaning towards each other is that she happens to be a little deaf. She had an ear infection as a child and it has left her a little deaf in her right ear.'

More was to come, he knew; a good deal more. From long experience he knew that these emotional fits had their own stages to complete before they came to an end. Why did she behave like this? By what peculiar throw of Fortune's dice was it that he had come to be married to such a bag of nerves? What was the original impulse that had brought him and her to a union?

'You have been writing poems about her. Do not deny it! I have read them! There they are!' She extended a shaking hand at the desk. ' "To Gertie"!'

Ah, so that was it. He did not attempt to deny the accusation; how could he have done so? The poems were there, an undeniable fact.

'I know that I should not have read them, but they have been on your desk, I could not help it. Probably the maids have read them too. Imagine what they must think! It is plain as anything. You are thinking of eloping with her! You cannot deny it. You are infatuated!'

Her eyes, burning with pain, sought out his. He avoided them, fiddling instead with the paper-knife.

'How could you? O, Thomas! It is so unnatural of you! She is married – married! – with a child, and you are running after her – why? I cannot believe it – I cannot,' she repeated, with even greater vehemence. 'I cannot. When I have given up everything to help you. I have given up everything!'

She now began to weep, as he had known from the outset she would.

'My dear, you are over-wrought,' he began at last, unable to conceal the resignation in his voice. 'You will make yourself ill again. Calm yourself.'

'How can I? How can I? When all day you sit here – thinking – only of *her!*'

Sinking to her knees and hiding her face in her hands, she sobbed that he had never truly loved her, that, if he loved her, he could not have written such things, and that he would not now be proposing to elope. 'I am so alone!'

So it had come to this, that he had never truly loved her: well, well. It was not the first time that she had laid this charge at his door; every few months brought a similar outpouring of pent-up emotion. How should he answer it? By declaring his love? He could not do it, not now, under duress; it would have been too false.

He spoke, nevertheless. As gently as he could, he tried to tell her that she misunderstood; that he had written the poems as literary exercises; that they were flights of fancy addressed to an imaginary woman. 'There is not the smallest possibility of my eloping with Mrs. Bugler.' O, he was being more than a little disingenuous; but if it would stop her weeping it would be worth it.

'Are you intending to publish these flights of fancy?'

'I have not considered. Probably not.'

'You cannot publish them. You cannot. It would be too hurtful.'

'Florence, you must not upset yourself so much over a few small, inconsequential poems. I repeat, they are not about me and Mrs. Bugler. You read too much into them.'

'How can you say they are inconsequential? You know how people will read them. You know what the newspapers are like. What will people in the town think? I can hear the gossip.'

'No one there reads my poems,' he said. This remark, although it contained a grain of truth, was not entirely true. However, what he then said was close to the truth: 'If these poems are about any one person, I assure you, they are not about Mrs. Bugler, but about Tess d'Urberville.'

She stared wildly. 'They are patently about Gertrude Bugler. "To Gertie"! It is plain to everyone. What has Tess to do with them?'

The old man said nothing. He had suddenly lost interest in it all; had retreated into some distant, safe region of the mind, from which he was able to see the present moment between himself and Florence as a small, insignificant ripple on the smooth face of existence. After all, the scene was such as he might have contrived for a novel many years ago: the wronged wife, her hot tears, her bitter accusations ringing about the ears of her husband . . . how many times, down the long centuries, had this encounter been played out, and with how many variations? Such was the thought that came to him as he sat at the desk.

He carelessly dropped a hand to touch the side of the dozing dog. The movement caught her attention; she jumped up, snatched the poems from the desk and flung them in the fire. 'O! O! O!' she cried. 'How could you be so cruel!'

She gave way to fresh paroxysms.

What did she expect him to do? He might have made some attempt to retrieve the papers before they burnt, but he did not stir. He might also have made some attempt to comfort her, rising from his chair, putting an arm round her heaving shoulders, offering her a handkerchief; even, perhaps, apologising, although he had done nothing for which he considered it necessary to apologise. Arguably he ought to have been capable of some such saving gesture, but an immense indifference paralysed his limbs, rendering him incapable of action. How safe, how remote, how tedious it all seemed! How little he cared!

One of the buttons on his waistcoat, he observed – the penultimate button, viewed in order of descent – was loose, hanging by a thread. He was fond of the waistcoat, which had been knitted for him by Emma.

He watched as the papers smouldered more strongly and then burst into flames.

She rushed out. The door opened and shut; the consequent draught blew through the room; but she was gone. A peace fell as he heard her rushing steps fade. Wessex, his slumbers interrupted, had gone too; and the atmosphere so violently disarranged by her emotion began to restore itself, to recover its former poise and composure.

The first of the poems that the old man had written to Gertie Bugler, and to which his wife seemed to have taken such violent exception, had been composed more than two months earlier. He could not now recall the spark which had brought it into existence, but there had been no deliberate decision. He had not woken up one morning and said to himself, 'Now I shall write a poem about her!' No; that was not how it happened, or not in his case. Perhaps it was so with certain poets, who wrote certain types of poetry; but for him a poem was generally an expression of an impulse of thought or feeling. In years gone by, especially in the dog days of August, he could remember lying on his back at night in order to watch for shooting stars. When such a meteor appeared it always did so without any warning; it burnt its way across his vision for a second, like a match lit in the darkness, and then was gone. The genesis of poetry, for him, was something like that.

So the first poem about Gertie had had its birth. It was a poem of regret, more than longing: regret that Fate had decreed that he and she, kindred spirits, were sundered by such an ocean of Time as to make their love impossible. The space of sixty long years lay betwixt them: was it that he had been born too early, or she too late?

In a second poem, they chanced to meet at a roadside inn. They talked of their love in hopeless terms. 'And I so much older in years, and so much younger in wisdom than she . . .'

In a third, he had imagined her mourning at his graveside, on a day of heavy rain. Her sodden hair dripped and her face streamed, while the rain penetrated the ground and sank to the hard box in which lay his corpse; yet his spirit was that of a bird, perched on the reddish bough of the yew that grew nearby, and singing loudly. She did not heed him, though he sang for all his might and strove to communicate that, for her, still, love's fire burnt in his crimson breast. O that, in her sorrow, she might have heard and understood!

In a fourth, they were both ghosts, lodged on some cold, astral ledge, reflecting on the distant world that they had left behind, and wishing they had known then what they knew now.

The fifth was the poem about the elopement, an idea that owed some of its inspiration to the example of Shelley. Undetected, after a surreptitious exchange of notes, he waited for her in the hour before dawn at Toller Down Gate, a lonely upland spot in the heart of Wessex. While a chill wind blew and the stars glittered in the spaces between the black masses of the clouds, the flock of ewes grazing nearby regarded him with a certain surprise, as if wondering what his business might be at such an early hour and so far from the nearest human habitation. He strained his eyes in the direction whence she would appear. Sunrise was the appointed time for their meeting. Would she come, as she had promised, or had she been prevented from doing so? Was she unwell? Was he waiting at the right spot? A dozen unhappy possibilities passed through his mind as the sky grew paler and the inky darkness began to thin by steady degrees, each minute allowing him to discern a little more than the minute before. At last, when the first tinges of pink were edging into the space above the eastern horizon, he seemed to make out the faint shape of a human form. For a moment he remained in doubt as to whether it was she or some other person, and then his uncertainties vanished. She ran panting towards him, and flung herself into his arms. Such had been the dreamt scene, such went the poem, such might have been the ends to which their thoughts and hopes had tended; but in the last lines of the poem it turned out that this scene was not the start but the end of love, for they were both married.

A sixth poem was a reflection on that lost autumn day when once she came to call, when the trees were shedding their last leaves and the light fading in the hall; there he and she sat and spoke of this and that for some short space while Time's chariot rolled on its heedless way. What remained after her going? A smear of lipstick on the cup's rim, a single strand of dark hair, and his overflowing heart.

In a seventh, unfinished poem, set far in the future – the poem on which he had been engaged – a man reading an old volume of Shelley's works discovered that same strand of hair pressed between the pages of 'The Revolt of Islam', and fell to musing whether the hair had come to be there by chance or design, and who the woman might have been to whose head it had originally belonged.

These were but seven of the poems; in all, he had written more than twenty in a mere month. It was much faster than his usual rate of composition, although there had been periods in the past when he had been equally productive.

He got up from his chair and used a pair of tongs to extract a surviving sheet from the fire, but it smoked so much that he put it back and let it burn. If necessary he would be able to write the poems over again, though he doubted that he ever would. To rekindle the original impulses that had brought them into being did not interest him greatly; besides, to bring them back would cause Florence even more pain. Again he heard her railing at him, again he saw her anguished face. You are infatuated, you are going to elope with her! How can you write such things?

If only she understood . . . why were women in some things so perceptive, and in others so lacking in perception? The history of relations between the sexes was, when considered with a dispassionate eye, one beset by unhappiness. 'Into the apple of love crawls the worm of distrust' – uninvited, a pleasant phrase came to him, and might have drawn him back to poetry, but the precious moment for literary composition had gone. The day seemed ruined. The insubstantial shadows of branches played over the desk, the paper, his hands and head.

Something niggled at his mind. He picked up the letter, which she had dropped. What were those strange, amber-coloured butterflies found nowhere else but on Egdon? Twice he read the letter, and then a third time.

Why had he ever written thus? He was not a lepidopterist – had never had the desire, one experienced by so many of his contemporaries, to collect butterflies and moths, skewering their bodies and storing them in cabinets. Yet he knew the heath intimately; as a small boy he had spent many long summer hours exploring its furzy secrets, following thin paths that wound erratically to and fro. On such walks one readily encountered paper-pale miller moths that lived in the dried bones of the heath and flew up in weak flurries when disturbed, but scarcely any butterflies, amber or otherwise, and of the species mentioned by the letter-writer, none was conceivable. The Lulworth Skipper was never seen on the Wessex heaths but was an habitué of the coast near Lulworth, exactly as its name declared. (And, like all the skippers, it was a shy little butterfly which would never have settled on a man's back.) The Small Copper, equally, rarely appeared on heath-land; thistles were its favourite food. As for the Fox Moth, he was not sure that he would have ever been able to identify such an insect.

Hoping for clues, he fetched a copy of the novel in question from a shelf. It was nearly the favourite of all his books, for it had been written at a happy time in his life, when he and Emma had lived in domestic harmony. He had not read it attentively for years. His eyes, rather like those of Clym Yeobright, were no longer good enough for prolonged reading, and anyway he was somewhat wary of looking too closely at his old stories, for fear that he would find phrases and sentences he might regret.

He turned the pages until he came to the appropriate passage, and at once found the answer to the mystery. This was, quite simply, that the amber-coloured butterflies did not exist, for his description of the heath had been a piece of poetical invention. He had been attempting, as it were, to conjure a jewelled vision of the rough heath, turning it into a place of magical beauty; hence the 'glittering point' of Clym's hook, hence, too, the 'emerald-green' of the grasshoppers which leaped over his feet, falling awkwardly, like unskilful acrobats, hence, even, the 'bright' of Clym's surname. The amber butterflies were part of that vision; they did not live beyond it.

Doubtless the letter-writer would be disappointed by such information; well, but it was the truth. Just like the butterflies, Egdon itself, that vast expanse of heath described at the start of the novel, did not exist and probably never had; it was a piece of fiction that stood at a certain remove from reality. He hated these literary detectives, who failed to grasp the nature of art: that it was a shaping of reality, not reality itself.

He was agreeably impressed to see that the passage began by introducing Clym as a 'man from Paris'. Within the novel, it was against the gaudy shows of Paris that this brilliantly jewelled heath stood. Country against city; that opposition was never far from his novels, with his implied view that happiness might more easily be found in the former than in the latter.

Yet there was something else. In those far-off days, amber had been one of Emma's favourite stones; its warm glow, she always felt, came close to matching the colour of her hair. Thick and luxuriant, tumbling in ringlets about her shoulders, her hair had unquestionably been her best feature. For that reason, at an early point in their courtship, when they had been so much in love, he had given her an amber brooch, oval-shaped. He could remember buying it, from a jeweller in Piccadilly. She had worn it often. His adornment of the heath with amber butterflies had a deeply private meaning, or so it seemed to him now.

This brooch must be in Emma's jewellery box, which he kept in a wardrobe in his bedroom. He wondered whether he might give it to Gertie. Slipping it out of his pocket at some suitable juncture, he would say, 'Gertie, I thought you might like this –.' Should he tell her that it once belonged to Emma?

It was not in doubt that he would have to act in secret. If Florence were to discover what he had done, he would never hear the last of it. But – he defended himself – it was his brooch, to dispose of as he wished. Unseen in the velvet dark of a jewellery box, it was wasted.

Might he post it to her Beaminster home? With a card: 'To the embodiment of Tess' –? Possibly. But if she were to write back, Florence would probably open the letter.

Thinking of the scene with Florence, he realised that it was not yet over. Her decision to throw his poems on the fire would, he was sure, have left her in agonies of remorse.

He wished it were not so. When he and Florence had first met, at a time when his marriage to Emma had been afflicted by one of its deepest frosts, his soul had been warmed by her devotional looks and her solicitude. He had convinced himself that she was a careful reader who might in time come to understand some of the deeper mysteries of his art. There he had been wrong; like Emma, even more than Emma, she had continued to read a poem as if it was a scientific tract. She was like the lepidopterist; every word and phrase that left his pen she interpreted in a literal fashion as an account of his inner self. She did not begin to understand, although he had tried to tell her, that he was not I, and I was not he. The relationship between he and I was close; they were blood brothers, but brothers often differ greatly. When he wrote a poem in which he contemplated an elopement with Gertie, it was nothing but a flower of desire.

Once again, he found himself thinking of Shelley's theory of the ideal woman who has the ability to appear in numerous guises. It perfectly seemed to fit his own dealings with the opposite sex, in and out of fiction. Who, after all, was the she in the poems to whom he had here given the name of Gertie? Who the shes of the novels and short stories? Behind each stood one even more mysterious, more alluring: a woman's shape veiled by shadow or mist, on the edges of vision, out of reach. If he tried to move towards her, she seemed to drift away.

His entire life had been spent seeking her, catching occasional glimpses of the same shape. During a sudden summer downpour near St. Pancras a slender girl in a fluffy blouse had taken shelter under his umbrella, and in the thick of winter he had recognised her again, stepping on to an omnibus that disappeared into the crowded Piccadilly dusk. Months passed, and she appeared on a woodland path, a freckle-faced village lass in a white smock reading a lover's letter under the boughs, and then she too went her way without a word. In her next incarnation she was a dark gipsy with ringleted hair picking blackberries from an entangled hedgerow, lips stained purple from the ripe fruits that she had consumed like a goddess in one of Keats's odes. Among these glimpses, of course, there was that of the dairymaid in the Stinsford water-meadows.

Of all such transitory visions, one held an especially strong hold on his imagination. As a boy of fifteen or sixteen he had been among hundreds of townsfolk who gathered to watch a hanging. It was late summer, and in the country that encircled the town the corn-fields were golden, but the day itself was one of heavy drizzle and a greying mist. The gallows had been erected outside the gates of the prison. Although he could not now remember whether he had been there by chance or deliberate intention, he remembered with great clarity the hour of the hanging and the murmur of excitement as the woman mounted the steps to the scaffold. She was not local, but had lived in a village in the west of the county, where she had been married to a man of no fixed trade or occupation. Her crime had been that of murder. Her unfaithful husband had come home drunk in the small hours, and when she reproached him he hit her with a horse-whip and kicked her hard; as he bent to untie his boots she split his skull with a hatchet. Some sections of local opinion felt sympathy for her and wondered whether she was guilty in the eyes of God, but others took a sterner view; at all events, the law had found her guilty and had determined that she should be put to death. Slight of build, with her hair pinned up, she was apparelled in a thin gown of black silk, and seemed so composed that she might almost have been some elegant woman of fashion there to admire the scenery from a new vantage point. Various figures attended to her dispatch, one tying her hands, another her feet, while the executioner, a thickset man with a big white beard, pulled a cloth bag over her head.

He was intensely interested, his consciousness alive to every detail of the occasion, which was not unlike that of a fair. Dogs and babies were present, and a good deal of lively conversation took place on matters entirely unrelated to the spectacle; very little of the respect that might have seemed appropriate was in evidence. Yet when the bolt finally slid back and the woman dropped, kicking and struggling at the rope's end, it was a shock; bystanders gasped, and a boy who had scrambled into the branches of a tree for a better view lost his balance and fell with a sudden cry. The moment failed to last; the body ceased its convulsions, and then someone spoke, someone sighed, someone lit a cigarette; he heard the scrape of the match and the faint crackle of the tobacco strands in the damp air. Someone else, at a remark unknown, gave a quick giggle: he turned his head and saw a pantry girl squirming in the embrace of a fat, red-faced man in a tailor's apron, and the man caught his eye and gave him a sly wink. Embarrassed, he looked back. The woman was now swaying to and fro with a graceful motion that reminded him of those tiny green caterpillars dangling from the branches of birch trees. Dazed, and disinclined to believe that he had seen what he had seen, the division of a human body and its spirit, he thought of the breeze, redolent with the scents of the fields and hedgerows over which it had passed in its invisible progress, now permeating the thin membrane wrapped around the corpse. The crowd slowly dispersed, but he stayed where he was – it was an hour before she would be cut down – and as the drizzle turned to rain, the tight black dress clung to her body and revealed her trim female shape, and the cloth bag adhered to her face and allowed her features to emerge for the last time.

Her name had been Martha. Martha . . . Tess . . . Gertie . . . he stared at the marks scratched by his pen. Ah, Gertie, Gertie. He dipped his pen in the ink-well, he turned the nib on the blotting paper and watched the ink spread through its fibres.

What should he do about her? He longed to see her on stage in London. Afterwards he would take her out to a fine restaurant – to the Savoy, no less – where they would drink champagne. Their glasses would clink, and he would toast her success, before escorting her back to her hotel. They would part in the foyer, beneath a glittering chandelier, and perhaps as they parted, she with a dazzling smile, he would give her the amber brooch.

Perhaps they would not part. Old as he was, and unlikely as it seemed, he refused to rule out the possibility of a romantic entanglement. Of one thing, at least, he was sure: that those philosophers who claimed that the passion of love was a matter that could be experienced in its fullness solely by the young, and in diminishing degree by those of more advanced years, were mistaken.

He opened the door softly. The stairs, the corridor, were empty. Listening for Florence, he heard only the heavy tick of the grandfather clock in the hall and the muted calls of the wood pigeons in the trees. He floated down like the spectre he was, one soft step at a time, a precautionary hand on the banister.

He was putting on his coat when he met one of the maids.

'Where is Mrs. Hardy?'

'She is away, sir. She said if you asked to say she would be away all afternoon.'

He paused, considering. 'In Dorchester?'

'I think so, sir.'

'Did she say why?'

'No, sir.'

Again a pause. 'Thank you.'

The girl was leaving for the kitchen when he remembered something else. 'Where is Wessex?'

'I couldn't say, sir.'

'Is he in the house?'

'I can't say, sir. He may be in the garden, sir. Would you like me to look for him, sir?'

'No,' he said, 'I expect he'll turn up. If you see him, keep him.'

'Yes, sir.'

This uninformative exchange over, he opened the front door and stepped out.

A portion of shadow awaited; he crossed it, and through a tangle of branches the winter sun burst upon him. He stood transfixed, not moving, adjusting himself to the sharpness of the light. The air was cold enough to make his breaths visible, yet the old sun warmed his mottled skin like that of a snake. At times like these, it was easy to understand how the pagans who had lived here more than two thousand years ago had worshipped the sun as a deity.

The sound of a cough reached his ears, and he turned his head: Caddy was halfway up a ladder, pruning one of the apple trees.

He spoke to the man: 'Have you seen Wessex lately?'

'Not since the mornin', sir. I seed them little rabbit again, sir, feedin' in the vegetables.'

'Ah. But still only one?'

'Yes, sir.'

'Well. Mr. Caddy – if you have a moment, if you would put the hens away, before it gets too dark.'

He walked to the end of the drive and, a trifle dizzy, rested by the gate. The view extended over grey stubble fields broken by dark hedges. Above, the sky was cloudless, but not blue as in summer; instead its hue was that peculiar admixture of rosy-pink and violet characteristic of hard winter weather, with the violet deepening, and growing progressively more intense near the horizon, around which it lay in a dark, concentrated band of smoke. A bitter night with another hard frost lay ahead, and already parties of rooks were straggling towards the wood that since time immemorial had been their nocturnal place of rest. The wood was only lightly shot, and rooks from far afield lived here in the winter months, gathering at dusk and crowding together for safety. If one entered the wood shortly after nightfall, as the old man had sometimes done, one heard the entire flock engaged in a conversation composed of squawks and shrieks, as raucous as parrots in a menagerie.

More and more birds came over his head, in long black strings which crossed the fragments of a large moon, shadowy and insubstantial. Was this the last time that he would linger, watching these quiet fields? Was this his last winter, was today, even, his last day, his final hour? Ever since Gertie's visit nearly a month ago he had had the sense of the approaching end, and standing here now he felt a certain sort of lightness in his body, as if without too much difficulty the northerly breeze might strengthen and, in a sudden gust, break his earthly moorings and carry him away.

The loud caws of the rooks receded, and in their place he was conscious of the distant puffing of a train as it gathered speed on the rise out of the town. It grew rapidly louder, for the line passed through a cutting no more than a quarter of a mile from the house itself. The sounds of such trains were part and parcel of life here, and not inherently unpleasant to him, but now he was made uneasy by the thought that Wessex might have strayed near the line. Years earlier, several of Emma's much loved cats had met their end in just this way. One particular favourite had been cut in half, and the discovery of its severed body on the rail had been deeply upsetting. A cat was only a cat; were Wessex to die in a similarly tragic fashion, Florence would be pitched into an unspeakable hysteria. Work would become impossible.

The train drew nearer, and louder, and then it had passed, leaving behind a trail of white smoky puffs which rose and began to disintegrate. His apprehension remained, though it was not, in truth, very great, and as he was walking back Wessex appeared from the skirts of the shrubbery. Grizzled, and a little stiff in the hind-quarters, but still very game, the dog seemed to stare as though puzzled as to his whereabouts, before identifying his master. He trotted over, tail twitching. Wessex, thought the old man: my friend, my ally. He could trust Wessex. He bent and stroked the dog, who promptly rolled on to his back.

An hour later, and he was again in his study. The day was failing, the light gradually easing as the earth spun away from the sun. Blackbirds around the house were making the loud clucking sounds that signalled the approach of dusk; amid their clamour he could hear the thin, wavering line of a robin's song. Such songs, he thought, such songs, issuing from such tiny, fragile scraps of matter.

The maids had not yet lit the lamps. He might have rung the bell and summoned them to do so, or he might have lit them himself, but for the moment he preferred to remain in the twilight. This was his favourite time of day, when the interaction between the physical and spiritual seemed strongest, when the barriers that were supposed to part the living and the dead dissolved into nothing. To say that at dusk he found himself able to conjure the spirits of the past was not entirely accurate, for often the spirits appeared unbidden in his inner vision, rising before him, beckoning, speaking.

Was he abnormal? he thought. Surely other men were like this? Yet he knew it was not so. Other men were not like him. Somehow, by temperament and training, his sensibilities had tuned themselves to a different key. At the drop of a hat he could change perspectives; could fly back to his childhood and become the boy he once was, or slip into the part of some other person, dead or alive. Equally, without difficulty, he could become a tree or a bat, or a bird. One effect of that daily relocating of the self was to loosen the ties that held him in the here and now, and set him free in a space of airy imagining.

Now, in this detached state, he indulged himself in a vision of his own funeral at Stinsford Church. It would be a winter's afternoon not unlike this, he felt certain; a chill winter's afternoon, a sharp breeze cutting from the north, and the light already beginning to leave the day, even though the hour was scarcely beyond two o'clock. There would be an excellent turn-out; many local people would come to bid farewell to the mason's son who had made good. All of the metropolitan crowd would be there; the train that morning from Waterloo would have been full of men in mourning vestments. The lane running down to the church would be lined by motor-vehicles and horse-drawn cabs.

He thought it likely that as many as five hundred might attend; far too many to fit in the church's narrow pews. He was a famous man; his death would have been reported in every newspaper, with long obituary notices and lavish tributes. Would any record the struggles of his early years? A country education had not given him the advantages that many men had enjoyed; denied the chance of university, he had had to tutor himself in Latin and Greek. Would any say how much doubt and uncertainty had dogged his footsteps, and how much determination and perseverance had been necessary to achieve what he had achieved? No, they would not say anything of the sort. How little they knew! And quite right, too: there was no need for them to know everything.

He waited by the grave; as they filed past, singly or in pairs, they averted their eyes. Among them was Gertie Bugler, beautiful as ever, a pair of long black gloves on her hands and a look of quiet intensity on her face; to his faint amusement, at the sight of her shapely calves and narrow ankles, he detected within himself a last quickening of desire. How strange! Yet there was no doubt that although corporeally he had no existence at all, some portion of his dwindling self desired her as his own, even now. More came. His brother, Henry; his sister, Kate. That saying about blood being thicker than water was a good one; during his life, he had never lost sight of the importance of family. Cockerell, of course; and who was that? Barrie! He was pleased by that; excellent that Barrie had bothered to come down, the old fox. There was Augustus John, looking his usual angry self, glaring at the universe. O, and Kipling, too, with a fat moustache, even fatter than Barrie's.

Some of the mourners he failed to recognise. Tradesmen, perhaps; journalists; acquaintances from times gone by? Others he recognised with acute surprise. What was Tennyson, whom he had met once or twice in London, but who had died at least thirty years earlier, doing in the ranks of the living?

He did not feel the slightest inclination to accompany them into the church. One feature of his personality was that he had always found himself to be most enamoured of churches when they were empty. The presence of other human beings, the troublesome nature of the liturgy and the turgid quality of the hymns distracted from the meditative atmosphere that had always appealed to him. He had not attended a service for years.

Once the heavy door was closed – by some miracle of compression, all must have crowded in, packing the nave and the aisles – his spirit remained outside to browse the familiar yard, with its yew trees and grey stones, and its uneven, mossy turf.

No doubt, he thought, a good many of those attending the funeral, especially those who had come from London, would have preferred him to be laid to earth in a more convenient plot. At one time he himself had entertained the merits of a larger church, that of St. Peter's, in the centre of the town and a short walk from the railway station; but it was a church for townsmen, not for a man such as he. Another church, even larger – the nearest church, in yardage, to the house, and the church that Florence sometimes attended – was Fordington St. George, but it was an edifice for which he no longer felt any affection, the vicar of the past two decades having carried out a piecemeal destruction of its glories in the name of modernisation.

In truth, only Stinsford – this quaint old place, a model of country reticence on the edge of the water-meadows – was possible. This was where his forebears were buried. His grandfather, his grandmother, his uncle, his father and mother: their graves were here, and here, and there, in the yew's shade. His first wife, Emma, lay here too, waiting for him in the pit, the stone temporarily put to one side. Dear Em: even if, in latter years, his and her relations had grown chilly, a matter that, inasmuch as he was at fault, continued to cause him regret, she had stood by him while he made his name in the world of letters. What times they had had together! Briefly, he contemplated the notion that their mortal remains would mingle in the cold Wessex loam. Would Florence, too, join them at the last? Tom with his two wives, one on each arm, travelling onward?

There was another poem here that he might have written, and without too much trouble: a last poem, 'The Three Ghosts'. How would it begin? Each silently rising from the ground in an inchoate cloud: first he, then she, and she, drifting, shape-shifting, gradually assuming the looming likenesses of their former selves. Old thoughts, and old, much-used rhymes – how often he had pressed them into reluctant service – but it was too late now for all that. A wave of self-pity broke through him as he faced the fact that he would write no more; his hand would cease to move, his fingers stiffen; all would cease.

The vibrating strains of a hymn emanated from the stone

interior. It was one that the old man seemed to recognise from childhood days; gazing towards the church, striving to place the tune, a picture of the scene therein rose in his mind. Stinsford, too, had not entirely escaped the indignities of over-zealous restoration. The works of eighteen forty had seen the loss of most of the high-sided oak pews from the Caroline and early Georgian periods, and those of eighteen seventy had needlessly destroyed a fine Tudor waggon roof, ruining the proportions between the tower and the nave. Yet it was easy enough for his imagination to undo those changes and to return the church to its former condition, with the old string choir – his grandfather on the 'cello, his father and uncle on the violin – playing a final encore in the west gallery.

As he gazed further, he found himself not entirely attached to the earth. The same sense of lightness that he had noticed earlier allowed the breeze to dislodge him from his stationary post and to set him in motion. He crossed the ground without effort, without a single step, his thoughts seeming to lead him invisibly on; there was a definite, steady pull, a current, carrying him to that part of the churchyard overlooked by gargoyles. When he had been a child they had frightened him horribly; clinging like misshapen bats to the roof's edge and with their faces drawn, as it seemed, from a nightmare, he had understood them to be souls in torment, facing the prospect of eternal damnation. Now he saw them otherwise, the expressions of horror and fear on their countenances deriving from contemplation of the terrestrial scene. For more than five centuries they had been watching affairs in this small space of earth; how much they must have witnessed of sorrow and unhappiness. Hopes dashed, love spurned; the best of intentions brought to nought. How short to them must seem the span of a human life! The chubby babe brought here to be baptised in the ancient font was, in a score of years, the proud bride walking to the altar; in another twenty, she was the doughty matron, attending her father's funeral; and in twenty more, the cold, wrinkled corpse borne by her sons to the grave.

The gargoyles themselves were badly eroded; they too would vanish in due course. Likewise, the lettering on most of the headstones had begun to fade. The stone invariably used by the Stinsford masons was not granite or marble but a variety of limestone from one of the local quarries, and a material far less resistant to change. Nature, in the form of rain, wind, frost and ice, soon attacked those upraised letters and chiselled edges, as if mocking their pretensions to immortality, and many of the older tablets were now blank faces covered in pin-cushions of moss, dew-soaked spider webs and the irregular, frilly growths of rusty pink lichens; long since, they had ceased to offer any clues as to the identities of the men and women in whose names they had been erected. Well; so it would be for him. In the end nothing would remain, save a few of his books, which might survive as his true memorials, although even they would eventually pass into obscurity. His life spread before him, set against the immensity of time, seemed a thing of utter insignificance, a speck in the firmament.

Which parts of his work would endure longest? That it would be his poetry he very much hoped; judged by the highest standards of art, his novels fell well short. They were workmanlike enough, but the early novels had been written in a hurry and crammed with incident in order to meet the requirements of the serial magazines, and even the later novels contained manifest faults of style and construction. And yet, as time had gone by, and as praise had come to be heaped upon them, he had noticed them steadily rising in his estimation. It still rankled that they attracted so much more attention than his poems, but perhaps they were not so bad; perhaps they would still be read a century hence, as accounts of a certain sensibility. People saw them as stories of country life, which they were, but they were also stories about love and its deceptions. Love, not the country, had been his true subject. And women? Women, too. Women were more fascinating than men, it seemed to him. The clothes they wore, the way they did their hair, their scents and voices, their music. He understood women more than men; when he examined his own self, he often felt that he had within him a larger than average portion of femininity.

Of course, he had been brought up by powerful women. His mother; his mother's mother. He recalled them vividly, conjuring his childhood in the little cottage with its dusky red walls. Even now, blindfold, he could have felt his way from room to room, up and down the creaking stairs, over the uneven floors. How long ago it all was! He was among the last survivors of a distant age; all but a few of those who had lived and breathed at that time now lay still, a fallen army. But the space between then and now shifted strangely, with Time compressing and expanding like a hurdy-gurdy. At one moment it seemed an aeon since the days of his boyhood, at another it was scarcely a day since he had danced and whirled to the fiddle's tune.

His mind projected into the future. Florence no doubt would stay here after his death, but the day would come when she too would die, and then his books, his furniture, his pictures, his notebooks – the careful accumulations and accretions of a lifetime's thought – would be dispersed. The house, too, would go under the hammer, or be sold by private treaty; another man would live there in his stead. It was an uneasy prospect. What would he think, this unknown occupant, of his distinguished predecessor? What changes might he make?

He drifted away. The crimped leaves of hart's-tongue fern gleamed in the damp corner at the base of the vestry door. Gradually the breeze bore him back to the open grave. Peering into the pit, he recoiled at the flat boards of Emma's coffin and the sludge of streaky grey clay.

If only he could have believed in God, or something of the sort! But what was the supreme being in which mankind was expected to believe? An old schoolmaster squatting on a cloud, flapping his hands, dispatching angels and thunderbolts – who could possibly believe that any longer? Had anyone ever believed that, in their heart of hearts? It seemed most unlikely. What was this world but a whirling body of matter in the immeasurable vacuities of space? If God was anything, surely, he was a ripple of birdsong, a pearl of dew, a flash of sunlight on the trunk of a tree! It was ironic to reflect that, as a young man, he had been an avid student of the Bible and had seriously considered taking holy orders.

But the service was over. The church door was flung open, and the coffin with its six pairs of dark legs and shining black shoes appeared like some giant beetle. To whom did these legs belong? Who were his bearers on this last, short journey? As the beetle turned towards him, the faces of those on the nearer side came into view. Lawrence was the first, and a good man to be carrying one's coffin. Then Cockerell, of course; he liked Cockerell, had often been charmed by him. Siegfried Sassoon, looking very pale and strained, was the third man in the line, and that pleased him, for Sassoon was a fine poet, with a highly developed literary sensibility. Who else? He was unable to make out the faces of those on the far side of the coffin, but no doubt there had been some considerable competition between writers for the honour. Well, it would not be for him to settle their petty disputes, though he sincerely hoped that it would not be Kipling. Once, years ago, he had spent several days trying to help Kipling find a house near Weymouth; but between them there had been too many differences of outlook and temperament for a true friendship to take root. The Nobel Prize had also come between them. He had never quite forgiven Kipling for winning an honour which he should have liked for himself and of which he believed that he was much more deserving. Every year for years he had been nominated, and every year he was mysteriously overlooked. He used to affect indifference, and as a joke, to cover his disappointment, say that he felt as if he had won the No-No-Nobel. But Kipling! It irked him, even now. What had possessed those Swedish greybeards?

The mourners slowly followed the coffin to the graveside. The men doffed their hats, while several red-eyed women, he was gratified to see, clutched handkerchiefs. It was a long procession; several minutes passed before all were assembled around the gaping ground. A month hence, he asked himself, how many of these mourning men and women would return in their thoughts to grieve him? How soon, how very soon, he would be forgotten! He looked for Florence. Ah, there she was, in that old cloche hat – and on the arm of Barrie! What did that portend?

The grave awaited, with its mounds of freshly dug earth. The sky was featureless, the colour of zinc. The breeze blew hard.

As the coffin was lowered, as it met the ground, the stays eased and creaked. The bearers stepped back, their work done, and the vicar intoned the last rites in a sonorous voice that rose above the breeze. Then a hush; no one moved or spoke; but a horse outside the churchyard gave an impatient whinny, and a thrush high in one of the elms, its pale breast shining, began to sing. Its musical notes rang out loud and clear, piercing the twilight, as if to defy the finality of what was ensuing below. And where was he in all this? Not in the box, on which the vicar had tossed a token quantity of earth; but somewhere nearby, on a convenient branch, head cocked to one side, observing and reflecting a little. So he had done in the course of his life: might it not be possible to continue the practice, for a fixed space, after his death?

He was aware of the metaphysical conundrum here. He had spent his professional life consorting with the dead, bringing them back to life in different fictional guises; yet he did not, when pressed, find himself able to believe in the existence of a permanent after-life, at least in the sense of an after-life that was a continuation of earthly existence. Against it too much weighed, despite the endeavours of the spiritualists. Yet the notion of a temporary lingering, of a gradual rather than sudden withdrawal into the shades, still appealed to him. At certain times, in certain places, he himself had felt so strongly the presence of the departed, just out of vision, that his breath had been checked.

As a boy he had been told more than a few stories about ghosts. Belief in hob-goblins, will-o'-the-wisps, witches and other nocturnal apparitions was common in the Wessex countryside, and his paternal grandmother had enjoyed herself in describing a spot on Egdon, by a clump of seven Scotch pines, where she had watched the walking ghost of a murdered man, a notorious smuggler, who had betrayed his comrades in crime and had been killed in consequence. If he had been deeply impressed by that, he was also curious, but whenever he questioned the aged woman (how many times had she seen it? what did it look like?), she refused to answer, merely pursing her lips into an enigmatic smile. The determination grew within him that he must see the ghost for himself, and late one summer's day he persuaded his sister Mary to accompany him there. He must have been six or seven while Mary was a year and a half younger. The pines stood on a knoll in a deserted part of the heath fully a mile from the nearest human habitation. He and Mary arrived soon after sunset, with the pines black against a sky that was rapidly shedding the last vestiges of light. With every passing moment their apprehension grew. The light dwindled further, the outspread body of the heath sank into darkness, and the legions of tiny, invisible insects that had remained silent during the day set about their usual droning. Then a nearby night-hawk began to utter its loud whirring call from the pines. Of all the heath's birds, none was so secretive nor so mysterious, and when it flew out of the branches and wheeled to and fro over their heads, clapping its wings, they fled for fear of their lives.

As he grew up and became exposed, through his reading, to the wider currents of rational and scientific thought that nowadays rule the Western world, he turned sceptic and dismissed all ghosts as fanciful inventions or tricks of the suggestive imagination. Then, one misty Christmastide, he had been visiting Emma's grave in this very churchyard when a man dressed in an antique military garb from the Napoleonic era stepped into view. He knew at once that it must be a ghost, chiefly from its insubstantiality of form, with the lower part of the apparition like a piece of gauzy tissue through which the solid facts beyond – the dark ground, the grey stones, the dripping trees – were still discernible. In a light breeze the figure of the ghost seemed to ripple.

After recovering from speechlessness, he had given a cough of inquiry. Good afternoon! The spectre raised its head and lifted a stiff hand before gliding – it would not be true to say that it walked – towards the church. Following uncertainly, he saw it thin and fade into its immaterial self.

What was all that? A piece of fancy? No: he did not think so.

He toyed with the thought that the world was full of ghosts but that only a very few of the living were able to perceive them. Or was it that ghosts, though generally invisible, occasionally attained visibility, perhaps when they chanced to draw near familiar scenes?

He toyed with another thought: that ghosts were able to perceive fellow spirits. Might two such, lovers in former times, meet, draw close, entwine? Might they kiss – their pale lips brushing – in memory of kisses shared during their earthly residence?

Were ghosts souls who had somehow failed to find the narrow way into heaven? (But he did not believe in heaven.) Or was it that the dead continued to live in the time in which they had lived when on earth? Where, after all, should they live else? Time, if so, was not, as commonly thought, a process, but a series of metaphysical spaces. Ghosts were seen when, for reasons unknown, they inadvertently slipped from their allotted time into the present.

Was it possible that some advance in science, akin to the discovery of X rays, would eventually allow the living to view a world crowded with noiseless, flitting ghosts?

He remained sceptical – it was impossible not to be sceptical – and yet he was also a romantic. He toyed with the notion of transformation. A man died to become the dust from which rose a tree, and in its green shade sat the man's grandson. Was this beyond all bounds of possibility? In a material universe – and, sadly, the evidence in favour of a material universe was very great – was this not the truest version of an after-life?

The service was over. The mourners were shuffling away, though Florence remained, her pale, powdered face deeply imbued with tragedy. She still clutched Barrie's arm, and the old man was glad of that. Let her find happiness where'er she might! Gertie was there too, with old Harry Tilley, dropping a small bunch of snowdrops into the pit. He liked the elegance of the gesture: what a fine creature she was!

Yet the one who caught his attention as the crowd thinned was a woman somewhat like Gertie but not entirely she, a woman whom he had never seen before, but whom he seemed to know with an intimacy which ran to the bone: the ideal woman, the well-beloved, the Shelleyan avatar of whom he had so long dreamed and who had haunted every novel he had ever written. Beneath a wide black hat she gazed into the grave before slowly raising her head as if to bid him a final farewell. Her precise features remained elusive, for her face was veiled, yet he had no doubt that she had full knowledge of his presence, and he would have liked to step forward, or to make, at least, some corresponding gesture, but found himself unable. Then she and all other members of the human race faded from view, and he was left alone by the yew tree, in the winter wind.

Something had changed during the service. His self was now light as a wisp of nothing, while his vision had dimmed. As through a darkening glass he watched a shadowy robin hop down to tug some invisible creature from the sodden earth by the edge of the pit. The earth bore the many footmarks of the mourners and bearers who in time to come, like him, would cross the gulf that lay between the living and the dead.

Presently he heard the sound of bells slowly rolling over the meads, through the gathering gloom, like waves at sea.

The light ebbed in the study. The dusk was dull and heavy. The birds in the garden had long ago fallen silent, retiring to their sequestered roosts.

A knock on the door.

'Yes?'

'Please, sir,' asked the maid, 'would you like me to light the lamps?'

'Thank you.'

So, from his meanderings in the future and the past, he was recalled to the present. He watched the girl as she made her way from one lamp to another. No doubt she knew that he and Florence had had an argument; the maids always knew. It would have been impossible to have run the house without domestics; yet, even after so many years, he had never quite managed to accustom himself to their presence.

'Is Mrs. Hardy back?'

'No, sir.'

'Not back?'

'No, sir.'

Not back, he thought: well. He blinked, but said nothing.

In the lamplight there shone on the pane before him the mask of his face, his cheekbones and eyebrows visible in upraised patches, the rest lost in darkness. My dead self, he thought: my spirit self.

The maid raised her arms to draw together the curtains.

'Will that be all, sir?'

'Thank you.'

CHAPTER IX

※ ※ ※

I am in a state of triumph. No, that is not it, but I am, at least, in a state of heightened determination. For I have become aware of something. My life does not have to be as it is. I do not have to submit, I can act to change the course of events. Why should I submit to his tyranny? Why does the woman always have to submit to the man? From now on I shall be no longer weak and self-pitying but strong and resolute. I shall no longer give way upon every occasion, I shall no longer submit to his silences. If only I were not so cold! Even in the taxi, even though I have a rug tucked round my legs, it is very cold. But I am confident and determined, and I have made up my mind how I shall deal with Gertrude. My stay will be short and brisk and business-like; I shall not take off my coat or gloves, and if she offers me tea I shall decline. No doubt she will put up some resistance, but I shall not enter into negotiations. Politely, calmly (it is most important that I remain calm), I shall say what I have to say, and take my leave. I am impatient to get it over and done with. Why is the taxi going so slowly? For some time we have been crawling along. We are barely moving at more than walking pace.

'Why are we going so slowly?'

'A lot of ice, ma'am.'

The back of Mr. Voss's solid neck bulges above his collar in three fat rolls. My mouth opens, shuts, opens again. We have taken nearly an hour thus far, and in this grey light it feels longer.

'Where are we?'

'We are on Toller Down, ma'am.'

Toller Down! Of all places! This is where they were to meet, according to the poem! A bare expanse of grasses stretching away, without a shelter in sight; even looking at it makes me feel cold.

'Will we get there before dark?'

After a long pause there comes his lugubrious reply: 'If it doesn't get any worse.'

Was it such a good idea to drive out here, on such a cold afternoon, on icy roads? There is no traffic; we have not met another car for at least ten minutes and it might have been better if I had written her a letter; after all, I am good at writing letters, stiff letters, I write them every day. But a letter would have taken time to reach her and it felt imperative that I should settle the matter now, that I should not have to face another night of worry. Worry is not good for me, not in the state of my health, although in truth for the sake of my health I should not be here, enduring this terrible cold. I have reached the conclusion that I feel the cold more than other people, more than Mr. Voss, I am sure, and certainly more than my husband, who hardly seems to feel the cold at all. Closing my eyes I try to pretend that I am at home by the fire with Wessie at my feet, but I am no good at this kind of pretence, and when the car begins to bump and rock I look up. The road is much steeper than it was, and to my alarm Mr. Voss is driving with one set of wheels on the road, the other in the verge. I lean forward.

'Mr. Voss, why are we driving half off the road?'

'Avoiding the need to brake, ma'am. The danger is, ma'am, the wheels lock and we go on sliding down. That's the danger.'

'If it is dangerous, you must say. If it's not safe we should turn back.'

Half of me would not care if we did turn back. I should be glad of it.

'It's not that much further, ma'am. It's the last part that may be difficult.'

I close my eyes again, but open them when Mr. Voss hoots the horn. Four large, bedraggled sheep — one with a long strand of bramble hanging from its fleece — occupy the middle of the road. He hoots again, and they begin to trot before us. We herd them on. O, we are going so slowly!

The sheep turn through a gap in the hedge; a car comes in the opposite direction, moving more quickly. Over frosted fields I make out the town, grey with smoke.

I know the name of her cottage, Riverside Cottage, but not the name of the street. So we draw up by an old woman carrying a bundle of wood. Gaunt, with hollowed cheeks, she is bent half double, as if in addition to the few miserable sticks in her arms there were an invisible heap of timber strapped on her back. Old village women must have looked like this since time immemorial. She is no use to us. She is deaf. When Mr. Voss speaks to her she merely shakes her head and shuffles off. There is no one else in sight, no one else foolish enough to be outside on an afternoon like this. A piebald horse — great cloudy breaths issuing from its mouth — stands in the shafts of a cart loaded with turnips, but there is not a person in sight. We drive up the hill to a little square with a stone memorial, and Mr. Voss climbs out to ask directions. He disappears into a butcher's shop. Pale, flayed haunches of meat hang outside, on hooks.

I wait, my knees pressed together, my whole self pressed tight. He returns. The cottage is somewhere down the hill, by the river. We drive down very slowly, and stop. A stream, half frozen, runs between the street and a small terraced cottage with a slate roof.

'That must be it, ma'am.'

Is this it? Is this icy stream supposed to be a river? I unwrap the rug and push open the car door. I cross the stream, using a short wooden bridge slippery with ice.

There is a knocker, but no door-bell. I knock, and then again, and wait, and when I knock again and again there is no answer I find myself confronting the possibility, one I had not contemplated, that Gertrude may be out. Perhaps this is for the best, perhaps I should retreat to the car; suddenly I am in dread of the conversation ahead. Then I hear a sound on the other side of the door.

'Mrs. Hardy!' Her surprise is complete. 'Do come in! Are you alone?'

'Is it a convenient moment? I am not interrupting anything?'

I cross the threshold and find myself unbuttoning my coat, which she hangs over the banister at the bottom of the stairway. Then she offers me a cup of tea. I accept, with a sense of growing dismay: why am I unable to stick to my plan? But already I am peeling off my gloves and following her into the kitchen. Her baby girl is sitting at the table, in a high chair. She has dark silky hair and fat cheeks. She has a towelling bib round her neck and a mouth covered in jam. At the sight of me she buries her face in her hands.

This is not the place that I had envisaged for our little talk. I had envisaged a suitably cold side-room, a rarely used front parlour – not this scene of easy domesticity, this warm, cosy, cramped kitchen with the laundry hanging on a rail above the range and the table cluttered with bread and butter and jam, and the other things that form part of her daily life but of which I know nothing. Until now it did not occur to me that she had a daily life. And then the baby – above all, I had not imagined such a fat, dark-haired baby. O, Florence! This is Gertrude's home, not yours! How could you have let yourself in for this? Clearly I am interrupting the baby's meal. But I steel myself. I am determined, I have not come all this way for nothing.

At her invitation I sit down. Gertrude puts the kettle on the stove and asks whether Mr. Hardy is well. (What should I say? That he is at his desk, writing her love poems?)

'He is very well, thank you.'

'I always think he is astonishing, for his age.'

'He is very good at putting on a show. He is frailer than he appears, I am afraid.'

No doubt she is wondering why I am here, but for all the

rehearsing I have done in my head I cannot think how to begin. It is the presence of the baby that disconcerts me so much. She is now peeping at me between her jammy fingers. Any moment she will probably begin to cry.

I wait. Gertrude and I exchange small talk about the weather, how cold it is, how long the cold will last. I compliment her on the baby ('How beautiful,' I say, 'you must be so proud of her') and she thanks me. Then the kettle begins to whistle. She lifts it off the stove, pours some boiling water into the brown pot, spoons in tea and leaves it to stand. She opens a tin of ginger biscuits and arranges them on a plate. She pours out the tea and sits down. She offers me a biscuit.

I can delay no longer. I take a deep breath and plunge like a swimmer into a pool, and rather to my astonishment the first sentences emerge with remarkable fluency. I explain that Mr. Hardy has been thinking about the Haymarket, and that he feels he may have persuaded her into something that she may come to regret, that may be against her best interests, that London is such a very unforgiving, lonely place, that the London theatre reviewers can be so cruel. Of course (I hurry on) the play may be judged a great success; if that were to happen, she might be asked to stay in town for a longer run. But (I point out), with her family down here, she could not possibly stay longer than a month. So, a little quicker than I should have liked, I reach my conclusion: 'You see what Mr. Hardy and I are afraid of. We feel, strongly, that it is a mistake, and that it would be better if you were not to do it, especially when your little girl is taken into account. That is the other thing Mr. Hardy and I feel so strongly.'

Gertrude is puzzled. 'There is nothing I want more than to play the part at the Haymarket.'

'Of course.'

'I am prepared for unfavourable reviews. And I am looking forward to staying in London.'

'Of course you are. But it cannot be right for you to abandon your family –'

'I am not abandoning them!' She draws herself up in her chair and repeats herself, very firmly: 'Mrs. Hardy, I am not abandoning them.'

'Maybe abandoning is not the right word. But you will be leaving them. And you will miss them so much when you are away, and they will miss you, so much. And I know that to you it is only a matter of weeks, but to her –' I smile at the baby, who is suddenly turning out to be very useful in my argument – 'imagine it, an eternity, without her mother.'

I am delighted with myself this far. I have expressed myself clearly, my tone has been reasonable and concerned and diplomatic, I could not have done it better if I had practised it a dozen times. I am so full of admiration at my performance that I feel like giving myself a pat of congratulation. All that is now required is for Gertrude to agree with me.

'Diana will be looked after very well, Mrs. Hardy; there is nothing for you or Mr. Hardy to worry about. I assure you I am not abandoning my family. My husband wants me to go to London.'

'But for a man – to look after her when she is so very young –'

'He is looking forward to it.'

'Are you sure?'

'I am certain.'

She is watching me closely – O, how difficult this is. I press on:

'Gertrude, if "Tess" is to be put on in London Mr. Hardy is certain to wish to go up to see it, and the air – the cold – the strain – the journey will be very injurious to his health. As I say he is quite frail. He is nearly eighty-five! Living quietly at home he manages well enough, but London would be too much for him, and yet if you are playing the part of Tess he will insist on being there.'

'Can you not stop him?'

'I cannot, I cannot, he is determined to go and I can do nothing. It is a very difficult position for me to be in. The truth is that I have come here in secret, I haven't told him, but it is absolutely necessary. You see, it is not merely that "Tess" has always been his favourite novel, but also . . . you must have noticed how fond he is of you. It is beyond anything you can possibly imagine. In the past few days he has even written some extraordinary poems . . . I am sorry but you must understand my position! I cannot allow it, I will not allow it! It will be too embarrassing, he will make a fool of himself!'

I am in full gabble, my voice has risen to a pitch of hysteria. I am aware of it but there is nothing I can do to stop myself. Gertrude is staring at me with those huge eyes of hers.

'What are these poems?'

'They are –' I hesitate. I should not have mentioned the poems; I had no intention of doing so. How foolish of me! But my voice hurries on. 'They are about you. That is what they are about, and other things, too. I have destroyed them, of course, I have destroyed them all. But, you see, this is what he is sometimes like. He is a very old man, he suffers from delusions, he thinks he's still thirty-five years old. He has a very loose grasp on reality.'

'They are about me?'

'There is a poem about meeting you at Toller Down Gate and eloping with you. I know – it is laughable! But to me it is intensely, intensely distressing. It is distressing and embarrassing! You must understand my position, I cannot have him pursuing you up to London!' I might also say how humiliating it is for me, how very humiliating it is for me. To have my husband, in his dotage, behaving like this!

'Mrs. Hardy, I am still not entirely clear. What is it you are saying?'

'I am afraid you must write to Mr. Harrison and tell him that you cannot play the part.'

'I must write to Mr. Harrison?'

'Yes. People will admire you for it.'

'Why will they admire me?'

'For putting your family first.'

She flushes, distinctly, and not only with shock. When she speaks her voice is much harder and angrier than I have ever heard it.

'Mrs. Hardy, I am not sure you understand my position.'

'O but I do, Gertrude, I do –'

'I'm not sure you can. When Mr. Hardy first talked to me about the Haymarket I didn't tell anyone except for my husband, in case it didn't work out. Since then I have told everyone. Everyone around here knows. When I take out Diana in the pram, people stop me to ask about it. Now you tell me that it is not possible, you cannot allow it, I must write to Mr. Harrison. What can I say to people? What can I possibly say to them? You say that people will admire me. They will not admire me, they will think I have been making the whole thing up. I will be a laughing-stock.'

'You will not be a laughing-stock.'

'Why can you not stop him from going to London?'

'I cannot! Believe me, Gertrude, I wish I could, but he pays no attention to me. I cannot stop him. He is the most obstinate of men.'

'And what am I supposed to write to Mr. Harrison? That I have changed my mind? I have not changed my mind. There is nothing I have ever wanted more than to act at the Haymarket.'

We are at an impasse. As our voices have risen the baby has been growing restless and now she begins to cry, a horrible sound in such a small room. Gertrude lifts her out of the high chair. 'Sssh, sssh, sssh. There. What's all this fuss about? Sssh, sssh. I'm sorry. Sssh.'

I say nothing as she cuddles and comforts the baby, but I feel such an intruder. To come here uninvited, forcing my way into the warmth of her home only to dash her hopes – how churlish and ill-mannered it must seem to her! If only she knew what it is to live with him, a man who cares more for the company of his pen than that of his wife, a man of such privacy that he keeps his wife at a chilly distance from his thoughts and makes her into an irrelevance, she might forgive me. How much I could tell her of my life and its unreal nature! But I have said too much already, to say more would be disloyal.

I watch her, joggling the baby in her arms. I ought to leave at once, and indeed I would like nothing more than to leave, but that nothing has been settled.

When the baby is quiet she turns to me.

'Mrs. Hardy, what would you tell Mr. Hardy?'

'How do you mean?'

'If I were to write to Mr. Harrison.'

'I would tell him that you had made the right decision. And he would respect you for it. He respects and admires you greatly. Believe me, Gertrude, I do know what a sacrifice I am asking you to make, but there will be another time for London, a better time; once he is gone, I promise you, I will make certain of it.'

'Have I any alternative?'

I can hardly believe she is giving way. 'Thank you, thank you.'

'I shall write tomorrow.'

'Thank you.'

I smile; she does not. She is desperate for me to be gone, I can see that. I am so sorry, I would like to say, can we not remain friends? But we have nothing left to say to each other. I pick up my gloves. Then there is a noise at the front door and to our mutual consternation in comes her husband, stooping under the low ceiling, a young man with a dark moustache and a face pale from the cold. What terrible timing! Two minutes later and I would have missed him! Now we have to be introduced to each other, we have to shake hands and exchange pleasantries about the weather. 'I do hope the little one hasn't been playing up too much,' he remarks, and I reply that she has been perfect. Gertrude is silent, with the baby in her arms.

He puts an arm round Gertrude and kisses the baby.

'Mrs. Hardy is just going,' she says.

'Yes, I must go, I must. How late it is.' I make my way to the door. She follows. In a hurry I put on my coat, and then the door is open. Darkness has fallen, the air is icy.

I totter over the little bridge and climb into the taxi-cab, which smells of cigarette smoke, and without a word Mr. Voss starts the motor. I wrap the rug around my legs.

And now I ought to feel relief, I ought to feel the glow of success, since I have achieved what I set out to achieve, yet as we crawl back along the same slow roads I feel nothing of the sort, only a kind of dull emptiness mixed with an extraordinary nervous fatigue. Why could I not have kept a better control of myself? Why did I tell her about the poems? O but she is more beautiful than I had realised. When she was on stage I never found her beautiful, but there in her own little kitchen, holding her baby, she seemed so beautiful. Am I jealous of her? I am, I am; ignoble as it may be, I cannot deny it, I am jealous of all she has, not only her beauty. The cottage was so much smaller than I had expected, and I can see that they do not have much money, but what does that matter? What does anything matter except love? I am the wife of an old man who happens to be a famous writer, a wealthy writer, perhaps the wealthiest writer in the entire country; it ought to be enough, and it is not. I ought to have been a mother, I ought to have had a baby of my own. I am living a life that I was not meant to lead.

The darkness slides by. Trying to conjure some familiar image to calm my distressed self, I am returned again and again to the ineradicable vision of Gertrude kissing her baby's head. I feel as if I was being driven through some other world or falling unchecked down a deep chasm.

Time passes in which I am scarcely conscious, but at last the car pulls up by the gate. 'Leave me here,' I tell Mr. Voss. 'I'd like to walk.' I pay him his money and give him a good tip. 'Thank you for getting me back safely.'

The sky is clear, the stars are thick. The cold is so sharp it seems to cut. The house will be cold, too. The ivy shines in the moonlight, and from each chimney there rises a pale curl of smoke.

CHAPTER X

❧ ❧ ❧

Dinner consisted of broth, followed by boiled eggs and toast. This was the standard fare of which they partook each evening at half past seven. They sat in the dining room, with two candles on the table and further light provided by a pair of oil lamps on the large mahogany sideboard.

Florence's head drooped. Only a few minutes had passed since her return from the town, and he and she had exchanged barely any words. Although neither seemed willing to refer to it, the altercation of the morning still cast a heavy shadow over the scene.

In his judgement, what had happened had happened, and as nothing could undo that it was best left to recede into forgetfulness. Since she was surely of the same mind, they ate in silence. The broth steamed, and the silver of the spoons shone in the candlelight.

He ate slowly and carefully. Mutton broth had long been one of his favourite soups, especially at this time of year. It was a nourishing winter dish; within the thick, salty liquid were small pieces of carrot, turnip, potato, barley and other vegetables, not always easy to identify. This evening he found a chunk of what he surmised, from its texture, to be parsnip, although upon further reflection he was not entirely sure. The beauty of the concoction was that the flavours of the different elements mingled to produce a harmonious whole.

Once he had finished, he pushed his bowl aside and turned to the eggs and toast. There were three eggs on the table, each in its own china egg-cup. At eighty-four, his appetite was not what it had once been, and as a general rule he had one egg, while Florence had two.

Having buttered his toast, he decided to break the silence. 'I told Caddy to put the hens away.'

She started. 'O! I'd forgotten!'

'As it was getting late.'

'Thank you; thank you so much; I'd forgotten.'

He tapped the top of the egg and began to prise off the end.

'They're good hens,' he went on. 'They must be happy to lay in this weather. It is a credit to the way in which you look after them.'

For a moment she did not respond. Her eyes seemed fixed on her bowl of broth, which he noticed she had scarcely touched. Then she said: 'I was thinking of getting a cockerel. They are so splendid.'

He raised his eyebrows. Cockerels crowed not only at dawn, as they were meant to. Some cockerels misjudged things, and inconveniently took to crowing in the middle of the night. Still, the field was a little way from the house, and if it was what she wanted, he was not going to object too strongly.

'They are your hens.'

'You don't mind?'

'Not at all.'

'Thank you. It would mean they could have chicks, which would be so nice.'

This small passage of conversation, insignificant in itself, seemed to him to mark a first step in the restoration of better relations.

He took a pinch of salt, and let it fall into the yolk. 'How was town? You were a long time. I was beginning to worry.'

'I ran into people.' She added, quickly: 'I didn't mean to be so long; I went into the church at Fordington.'

So that was it; she had been on her knees for hours. No wonder she was exhausted. He imagined her praying in the cold church and felt sorry for her. He understood, of course, why she had been praying; she felt guilty about her earlier behaviour, and about throwing his poems in the fire. He was tempted to say that there was no need and that he forgave her, but he was wary of reopening the wound. Instead, largely to keep the conversation going, he asked her whether the restoration at Fordington – a restoration which had been in fitful progress for about twenty years – had been completed. At this she seemed flustered and said that she had not noticed.

'I shouldn't think it'll ever be finished,' he remarked. 'That vicar . . . from what I hear he's lost the support of his flock.'

'Sometime it will be.'

'What?'

'Sometime they must finish it.'

'I doubt it. The trumpets will sound, and they'll still be fiddle-faddling around.' He put a spoonful of hot egg in his mouth. 'The best thing for that church would be for him to die. Wessex, behave yourself.' The dog was gently scratching his trouser leg. 'Stop it. Stop begging.'

'Thomas – when I was in the town I happened to meet Mrs. Bugler's father, Arthur Bugler, in South Street.'

He waited.

'She has changed her mind. She has decided not to play the part up in London. She has decided, after long reflection, that it would not be right. I am sorry, Thomas.'

He put down his spoon. He stared down the length of the table, between the two candle flames. 'Mr. Bugler told you?'

She raised her eyes to his. 'She is writing to Harrison.'

The old man said nothing.

'And, you know, I do believe that she has made the right decision. She is acting in a selfless way, as she should. It is the right decision. I admire her for it.'

How had this happened? How had this happened, and why?

When everything had been arranged, for this to happen, and without any warning? If she had serious reservations, why had she not come to talk to him? He would have stiffened her resolve.

'When did she decide this?'

'I don't know. Several days ago, I think.'

'So she is writing to Harrison?'

'Yes. And to you, I expect.'

There was a lengthy pause, while he pondered. 'Did he explain why she had changed her mind?'

'I should have thought it obvious. She has come to the conclusion that she should put her husband and baby first.'

Another lengthy pause. Was that it? Or was it that she had suddenly taken fright at the thought of London? It was a mystery; she had never given the slightest indication that she was in two minds. She had always seemed so certain of herself.

'Her father did indicate that he thought she was right.'

'In what way, right?'

'I don't know. To put her family first.'

It was not hard to find one possible cause of her volte-face. Gertie's clodpole of a husband had made clear his opposition, and had forbidden her to go. If so, how selfish of him to stand in her way! How petty and small-minded!

'I think it is all for the best,' Florence said. 'I know it is disappointing for you, but what it does mean is that Sybil Thorndike can play the part, and she will do it so well. She will be a different Tess to Gertrude, but a very good one. Everyone who saw her in "Saint Joan" said she was quite wonderful. She will bring a true professionalism to the part.' She carried on in this flurry of enthusiasm, saying how the critics adored Sybil Thorndike, how Sybil Thorndike was a vastly experienced, accomplished actress, incomparably the best actress in England, how the theatre would be full of people wanting to see Sybil Thorndike.

Noting the unmistakeable triumph in her voice, his feelings turned to bitter resentment. She had never believed in Gertie; she had wanted Sybil Thorndike from the start. Well, it was his play, and it was not going to happen; not in his lifetime, anyway. Better that there should be no production at all than have Sybil Thorndike, a woman in her mid forties, a woman who would be incapable of managing the Wessex accent, in the role of Tess. What a grotesque mis-casting! She was the same age as Florence herself!

He let her run to a halt, waited a moment, and then said, in the most brusque tone he could muster: 'Sybil Thorndike is too old. I am not having Sybil Thorndike playing the part. Let there be no more mention of it.'

Calmly he finished his egg, pushed back his chair, patted his mouth with the napkin, and departed the room.

That evening he was due to have a hip-bath in his bedroom, as he did every Monday evening, winter and summer alike. There was a large enamelled bath with claw feet which, several years earlier, at great expense (an expense that had appalled him), Florence had had installed in a room on the ground floor, and to which water, both hot and cold, was delivered by pipe and tap; but, perverse as it probably seemed, he preferred to do as he had always done. So, after the grandfather clock had struck nine, the two maids carried the jugs of boiling water from the kitchen up the narrow twists of the back stairs, poured their contents into the iron tub, arranged a flannel, a sponge and a cake of coal-tar soap on a side table, and hung a towel on a nearby towel rail.

Once they had gone – once the door was shut and he was alone, save for Wessex, who always seemed to enjoy watching him take a bath – he began to undress, removing his jacket, tie, waistcoat and other items of clothing. The bath had been drawn close to the stove; even so, on a winter's night such as this, the water tended to cool with some rapidity, and he hurried a little, fumbling the buttons of his shirt, although before committing himself wholly to the water he took care to test its temperature with a foot. When he entered the bath he sat still, allowing the heat to communicate itself to his various limbs and extremities.

Here and now, his physical decline was inescapable. Studying his legs, he was struck by how thin they were, the muscles of the calves and thighs having wasted away for lack of use. They bore fewer hairs than they had once possessed, and on the edge of the left shin there was an irregular inky stain, the memory of a moment one night when Florence was in London; answering an urgent call of nature, and confused by the darkness, he had walked into the side of the door. Bruises had once cleared up in the space of a few days, but this one showed no sign of fading, and probably would still be there when he died. With a sense of revulsion he foresaw his corpse stretched on a thin table, under a white sheet. The dead were at the mercy of the living; how many strangers would pull back the sheet to stare at his flaccid arms and skinny shanks?

He wetted the sponge and rubbed it against the cake of soap. Slowly he wiped his chest and the folds of his stomach. As the warm water lifted a musty smell off his skin, a line drifted into his mind: 'Let me wipe it first; it smells of mortality.' That was Shakespeare: the aged King Lear, responding to Gloucester's proffered hand.

He dangled his own hand towards Wessex, who licked the skin with his rough tongue and gazed at him with blue-filmed eyes. 'O, Wessex, Wessex,' he said. 'What is to be done? What will happen next? Hmm?'

He felt unaccountably tired. Or rather, not unaccountably: Florence's tantrums always drained him of energy.

His thoughts drifted indistinctly while the water cooled further. An owl was hooting loudly in the trees, and another owl, somewhat further away, near the railway line, hooting in reply. Owls were particularly vocal on frosty winter nights, especially in the early hours and towards dawn, the intervening passage of time being presumably devoted to the pursuit of voles, mice and other delicacies necessary to the sustenance of life. Briefly he imagined the moonlit bird on the sturdy branch of one of the pines, calling and then listening to the reply that it received from its neighbour. There was a third owl in the vicinity, and possibly even a fourth, also uttering a series of short, piercing shrieks, although as the various calls conjoined and overlapped it became hard to distinguish one from the other. Since boyhood he had enjoyed the hooting of owls: that fluttering, haunting sound, that 'wild hallooing . . . a jocund din . . .'

With an effort of will, he climbed out of the tub, dried himself by the stove, and pulled on his night-shirt. The shirt, newly laundered and ironed, smelt slightly burnt.

At which Florence entered the room, carrying his nightcap. She seemed even more nervous than usual; her eyes loaded with anxiety, her face expressive of much apprehension. It was this nervousness that, perhaps, irritated him more than any other single thing; yet his irritation was what made her nervous, as he was well aware. She is not happy, he thought to himself, she is never happy. Why are you never happy? he might have asked her. Are there no happy memories, no memories of your early life, to which you can return at moments of strain?

He put on his dressing gown, knotted the cord around his waist, and slid his feet into a pair of leather slippers. She put the glass of whisky on a side table and began to pick up the clothes that he had left scattered on the floor.

'Leave it to the maids,' he said.

'They cannot do everything,' she seemed to reply, but in a voice so quiet that he was unsure whether he had heard correctly.

He helped Wessex on to the bed, for the old dog had lost his spring and was no longer capable of climbing there himself. As he did so he found a burr lodged in the dog's nether quarters. 'What's this? A burr? He needs a good brush.'

'I brushed him this morning.'

Why did she react so? 'My dear, you misinterpret me – I am not reproaching you.'

'I brush him every day. Every day. I always brush him. I've done it for years. You know I always brush him.'

He did not know and, as so often nowadays, felt himself at a loss. 'He's a very lucky chap.'

'I always brush him,' she repeated, tightening her lips.

He examined the dog and found a second burr, this one deeply tangled. Wessex quivered his muzzle and bared his teeth as the old man pulled it out. 'Wessex, stop that,' he said.

Then he had the two hairy burrs in his hand.

'Thomas, give them to me,' she said impatiently, and with a quick movement she threw them in the unlit fireplace, an action that at once recalled the way she had thrown the poems into the fire in his study.

But then she rang for the maids. They must have been waiting nearby, for immediately they came into the room. One at either end, they carried out the tub with its swill of dirty water.

Florence sat in a chair, tucking her rug under her legs and tightening her stole around her neck. She opened 'The Georgics' at the point where she had left off the night before, midway in Book Two. He feared that she might be in too emotional a state to read properly, and her first words were shaky, but she steadied herself, to his relief. All was well. All was well.

He sat motionless by the stove, both hands holding his glass of whisky. 'The Georgics', in Dryden's sparkling translation, was a work that he admired greatly. It was the great paean in praise of rural life, much of it being a poetical guide to practical husbandry: when to plough and sow, when to reap and thresh and winnow, when not to do these things. Prosperity, according to Virgil, depended on hard work and perpetual vigilance; a farmer needed to watch the weather, keep an eye on the moon and stars, and pay tribute to the gods. Sometimes storms would blow up, sometimes crops would fail, but such troubles were to be expected, part of nature's cycle; next week, the sun would shine from a clear sky, next year, the harvest would be a good one. Despite the uncertainties, the earth was a good place to live.

Was it true, he wondered. Was the earth a good place to live? How simple it seemed in those innocent days, how very much harsher and more complicated Life had become. But perhaps it had not been so innocent, even then; Virgil, he reminded himself, had been writing not for farmers, but for the sophisticated men and women of imperial Rome. The poems were there to feed the dreams of the city.

After a time he ceased to listen to the meaning of the words, and instead, while taking the occasional sip of whisky, allowed the sounds to play loosely around the crevices of his mind, disturbing little stones and pebbles of memory. The metaphor interested him; the thought of memories laid down in geological strata followed; thence he found himself contemplating a vision of the bay at Ringstead with its slate-dark cliffs, and how he and Emma, one sultry day in the early part of their marriage, picked their way towards a recent landslip in the hope of finding fossils that had been freshly exposed. They passed a family of four picnickers, a husband, his wife and their two young children, and later an elderly geologist, equipped with hammer and chisel, who gave them a suspicious look, as if fearing that they, not he, might discover the best of the ammonites. There were few other people, if any, on the beach that day. When they were several minutes beyond the geologist, they halted and sat on a conveniently flat rock, side by side. The rock was hot in the sun. Gazing over a milky sea, he slid his hand up one of her legs and slowly toyed with her sex while she unbuttoned his flies and gently caressed his penis. The waves came in, broke, sent little frills of bubbling lace over the pebbles, a gull or two floated by, and their mutual pleasure grew until both were on the point of ecstasy. What a moment that had been, beyond anything he could ever have dared to put in a novel! How happy he had felt as they walked back along the sea-shore! 'Do you think we have been very common?' she murmured, and of course their conduct was very far from what, according to accepted standards, befitted a lady and gentleman. But he was the son of a country mason, she of a vicar: respectable antecedents but not enough to put either of them near the level of gentry. As he now perceived, their relish derived from the knowledge that their behaviour carried a certain danger; if they had been discovered, if the fact that they had engaged in such a coarse act had become public knowledge, the scandal would have haunted them for ever.

Looking back more than fifty years, he found himself shifting positions in his usual manner. From a close distance he watched the young couple walking over the grey pebbles, the man in a dark suit, the woman in a light dress, with a straw hat on her head, against the backdrop of the ocean. They passed the hammering geologist and sat on the flat, hot rock, facing away from him. Invisibly he approached; he stole up and hung behind them as their breathing quickened. When they strolled back barefoot, hand in hand, he had withdrawn a space. Then Time's telescope underwent a reversal, and glancing up, they spied a mysterious, white-haired old man against the darkness of the cliff.

It was hard to be sure that he had remembered correctly. Such an outrageous incident: could he have imagined it? Without Emma, there was no one to provide confirmation.

He thought gloomily: what happened that afternoon only she and I ever knew, and she is dead and buried, and when I am gone the memory will go too. At a man's death, all the memories of his existence on earth, all those fragments of time stored and sorted, visited and inspected, all die with him. He could tell no one, certainly not Florence.

But she had stopped reading, and was closing the book, doing so with a soft but decisive clap. He stirred in his chair. The owls had long ago ceased their colloquy.

'Thomas,' she said.

He was appalled. After all, he had not escaped. The peace that the poetry had given him was about to be blown away. 'Not now,' he said quickly.

'I must speak.'

'No.' He lifted a hand. 'Florence, I understand what must have happened. It is crystal clear. She must be expecting a child.'

This conclusion was one that he had reached shortly after dinner. Gertie was pregnant again. Why else would she have changed her mind so precipitately?

Florence gave a gasp. 'I don't know –'

'There is no other possible explanation.'

'Thomas –'

'She has only herself to blame.'

'Thomas!'

He waited.

'I am so sorry about your poems!'

'O –' he made a dismissive gesture.

'I should not have done it. I should not have!'

'Let us forget it and go to bed. Let us forget it, please. They were no good; the fire was the best place for them.' He was not far short of desperation. 'Read some more, please.'

'Will you ever forgive me?'

'My dear, there is nothing to forgive. Read something else.'

'What would you like? More Virgil?'

'No – something else – anything.'

'What?'

For no reason that he could have clearly expressed, save that it was one of his favourite poems, and that he had not heard or read it for many months, and that it was not too long, and also that it seemed appropriate to the moment – the hour being late, and a hard frost certain – he named Samuel Taylor Coleridge's 'Frost at Midnight'.

She fetched the volume of Coleridge's poems from the shelves, opened it, and began to read in a shaky voice:

> The Frost performs its secret ministry,
> Unhelped by any wind. The owlet's cry
> Came loud – and hark, again! loud as before.
> The inmates of my cottage, all at rest,
> Have left me to that solitude –

Here, to his surprise, she broke off. 'O dear me,' she said with a sob. 'Dear me.'

He reached out, put a hand over the page. 'It is all right – stop – Florence – there is no need to read anything.'

'No. No.' She pulled the book from under his hand, and read on:

> – that solitude which suits
> Abstruser musings: save that at my side
> My cradled infant slumbers peacefully –

before bursting into sobs through which he made out her impassioned words: 'I am sorry, I am sorry, I am sorry.'

'There is nothing to be sorry for. Let us go to bed. We are both tired. Wessex is tired too. We should go to sleep.'

'No! No! Thomas! I must speak! I must speak! I have been your wife for eleven years. I have lived for you, cared for you, done all I could do to help you, and to make you happy. If you are not happy, it is not for lack of effort on my part. I have served you constantly. In marrying you I have abandoned my hopes, my dreams . . .' Her voice choked in bitterness. 'O, Thomas! Can you not see?'

She had been preparing this speech, he thought. He had heard it before.

'I have lost my youth. I have lost my youth, living here. I am old already, in my heart –' and she rapped against her heart with a fist. 'I used to be able to write,' she went on. 'I am a human being too.'

He had always been embarrassed by her writing. When he remembered those trite, whimsical verses about bunny rabbits and fox cubs – when he remembered how he had encouraged her, and for motives that were patently self-serving, he was ashamed of himself.

'Florence,' said he, and he put down the glass of whisky, 'of course. Of course. Of course. We are all older than we were, unfortunately.' Was he now expected to make a declaration of love? 'My dear, I have always considered that, as marriages go, ours has been a very successful one,' he said, aware that this was, by any measure, a fairly feeble effort, yet unable to find any stronger words.

'And so have I,' she brought out, in a whimper. 'And so have I. But you are not happy!'

He considered this with some puzzlement. Was he not happy? He was happy enough. She was the unhappy one.

'I am not unhappy,' he replied. 'In general I am happy. I should be happier if the world were a happier place, and I should be happier if you were happier. But we are in many ways fortunate.'

She said something he did not catch.

'What, my dear?' He leant forward, so as to hear her words more distinctly.

'We ought to be happier.'

'Perhaps. But I have come to believe that the secret of happiness generally lies in lowered expectations. It is a mistake to expect more than a little out of life.'

She seemed to stifle a sob. 'If we could only have had children. Just one child, just one. I am sorry, so sorry.'

The old man was taken completely by surprise. For a moment he could not think what to say. Then he took her hand.

'You should not have married me. I needed you, and I am very grateful to you for marrying me, and for all you have done for me; but you should not have done. I was too old.'

She gave a moan. 'No, no, no.'

'I was. You should have married someone younger. When I am dead and gone, when I am dust – marry again. You are still an attractive woman. Marry a young man.'

'O, Thomas, Thomas, it is too late for that, far too late.'

'Nonsense. There are many men who would like to marry you. You will be a woman of substance, when I am gone.'

'I mean it is too late for children. I am forty-six. I am past child-bearing.'

She stared at him, her eyes welling with fresh tears.

His eyes had not filled with tears for many years; age had dried up the fluid capacity. Yet if he could have done, he would have wept too. Children; yes; if they had only had children. A child would have made all the difference to her – and to him, too. How many times had he thought as much! How many times had he reflected on the fact that he would die without issue! Once he was gone, the long line of Hardys, like the long line of the d'Urbervilles, would reach its end.

He had failed his ancestors. Grim-faced and condemnatory, their ghosts watched him and shook their spectral heads.

He might have had a child with Emma, but when, in the first few years of the marriage, she had talked about her desire to start a family, he had always fought shy, saying that it was too early. He was trying to make his way as a writer, and they were not financially secure; he was not sufficiently established to be able to afford a family. If they had had children, would he have been able to justify the hours that he had spent at his desk without any certain prospect of financial reward? No. His writing would have come to a halt, and he would have fallen back on his work as an architect. It was too early – and then, or so it seemed, it was too late. A chill set in; and for the last twenty-five years, by common consent, they had slept in separate bedrooms, a floor apart.

And with Florence? Again it seemed too late. Far too late, at least for him; he had been past seventy when they married. To father a child at that age would have been judged irresponsible, and he had never even dreamt of it. Still, perhaps it would have been possible, if they had tried harder, if he had tried harder. She might have become pregnant. Certainly she had been sufficiently young to bear a child.

Now she was not. She was barren. That much was unalterable. Now, beyond a doubt, it was too late. He felt the deepest sympathy for her.

He found himself on the point of telling her that children were not everything, that there were many paths to self-fulfilment other than reproduction; that, in all conscience, it was not morally right to bring another human being into a sorry world such as this. We live in a vale of tears! But other words came from his mouth.

'We have Wessex,' he said.

'O yes.' She seized on the thought. 'Yes. Yes. We have Wessie. Dear Wessie. Dear, dear, darling Wessie!'

Her face streaming, she flung herself on the dozing Wessex.

He watched. He watched.

Weary after a long day, wanting only to sleep, Wessex uttered a long, heartfelt sigh, expressive of the desire to be left alone, and curled himself into a tighter ball on the bed.

Still on her knees, Florence lifted her head. Her hair had come loose, and her face, blotchy and swollen with tears, stared at him. 'O Thomas, Thomas! What will become of us?'

As to her precise meaning, he had no idea. He reached forward, and laid a hand on her shoulder. 'Nothing. Nothing will become of us.'

'Living here, in this house —' she broke off, then resumed. 'It wears me down. It has worn me out.'

'We need another maid. The maids are useless, both of them.'

'It is not the maids, it is not the maids, it is nothing to do with the maids. Thomas, we must do something about the trees! Everyone agrees! It is so dark.'

The trees, again; always the trees. It was an illusion, he knew, that cutting down the trees would make any difference at all to her mental state, and almost at once he seemed to drift away, detaching himself from the moment and observing from a distance. The man and woman, the husband and wife, he and she. Was it possible for a marriage to exist without difficulties? Was it not obvious that marriage brought to the surface difficulties which would otherwise have remained hidden?

'The trees are what make me ill,' she brought out. 'I know they do. The spores . . . the mould . . . the air . . . I breathe it in. I am blighted! They are an evil force!'

'I am sure they are not.'

'Mr. Sherren says so! He agrees with me! They are cancer-inducing!'

'Let us talk about it later,' he said. 'Later. Florence, I beg of you, not now – you are overwrought. This is not the time.'

'You always say the same!' she cried. 'It is never the time! It is always later!'

'In the morning,' he insisted. 'We will talk in the morning, I promise you. We will talk over breakfast. But now . . . now we must sleep. Sleep is the thing, blessed sleep. Tomorrow will be better.'

'But will it? Will it?'

'It will.'

'I do so hope – I hope so. They do worry me so much.'

'You exhaust yourself over nothing. You should rest more. You need to sleep.'

'I cannot rest. I cannot sleep. I can never sleep.'

'You must sleep,' he said firmly. 'You will sleep, I am sure. If you believe you will sleep, you will sleep.' Thus, by sheer repetition of the word, he hoped to help her. As a general rule, he himself slept like the dead – or so the phrase went. But who knew how the dead slept? Who knew if the dead slept at all?

Something occurred to him. He took her hand, and caressed it gently. 'My dear, I was thinking. When I am gone, I shall be buried with Emma, I expect. Presumably, in the fullness of time, you would like to be there also?'

She blinked at him, her eyes bloodshot.

'Not for many years yet, of course,' he added hastily. 'But in these matters it is always as well to plan ahead . . .'

'Will there be room for three?' she asked in a mouse-like squeak.

'O, yes. I am sure there will be.'

'Would you really like me there?'

'Very much. Of course. If you would like to be there.'

She seemed to nod.

He squeezed her hand, in a gesture of affection which was also intended as a sign that they should, now, say goodnight. 'Sleep,' he said, and as if to a child: 'Bed-time now. Bed-time now.'

But she lingered. Her weeping recommenced, and grew in intensity. Bending over her knees, her hands pressed into her face, her entire body shook with sobs. The fox stole slid off her neck and lay glassy-eyed on the floor. At last the convulsions diminished in force.

'I am so sorry. It's just this winter . . . fighting with the cold . . . I am so very tired. '

He offered her a handkerchief, to dab her eyes. She thanked him. He waited a moment. 'How is your neck?' he asked, for that, surely, was what this fuss was all about.

She put up a hand. 'If only it was not so obvious.'

'One can hardly see anything,' he lied, though the jagged red line of the scar that she had hidden from him for so long was clearly visible. It shocked him. 'Mr. Sherren did a good job.'

'I am so afraid it will return.'

'It is done, it is done; there is nothing to be afraid of.'

She wrapped the stole around her neck again. 'What if it does return?'

'My dear, it will not return. Of that, I am certain, inasmuch as one can be certain of anything in this life.' He hunted for something more to say. 'You know, it may be winter, but spring is never very far behind.'

The reference to Shelley was a famous one. Whether she

recognised it or not, the old man could not be sure; but she managed a timid smile. 'Thank you.'

She had got to her feet, and was about to go, when another thought struck him. 'O – Florence – here – if you see, there is a button loose –'

She picked up the waistcoat. 'I'll get one of the maids to see to it. Good night, Thomas. And thank you for putting away the hens.'

'Good night, my dear. Good night.'

So she left him, retiring to her own, cold bedroom. Wessex aside, he was alone with his thoughts and a single lamp. Alone: as he had always been. Alone we come into this world, alone we depart: a truism. Well. He was accustomed to being alone. He did not dislike solitude.

He turned off the stove, removed his dressing gown and climbed into bed, partly dislodging the dog. The day had been a vexatious one, all in all. The burning of his poems did not, he found, bother him very much, for he could easily rewrite them, if they were worth rewriting; but the news about Gertie was a bad blow. She would have done it so well! There would never be another Tess half as good; no, not one quarter.

This was part of his disappointment, for he had set his heart on seeing her on stage at the Haymarket – had imagined her intense and vivid, her red lips, her wide eyes and lush hair, in every scene, down to the final curtain. Yet he was also disappointed on her behalf. She was such a thrilling woman; in years to come, buried in Beaminster (he had no romantic illusions about life in Beaminster), how would she be able to escape a sense of regret at what might have been? The opportunity of a lifetime – an extraordinary opportunity – lost! It had seemed her destiny. How foolish of her, to allow herself to become pregnant at such an important time! What a curse!

And yet he knew, even at this moment, that another view on the matter was possible. The critics might well have brought her down, if they had a mind to. She was an unsophisticated country-woman, born and bred, and there was something about the thought of her in London that disturbed him. How might London have changed her? He had met a few London actresses – affected crea-tures, full of extravagant airs: he would not like her to turn into one of those. Virgil's counsel, with an eye not to ambition but to happiness, would have been for her to stay in the country.

He extended his legs further, accidentally kicking Wessex off the bed. The dog fell heavily, with a thud and a small groan.

Needing to settle his mind, he turned up the lamp so that it shone more brightly, and opened the volume of poetry. Although his eyes hurt, by holding the page close and using a magnifying glass he was able to read the rest of Coleridge's poem, a young man's passionate expression of love and hope, one fine winter's night, for his infant son and, by extension, for the whole earth.

It moved him greatly, although he knew it so well. It was a poem of pure, transcendent optimism, to a degree that lay beyond him; even in his youth he had never had such a degree of faith in the future. The final incantatory verses, a blessing on the little boy, roused him so much that he could barely bring himself to read to the last image, that of the silent icicles quietly shining to the quiet moon.

The moon had risen here too. The same radiant moon that had shone on Coleridge, more than a century earlier, now shone through the gap between the curtains, through the weave of branches, a goddess encircled by an iridescent double halo. Likewise, the same frosty agency was at work, stealing through the starry night, stiffening the bents and grasses of field and meadow, crisping the fallen leaves in wood and copse. Droplets of moisture were turning to jewels, puddles shivering into stillness, ponds and lakes taking on a glassy sheen. Beneath the eaves, in cottage after cottage, in village after village, an armoury of spears and lances glittered in the lunar rays.

One such was the cottage in which he had been born, on the

heath's edge; how often had he lain in bed and watched the translucent ice hanging from the thatch! How often had he leant out to touch! The icicles would be growing there now, this very moment – if he were there he could have pushed open the window and snapped one off, licking the tip, just as he had done when he was a little boy! But, even as he pictured himself with the icicles, other places dear to him from a long life were appearing in their wintry vestments. The height of Bulbarrow rose like a mountain in the moonlit dark, the Vale of Blackmoor extended itself in a sheet of latticed pearl, and the pillars of Stonehenge laid their shadows sharp as knives on the hard ground. At the base of the Beeny cliffs wave after wave burst on the black rocks and sent up clouds of luminous spray, and at Sturminster the river poured in silver torrents under the arches of the old bridge. Patches of clotted froth bobbed whitely in the frozen reeds. The scenes came in rapid succession, until at last he found himself in the churchyard at Stinsford, where the ancient yews spread their berried boughs over the graves of the once living. There, too, in the fissures of each tomb, minute crystals were being born from the cold air.

So it was all over England. So it had been for ages past: so it would be for ages to come. Why then was it impossible for him to feel, like Coleridge, confident in the future? Why rather was he affected by such a profound sense of foreboding?

The old man shut the book and extinguished the lamp. He lay, watching the pale slab of moonlight on the uneven wall, and waiting for sleep to come to him. If he did not sleep, he knew, he would find it harder to work in the morning. He had closed his eyes and tucked his hands under his chin, his usual sleeping position, when a series of sharp noises, not far off, the urgent shrieks of a vixen calling for a mate, tore through the stillness of the night. She called repeatedly for several minutes, before falling silent.

❧ ❧ ❧

CHAPTER XI

My husband sleeps easily; nothing ever disturbs him. I do not sleep. I huddle in bed, under a heavy eiderdown and four blankets that weigh me down like a body of earth. Despite socks and a hot water bottle, my feet and ankles are frozen. What is wrong with my circulation? As the cold presses in, so does the darkness; so do the trees. Their twigs scrape in an uneasy breeze. Before long, they will be tapping on the panes as they do in 'Wuthering Heights', and the ghostly shape of his first wife will loom at the foot of the bed.

This is not a comedy: it is a slow tragedy. Look now in the glass of my imagination and the life I have never had stares back and haunts me with what might have been, had I acted differently. I did not, and it is as a consequence that I find myself where I am, in a winter of frost and ice, of damp and draughts, of chilblains and aches. Stains spread down the walls, and blue moulds speckle shoes and belts. My mind is thick with mould. My life is thick with mould.

Truly, this is not a healthy house, engulfed by these dark trees. Thomas, I have told him on countless occasions, we must cut back the trees! The trees must be cut back! If only the trees could be cut back a little! I beg of you, on my knees! This one thing, this one small thing, to make me happy, to brighten my spirits. If you love me, if you did ever love me, Thomas dear, let the trees be cut back!

But, no. Thomas does not love me, and has never truly loved me. What he feels for me is gratitude and affection: a great deal of gratitude, and a considerable, comfortable affection. It is not love. I know this, I know what love is, I have seen it with my own eyes, lovers in the streets, hand-in-hand, each engrossed in the other, oblivious of anything else, their faces flaming. Gertrude, her husband and their baby – they stand in a triangle of flames. That is love, a white heat, a blazing fire! It is not gratitude, it is not affection!

When Thomas writes about love it is always about love lost, never about love that endures. He does not believe in love that endures because, for him, it never has endured and never will. I see that now. 'You should not have married me – you should have married someone younger –' but there was no one younger. No one had ever come close to asking me. I loved him and still do. Was I so wrong to hope that he would come to feel love for me? Is it possible that he does love me, but finds himself unable to express it? But if he loved me, he would let the trees be cut back. How circular my thinking is; every time it loops round to the same thing. The circles grow shorter, and tighten, and become a knot, and when I put my hands round my neck and squeeze I feel the pulse of constricted blood. Can one strangle oneself with one's bare hands?

Leave him, Eva says. Leave him, Florence. But I cannot. I am too frightened. I do not have sufficient courage or independence of spirit to face the world, or to face myself, if I were to leave him.

This is my situation, then, and yet I cannot accept that my life is over. He has told me – Cockerell has told me, too – that I shall have plenty of money once he is gone. So in my mind, lying here in the cold and dark, I comfort myself by planning my after-life. On the morning after his death I shall burn his old shawl and laugh at his first wife as I do so, and then I shall set a team of wood-men to work, and calmly watch as one tree after another crashes to the ground. I shall have the chimneys swept. I shall clear the shrubbery and plant it with roses. I shall buy myself a motor-car and employ a chauffeur, and I shall ride in an aeroplane (giggling like a little girl as we loop the loop). Perhaps I shall buy myself a London flat, and attend theatres, and visit art galleries and museums! This is how I see myself in the summer months, in light summery clothes, in the summer of my life. But I do not intend to give myself up to frivolity; I intend to do good, quaint as that may sound in this modern age. If Life has any purpose, it must be to do good to others, and being well-off I shall do what I can to help orphaned children in the slums.

In the winters, I shall leave England and stay in the south of France, on the Riviera. The air is soft and balmy, and the sea a deep, turquoise-blue, as I am told it always is in the Mediterranean. There are no frosts here. The hotel gardens, which my room overlooks – I stand on the balcony and gaze at them in the early morning light – are full of palms and other tropical plants. I eat my breakfast in a dining room ornately decorated with mirrors and chandeliers, and make new acquaintances among the other residents of the hotel; we stroll along the promenade, and enjoy interesting intellectual conversations on safe topics. Every evening after dinner we play cards, or dance in the hotel ballroom. It is such a long while since I danced that I am a little apprehensive and self-conscious, but I soon get into the swing of it, as the phrase goes. Slowly but steadily my health improves. I forget my neck, and my nerves repair themselves. Fully restored, I return to England as the first daffodils are coming into bloom and the first leaves opening on the chestnut trees.

In this way my long existence in the depths of the countryside gradually recedes, taking on the quality of a dream. Emboldened, I write the story of a young woman who sacrifices herself by agreeing to become wife to a great writer, and whose story, in its turn, wins acclaim. Thus I reclaim my destiny. Thus my voice, my true voice, is heard at last.

Shall I go further? Shall I dare again to mention the word love? Shall I allow myself to believe that the fire of love will blaze within me, even at this late hour of my life, and that I shall marry again? With every fibre of my being I hope that it will be so. Indeed, when I try to picture the unknown man who will become my new husband, the kind, handsome face of someone very like Mr. Sherren comes mysteriously into my mind. It is not impossible, or so I persuade myself (drawing the back of my wrist across my lips and feeling the hardness of his lips on mine), that I may end up as Mrs. Sherren.

I know that all this is in abstract, a phantasm of a merely possible future among other possibilities. The present remains, and with it my scarred neck, which frightens me, my headaches, which plague me, and my domestic duties, which bore me. Above all, there is this long and hateful winter, hard as stone, cold as death, and in its train the terror that I am deluding myself and that I will never be entirely free; that either I will die first, or that, if I survive him, I will nonetheless remain here, in the same dark, icy house, with servants who despise me, and with his ghost and the ghost of his first wife for company.

Nothing changes in this vision. Even summer is winter; and I live a lonely life safeguarding his memory. After seeing his biography into print (having cut from it all references to Gertrude Bugler), I organise the transcription of his notebooks, negotiate with publishers over future editions of his works and answer letters from scholars and historians. In every detail I ensure that his study is maintained as it was on the day of his death. When visitors call, I lead them up the stairs and show them the hallowed place where he worked and brought into life his novels and poems. Behold the scene of Creation! Behold the paperknife, the pen, the ink-well, the draft of the last poem, unfinished – all exactly as they were on that fatal day! I shall change one thing only. The pages of the calendar will be turned to rest on the twelfth of January. If the visitors ask – I shall not tell them unless they ask, but if they do

– I shall proudly tell them, 'Yes, it was the most important day of the year for him, my birthday.'

I am not unaware that there is a certain heroism in the role of devoted widow, and that it is one which appeals strongly to the melancholic side of my nature. Many years ago in London, when I first met him, I used to go to the British Museum and ferret here and there for historical information on his behalf. My research concluded, and with little else to occupy myself, I would wander round the Museum, studying its various treasures. In one room there was – and probably still is, for all I know – a large stone bas-relief from Assyria on which four soldiers, wearing helmets and breast-plates, and with swords drawn, stand guard over the tomb of their emperor.

Picturing myself thus, I feel a warm glow. Yet who will be there to stand guard over my tomb?

PART FOUR

CHAPTER XII

❦ ❦ ❦

In the period after my last visit to the Hardys a sense of unreality began to overwhelm me. Life in Beaminster went on much as always, and yet every day brought me nearer to the moment when I would be on stage at the Haymarket. The time went quickly – the first performance was to be on April the eighth, but rehearsals were due to begin a month earlier – and I began to get anxious about things like clothes. One morning, having left Diana with Ernest's mother, I took a train to Exeter and bought a skirt and cardigan, and a lovely elegant dress in emerald-green chiffon. I still remember the dress. The hem was quite high, not much below the knee, and it wasn't the kind of dress anyone could possibly have worn in Beaminster, not in the nineteen twenties. I put it on to show Ernest; I twirled like a model and he whistled admiringly and said I would turn heads, but I could see from his face that he was a little uneasy. In hindsight I know why, and it wasn't the hem length: he was worried that London would change me, that I would become someone other than the country-woman he had married, the woman who would be the farmer's wife. There were times that winter when he seemed to withdraw into himself, and more than once I said to him: 'You do want me to play Tess, don't you?' He always gave the same answer. 'All I want is what you want, Gertie.'

It was a very cold and gruelling winter. Probably the really cold spell lasted for only a few days in February, but in my memory it seems longer. All round Beaminster pipes were bursting, and the edges of the stream that ran down Prout Hill crisped with white ice. When Diana and I went out with the pram, I used to pile so many blankets on her that only the tip of her nose stuck out. What kept me warm was the thought of the Haymarket.

Mrs. Hardy's visit came on one of the coldest days of all. She arrived when I was about to give Diana her tea, and the cottage was in a terrible mess, with clothes hanging on the rack over the stove. I wasn't a very good housewife, I'm afraid; I wasn't then, and I never have been, but I was embarrassed that she should have seen it like that, although perhaps she didn't notice. She was in an extraordinary, hysterical state, but very determined; she had come to bully me. It's hard for me to describe what I felt immediately after she had gone. Stricken, I suppose; stricken. I was devastated. If all my hopes were a pane of glass, she had punched a hole in it. Ernest had come in only at the last moment and had missed what had happened, and when he put his hand on my shoulder and asked if I was all right, I burst into tears. I always made it a rule not to cry if Diana could see me, even when she was very little, in case I upset her, but just then I couldn't help myself.

When I did manage to tell him, he was furious. 'If only I'd been here! If I'd come back a few minutes earlier, I'd've told her where to go!' – 'It wouldn't have made a ha'pennyworth of difference,' I said, and I went upstairs and washed my face and wrists. The water was close to freezing, which helped; when I came downstairs again, I felt much calmer. Ernest was still very angry. 'How dare she? What a nerve! Didn't she even say she was calling?' – 'No,' I said, 'she just turned up.'

He didn't believe the story that Mr. Hardy was infatuated with me, not for an instant; as for eloping, that was laughable. There had to be some other reason for putting me off. 'Do you think they've got someone else lined up? I bet that's it. What a low trick. They've offered someone else the part, someone famous.' I sat down at the kitchen table and burst into tears again.

'You know,' he said, 'you don't have to write to anyone. Don't write. There's no need. Just write to her and tell her that you're still doing it. Gertie? Look at me. Gertie!'

I looked at him. 'Ernest, how can I?'

'Course you can. You write and tell her. Or I'll write for you.' He took my face in both hands and smiled at me. 'That's settled, then. Agreed? I'll write and tell her. The old bitch.'

'But if the part's already been offered to someone else –?'

'They can only offer it to someone else if you withdraw from it. You've been offered it, you've accepted it. They can't stop you. I think she's got a nerve.'

'Thank you,' I said, 'but if anyone's writing, I'm writing. I'm perfectly capable of writing a letter. But it's not a matter of writing to Mrs. Hardy, it's a matter of whether I write to Mr. Harrison. Do you think the real reason may be that they think I'm not good enough? I don't want the part if they don't want me to have it. If they don't think I'm good enough, I'll withdraw.'

'If they think that, they're mad. Everyone knows how good you are.'

'Do they?'

'Gertie,' he said, 'it doesn't make sense. Why would they have offered you the part in the first place if they didn't think you were up to it?'

I wasn't easily persuaded. Maybe Mr. and Mrs. Hardy had offered me the part out of kindness and then had changed their minds, or maybe Mr. Harrison had only agreed that I should play the part as a special favour to Mr. Hardy. I remembered how, at one stage, Mr. Hardy had mentioned the idea of Sybil Thorndike playing the part.

I heated the water for Diana's bath, I bathed her and dried her and wrapped her up tight and carried her upstairs to her cot. I always loved settling her at night in those early months, singing to her and watching her slip off to sleep, however long it took. She was so small and vulnerable, and so utterly trusting, and as I watched her getting drowsy, her eyelids growing heavier and heavier, I began to think how precious this time was, and how it wouldn't last very long, and that I needed to make the most of it while I could. Once she was sound asleep, I went back downstairs. Ernest was in an armchair, reading my scrapbook of newspaper reviews.

'Look at these,' he said. 'Look. It's nothing to do with your acting. You're bloody brilliant; they all say so.'

'Ernest,' I said, 'you don't really want me to go away, do you? Honestly? You'd rather I stayed, wouldn't you?'

'No,' he said, 'I wouldn't. I want you to go and do it. And I'm going to come and see you.'

'But how are you going to manage here?'

'Gertie, we've been through all this a dozen times. We'll manage very well. You're not going for very long, are you? It's not that long!'

I sat on his lap, with my legs over the arm of the armchair. 'I don't want you to have to manage.'

'Gertie, you want to be up on that stage at the Haymarket. It's what you've always wanted, what you've always dreamt of.'

I cooked some supper and we went on talking about it. Despite what Ernest said, I didn't like the idea of him by himself every evening, tired after the day's work, having to cook himself a meal, and I knew how much I would miss Diana. I also thought about Mrs. Hardy. I'd given her my word, and that was that, really; I couldn't go back on it. Besides, if I didn't write to Mr. Harrison, she would have done. That was what she'd said.

The next day I withdrew from the part. In my letter to Mr. Harrison I avoided any mention of Mrs. Hardy, and simply said that after a lot of consideration I had decided it was best for my family. Heaven only knows what he thought of me.

Telling local people was very hard. No one understood, and

why should they have? Despite the temptation to explain what had really happened, I bit my tongue, at least at the time. Close friends and members of my family rallied round and did their best to console me, although my little sister, who had been going to keep me company in London, was very cross. While she was cross with Mrs. Hardy, she was also cross with me for being feeble. I said to her: 'You have no idea what she was like.'

Mrs. Hardy wasn't a well woman, and when I think of her now, it's always with that horrible stole round her neck, and those strange lemur-like eyes. I should make allowances, but I do find it hard. She never bothered to consider the matter fully from my point of view, or maybe the truth is that she wasn't capable of doing so; either she was cruel, or she lacked imagination. At the bottom of it all lies the fact that she did not like me; that is what I now believe. I still do not know why she disliked me, but I am sure that lay at the root of it all, and I am afraid that, although I dislike disliking people, I did come to dislike her with a passion. It is very hard not to dislike people who dislike you. When, only a few months later, I happened to hear that 'Tess' was to be produced in London with another actress, not Sybil Thorndike but someone else, in the title role, as Ernest had predicted, I did feel bitter.

I never saw Mr. Hardy again. He died three years later, and had two funerals at the same time, one in Westminster Abbey, where they buried his body, and the other in Stinsford, where they buried his heart. I went to the heart funeral, and hated it from start to finish. I hated the thought that his heart had been cut out of him, it seemed such a barbaric act, and I hated Mrs. Hardy for agreeing to it. There wasn't a proper coffin, only a little casket, and it was impossible when you saw the casket not to think what it contained. Someone had cut him open and dug out his heart – it was a piece of butchery. To make matters worse, a woman turned up in her hunting clothes, bright scarlet, and spattered with mud. She must have come straight from the hunt, and it seemed so disrespectful of her; he loathed fox-hunting, as I do too. During the service she was in one of the pews near me, and when it came to the interment she forced her way to the front, as if she knew him well and had a right to stand on the edge of the grave. The sight of her upset me terribly. That said, it was a very solemn and sad occasion. All the shops in Dorchester closed as a mark of respect. The service was taken by the Reverend Cowley, who had married Ernest and me.

Mrs. Hardy wasn't at the heart funeral – she must have been up at Westminster Abbey. I think she felt guilty on my account, because some while later she arranged for me to play Tess at the Duke of York's Theatre in London, with a professional company. I met her again then, twice, and we were both extremely polite to each other. Of course, it wasn't the first London performance of 'Tess', and although the reviews were good, if I'm honest they weren't quite as good as they might have been. The other actors and actresses were great characters and I did love the bright lights of London, but I always knew that before too long I'd be pleased to be home in Dorset. Once I was back, I had most of my hair cut off. I was too old to have hair down to my waist, blowing this way and that in the wind. Very long hair is for girls, not middle-aged women. Diana didn't recognise me for a moment, and I hardly recognised myself. How light my head was!

So I gave up my dream of becoming a professional actress. I became a housewife. Well: what's the use of an unfulfilled dream? I didn't do any more in the way of amateur acting, either. The Hardy Players disbanded after 'Tess'. My sister also blames Mrs. Hardy for that, but in all fairness I don't think it was entirely her fault. Any play after 'Tess' would have been a let-down. '"Tess" was our swansong,' as Mr. Tilley said – God bless him. 'And it wouldn't be the same without the old boy watching, would it?'

Dear Mr. Hardy. I still have the silver vase that he gave me, and the books and the letters, and my scrapbooks; and occasionally, when I'm by myself, I have a little peek and think about what might have been, as I did after that talk at the W.I.

Ernest wasn't able to fulfil his dream of becoming a farmer, either, and we stayed in Beaminster. He never came to terms with being a butcher, just as he never quite got over what happened in the War. It came back to him when he was dying; he talked a lot about it then. As I say, the past stays alive, however much you would rather it didn't.

More than forty years have passed since the events that I have described, but last week I suddenly knew that if I ever wanted to bring my thoughts into a proper order, I needed to see the Hardys' house again. So on Friday I went back. I went by myself and I didn't tell anyone else. I caught the bus to Dorchester and walked up the hill. The weather was ordinary, nothing to speak of for the time of year, a plain grey sky, cool, light air. Autumn. An ordinary autumn day in England.

Well, dear me. It's not like it was. The town has grown and grown, and the house, which used to be out in the fields, in clear countryside, now feels quite suburban. The new bypass is a hundred yards away in a cutting, and where the allotments used to be a housing estate is being built. The noise is really what struck me. When I visited in the old days, it always felt quiet and secluded, but now you hear the racket of traffic all the time, and aeroplanes go over, and there's the crash and bang of building work. Mr. Hardy would be horrified, without a doubt.

I stood for a while by the gate, thinking to myself. The white paint was peeling off the gate, there was moss on the drive, and leaves were falling from the trees. I did feel sorry for the house, inasmuch as one can feel sorry for a house. Whether anyone lives there permanently I am not entirely sure. Probably there is a caretaker or someone who calls by once a week, but the gardens are in something of a mess; not a total ruin, but slipping that way, neglected, a little forlorn. The gate wasn't locked, and I could easily have walked up the drive for a closer look, which was what

I had originally intended to do, and I nearly did; I opened the gate, and took a few steps, and then I stopped myself. I was frightened, in a way, that I might see something I'd prefer not to see, that I might damage the memories I have. So I went back to the gate and thought how honoured and lucky I was to have known him, and how odd luck was, because I so easily might not have known him. I tried to remember the various occasions when I'd been to the house, and the one that stuck in my mind, more sharply than any other, was the last time, that foggy afternoon when he walked me down the drive to the very same spot where I now was and told me to think of him as my friend. He had stood there, on that patch of ground, and I had stood here, on this patch of ground, beneath the same trees; both of us alive, breathing. The memory was so very concrete that I felt quite dizzy; my mind seemed to turn in on itself, and take me back to the moment itself. I could see him clearly, looking at me over his moustache with a doubtful, yearning expression, and I couldn't help but wonder if he truly was as infatuated with me as Mrs. Hardy said, or if she had made that up. Did those poems that she mentioned ever exist? Did he really write a poem about eloping with me? I would love to know, but I never shall.

After Mrs. Hardy's visit to the cottage, that winter's night, Diana woke in the small hours with this piercing scream. I jumped at once – I always slept lightly – and she was lying in her cot, stiff as a board, with her eyes wide open. She had kicked off her bedding and she was freezing. I picked her up and for a moment she stayed stiff, and then she came to and began sobbing. I nearly brought her back to bed but I thought that would disturb Ernest, and so I gave her a big cuddle, and told her that there was nothing to cry about and that everything was all right and that I loved her – over and over again. It took a long while, but eventually she calmed down. However, as soon as I tried to put her back in her cot, she cried out and clung to me. This happened I don't know how many times. She had a tight grip on some of my hair, and she had no intention of letting go. It was such a cold night and I needed to get her back to bed, but she wanted to be with me.

Of course, I may not be remembering it exactly as it was. She wasn't a very good sleeper, and I had a lot of broken nights. But I do remember that night well, and how light it was. When I took her to the window and we looked out, it wasn't dark; not at all. There was a moon high in the sky, and everything was very bright and very still; the road was glistening with ice, and all the shadows were a sort of smoky grey. Diana's eyes were wide open, shining in the light of the moon. She still clung to me. And although I was longing for bed, I don't know if I wanted that moment to end. I didn't want her to grow up, ever. There were various emotions in my heart that night, among them sadness at the thought that I would never play Tess at the Haymarket with Mr. Hardy in the audience, but I was happy too. I have had many happy moments in my life, but I think that was one of the happiest, with Diana safe in my arms, looking at that still moon and the empty, icy road.

She fell asleep soon after that. I lowered her into her cot, tucked the blankets tightly round her, and went back to Ernest. As I climbed into bed – letting the cold air in, I suppose – he gave a little groan of protest. 'What's going on?' He was too drowsy to wait for my reply. I was chilled right through, but his body was giving out plenty of heat, and I pressed myself against him and warmed up, and fell asleep at last.